THE WHITE GARDEN

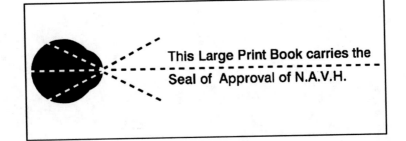

This Large Print Book carries the
Seal of Approval of N.A.V.H.

THE WHITE GARDEN

A NOVEL OF VIRGINIA WOOLF

STEPHANIE BARRON

KENNEBEC LARGE PRINT
A part of Gale, Cengage Learning

GALE
CENGAGE Learning·

Detroit • New York • San Francisco • New Haven, Conn • Waterville, Maine • London

GALE
CENGAGE Learning™

Kennebec Large Print® Superior Collection.
The text of this Large Print edition is unabridged.
Other aspects of the book may vary from the original edition.
Set in 16 pt. Plantin.
Printed on permanent paper.

LIBRARY OF CONGRESS CATALOGING-IN-PUBLICATION DATA

Barron, Stephanie.
  The white garden : a novel of Virginia Woolf / by Stephanie
Barron.
    p. cm. — (Kennebec Large Print superior collection)
    ISBN-13: 978-1-4104-2387-0 (pbk. : alk. paper)
    ISBN-10: 1-4104-2387-5 (pbk. : alk. paper)
    1. Woolf, Virginia, 1882–1941—Fiction. 2. Women authors,
English—20th century—Fiction. 3. Large type books. I. Title.
PS3563.A8357W47 2010
813'.54—dc22   2009044921

Published in 2010 by arrangement with Bantam books, a division of
Random House, Inc.

Printed in the United States of America
  2 3 4 5 6   14 13 12 11 10
ED074

For Leslie, with love

PROLOGUE

It was chillier than she expected that morning, and a stiff wind shuddered through the apple blossoms — penetrating even to the desk in the Lodge at Rodmell, where she preferred to write. The wind formed a background to her stuttering thoughts, not unlike the sound of airplane engines cutting out overhead — there had been so many engines in recent months that she'd stood beneath them as they passed, her bony fists clamped to her jutting hips, staring upwards from the back garden. So many planes. So many bombs that one had actually fallen near the house when she wasn't looking. The river dykes were smashed and the water crept over the flat Sussex meadows as steadily as infantry.

She had hoarded poison against the coming Germans and made death pacts — she would not be taken alive. But by winter the planes had dwindled, predatory birds bound for harsher climes. Leonard hid the poison very secretly while she was in London one day.

And so she was forced to make other plans.

She wrapped the wings of the ancient cardigan closer about her wasted frame and began to write.

I feel certain that I am going mad again; I feel we can't go through another of those terrible times. . . .

He never used the word *mad,* Leonard. He was infinitely careful in his choice of words, as befit a good editor. *Your health,* he would say; *your nerves. You must think about a rest. Now that the book is finished.*

The book was called *Between the Acts* and she thought it was probably her worst, but then she always thought that when she had finished something — drained of the dream phrases that had gripped her for months, she was light-headed and exhausted and immeasurably depressed, as women are who have given birth. In the weeks after writing *The End* she would refuse to eat. Loiter in doorways. Crave kind words, like a whipped dog.

I begin to hear voices. I can't concentrate.

Leonard was at his most brisk during such periods. He would leave his work in the garden or the typeface he labouriously set on the hand printing press and shepherd her towards a chair, offer the bulk of her knitting, employ the hands that no longer held a pen. He would urge endless glasses of milk down her throat and forbid visitors. Keep her from travelling to London — although it was the bombs that had taken London from her now, the house in Tavistock Square cratered to its foundations. Leonard wanted the best for her; Leonard manufactured peace.

You have given me the greatest possible happiness. . . . I don't think two people could have been happier than we have been. . . .

Squandering their rationed petrol, he had driven her across the countryside to Brighton yesterday, so that Octavia might look at her.

The horror of unbuttoning her blouse before the woman doctor; the ugliness of her rib cage; the sag of nearly sixty years. She had answered Octavia's piercing questions in monosyllables. *Yes. No. I'm not sure.* And then she choked out what was most important: *Don't force me to take a rest cure.*

Now she signed her farewell and put down her pen. She did not look back as she left the Lodge in the garden.

■ ■ ■ ■

Later, in her fur coat and galoshes, her walking stick in one hand, she traversed the drowned meadows to the river.

A bird was perched on a fence-post, not ten feet away, trilling despite the bombs: *Life! Life! Life!*

Even as a child, she had dreamed ecstatically of drowning. Water had an inexorable pull: at the sight of it, she was dizzy with longing and vertigo. To stand on the bank of the River Ouse was to grip the edge of a volcano: she could hardly keep from hurling herself in. The current was nothing, close to the edge; a few days before, when she had ventured out, the ripples quickened at her knees, then sucked at her thighs, a lover dragging her to a sticky bed. Then she'd surrendered to it, sinking down until an unexpected claustrophobia overwhelmed her — the water slamming on her head like a cupboard door. She fought her way out, arms flailing and feet stumbling, her skirts dragging her back.

She told Leonard she'd slipped into a dyke. A bit of weed twined around one leg.

If she were to try again, she thought, it would be important to find some stones.

She picked up a few beauties as she trolled along the riverbank. A chunk of granite; a sharp slate knife. The bird sang past her as the water eddied in the stiff breeze.

Life! Life! Life!

In Latin, the word would be *vita*.

CHAPTER ONE

October 2008
Kent, England

Jo Bellamy eased her rental car cautiously into the Slip Road roundabout, every fiber of her body braced for the shuddering crash that must surely come, and when it didn't — when the circular bit of carriageway remained miraculously free of maddened English drivers on this late October morning — she darted a glance in the wrong direction, cursed softly, then searched over her left shoulder for the first available exit from this particular rung of hell. She was looking for something called the A262, which ought to lead straight to the castle, but after an hour and a half of descending from London's Victoria Embankment through the Blackwall Tunnel, not to mention Margate and Maidstone, her patience was frayed and her calf muscles cramped. She was a brown-haired, crinkle-eyed

American woman, thirty-four years of age, and this was her first visit to England — which sufficed to say that she had never driven on the left side of the road before. She had *particularly* never driven a stick-shift transmission on the left, and both her feet and her hands were disobeying her rational mind's orders. She had stalled twice, clipped the left side of the car with an errant curb (or kerb, as they insisted on spelling it here), and was desperate for a stiff drink, although it was only eleven o'clock in the morning. If she did not find the castle soon, she intended to drive the darling little Mini straight into one of the massive oaks that lined the carriageway, and walk to Sissinghurst.

And then, quite suddenly, the tower rose up from the sheep pastures and tilled fields and she felt her pent-up breath exhale slowly from her lungs.

For years she had read about Sissinghurst, in textbooks, magazines, and glossy coffee-table volumes her grandmother kept in her small house back in the Delaware Valley. She'd known what to expect: Elizabethan tower of rosy brick, rising some five stories with a weather vane on top, lapped by the burnished farmland and woods named the Weald of Kent, or what remained of it. The tower was almost derelict when the Nicolson family bought it in 1930, and they had set about clearing the weeds and neglected cottages at the tower's foot until a courtyard and a clutch of buildings remained. These they knit into a minor paradise with a series of gardens, as though tower, cottages, sweep of lawn, and surviving moat were a single house, half of it exposed to sunlight and rain. The Nicolsons took their meals in one room (outdoors) and made their beds in others; but the tower had been the sole province of Mrs. Nicolson: Vita Sackville-West, the writer.

Jo frowned at her choice of words as she steered the Mini recklessly into the National Trust car park. *The writer* was one way to describe Vita Sackville-West, but *the gardener* was another. The woman had written about gardening as much as anything else, because the act of plunging her hands into dirt and making things bloom had been as intimate as sex for Vita — and she always wrote about what was most intensely intimate, including sex. She had had a good deal of that in her lifetime, with both men and women, and for this, too, she and Sissinghurst were famous. The castle was a place where genius and wild beauty were cultivated, a proving ground of eccentrics, and as Jo stopped in her tracks to stare at Vita's tower, gazing raptly upward, she felt suddenly and profoundly unworthy. Ordinary. A *visitor*.

God help her, an *American*.

No, she told herself firmly. *You're a gardener.* She braced her shoulders and strode in the direction of the nursery greenhouses, her shoes scuffing the gravel.

Imogen Cantwell had forgotten that the woman was coming. It was Thursday, which meant the garden was closed to visitors, and the equivalent of a Friday Tidy was under way all over the plots of Sissinghurst — the Purple Border in the Top Courtyard dwindling now that it was October to a few shafts of cardoons and late dahlias, her staff busy mowing the grass paths along the Moat Walk. She herself was examining the ratio of rose hips to lingering blossoms in the Rose Garden, her eye wandering inevitably through the Yew Rondel toward the statue of a bacchante in the Lime Walk, one of Sissinghurst's glories. She found it impossible to keep her mind on work — the air was delicious, and the fact that it was a Closed Day meant that she had the garden to herself. No hordes of motor coaches lining up in the lower car park to disgorge a

15

portentous group of elderly Garden Club enthusiasts, many of whom had been coming to Sissinghurst for forty years and felt entitled to inform the Head Gardener (as Imogen was) of the atrocities they felt had been committed in the name of Progress — some of whom, indeed, had actually known *dear Vita* as they chummily called her, or worse yet, *Pam and Sibylle,* the previous pair of Head Gardeners. It was complete bliss to be left to herself to contemplate the art she had grown and nurtured, and she felt a surge of grumpy ire at the sight of the unknown brown-haired woman moving purposefully toward her from the Powys Wall, her stride occasionally faltering as she plunged her nose deep into some remarkable specimen — the Hybrid Musk Vanity or Pax, each remontant in autumn. Vita had loved and collected old roses, most of which bloomed only in midsummer; the garden was a trifle thin by now, but still felt right. As it should. Except for this stranger drifting down the central axis —

"Bloody *hell,*" Imogen said aloud, and stumped forward to block the interloper, this canker in the rose of her day.

"Ms. Cantwell?"

An American. Of *course.* Americans never respected Closed signs; it was enough that

16

they had flown the Atlantic, that their schedules demanded they visit Kent on a Thursday, for them to presume that Closed meant Except For You. This one did not look the type to wave a fifty-pound note under the Head Gardener's nose, as a special plea for admittance, but one never knew. The functional Merrells and the corduroy jeans, the light cardigan and the hair cinched with elastic, might be merely the protective cover of a rapacious hunter, the kind that snatched cuttings of Sissinghurst flowers and smuggled them home in her Vuitton suitcase. Imogen prepared to be at her most British, her vowels forming plummily even before she uttered them, her Lancashire childhood receding before the Enemy.

"I'm dreadfully sorry, but actually the garden is *closed* on Thursdays for general maintenance. How did you happen to get in, I wonder?"

The woman looked bewildered. "I was told to stop at the Head Gardener's office, down by the service area, and one of those people sent me over here. Is Ms. Cantwell around? My name is Jo Bellamy. We were supposed to meet this morning."

"Bugger," Imogen said, in two short, explosive syllables. "Of course we were!

Forgive me, Miss Bellamy — I'm in full-blown menopause at the moment and my mind is a treacherous sieve. You wanted to see the White Garden, am I correct?"

"Yes. If it's okay. If I'm not —"

"People always do," Imogen said briskly. "I'll wager it's the most admired bit of ground in Europe, and the most copied — although rarely with success. That's why you're here, isn't it?"

It was all coming back, now, as she swung into the Yew Walk — which was heavily shaded, claustrophobic and narrow, like some sort of Gothic tunnel to the Under-world, so that Jo Bellamy fell into step behind her rather than attempting to walk abreast. Imogen had received an email from the woman in September, with a request that was tediously common: some rich client in New York with pretensions to Olde World Grandeur had decided she *must* have the White Garden in her backyard, and had sent Jo — who claimed respectable-enough credentials, a degree from the School of Professional Horticulture at the New York Botanic Gardens, an M.A. from Longwood — to study Sissinghurst and carry it whole-sale back to the potato fields of Long Island. Infuriating and pathetic, as all Garden Plagiarism must be, but not particularly against the law. Imogen usually presented a quelling façade of unwillingness that the humble supplicant from Abroad was forced to overcome, inch by inch; relenting at last, and granting access to the Inner Sanctum — the closely guarded cultivation secrets, handed down from Vita to Pam to Sibylle to Imogen — only after a substantial but *sub rosa* donation was tendered to the National Trust, earmarked for the preservation of Sissinghurst Castle Garden. Jo Bellamy had jumped through these hoops intrepidly, on behalf of an unknown Mrs. Graydon Westlake, of East Hampton; she had written intelligently of cultivation standards and soil composition in New York; she had even invoked her English grandfather, a Kentishman. And Imogen had made this appointment she promptly forgot.

A sudden break in the yew, a bright doorway of sunlight; the Lower Courtyard, flashing past. The end of the walk loomed. She turned left through a second gap in the yew, into the dazzling flood of the White Garden, and stopped short abruptly.

She could feel the American standing wordlessly behind her. Neither of them spoke for an instant. Then Imogen said, "It's a bit past its prime, this time of year.

19

Although still lovely, of course." And regretted the words as soon as they were spoken. The British recognized self-deprecation for the subtle pride it was. Americans always mistook it for lack of confidence. And the White Garden had no reason to apologize.

A large rectangular space divided into two parts by a crossing of main paths, and a rose arbor in the center. To the left, a quartering of beds, filled to bursting with every conceivable arrangement of white and silver flowers; to the right, a boxwood parterre, severe and formal, its lines relieved by the lushness of its plantings. Jo Bellamy walked tentatively forward on the path, her eyes searching the beds. "Is that John Huxtable?" she asked, her gaze fixed on the clematis engulfing a pillar. "You must cut it back hard, each spring, to make it bloom so late."

"We do," Imogen agreed. "It's always a challenge to keep the works going until closing day, but we manage."

There it was, again — the false apology — but the American merely nodded. "You do a magnificent job. Marguerites, of course — they'll soldier on until frost — but the thistles are a surprise. We view them as weeds, where I come from. I'll have to educate Mrs. Westlake on the subject of five-foot-tall onopordum. Is that Spirea 'Arguta'?

You're deadheading the antirrhinums with a vengeance, I imagine. . . ."

It was remarkable, Imogen thought, how competent a gardener became within smelling distance of the soil. Even a woman like this one — not a pushing sort of person at first blush — became ruthlessly authoritative on the topics of hothouse seedlings and the proper batter of hedges. They moved slowly among the beds, looking and talking, the American avoiding the mistake of pulling a tablet of paper or a digital camera from her pocket; she conveyed the impression that there would be time for more sordid studies, more wholesale theft, later. For now, she simply enjoyed the garden in Imogen's company. When they had exhausted the tendency of foxgloves and lupines to sport, and the necessity of extensive hawthorn staking, Imogen glanced at her watch.

"God! It's gone past one. Have you eaten? Can I offer you something? A cup of tea?"

Jo Bellamy hesitated. "I hate to take more of your time. And I should find a room nearby, if I'm going to stay —"

There was a question implicit in the words. Imogen studied the woman: brown eyes crinkled from constant work in the sun; hands weathered by soil and exposure. A

21

pretty face and a self-assured air — but no pretense, no drama. A *gardener.*

"They might have a room at the home farm," Imogen said. "I could ring. Or there's a much posher place in Cranbrook called the George. Flat-screen telly, and all that. How long do you reckon you'll stay?"

"A few days."

"You'll want to draw up a plan, I expect — consult our records for the past several seasons, take pictures and measurements, and so on?"

"If you'll allow me." Jo peered under the rose arbor at the elaborate mesh of trained *Rosa mulliganii* canes, intersecting to form a perfect pyramid. "It's going to be a bear to maintain this garden once we plant it. The Westlakes, of course, have no idea what they've asked for. How many people do you employ?"

"Eight actual gardeners," Imogen answered. "But that's National Trust funds, and we cover the entire six acres, not just the White Garden. Vita and Harold — her husband, Harold Nicolson — made do with two. But they also worked the place themselves, of course. Your Mrs. Westlake —"

"— Never gets her hands dirty. These beds must glow like stardust at night. Did the Nicolsons ever see *the great ghostly barn owl*

22

sweep silently across the pale garden?" Jo asked, ducking from under the arbor.

Imogen stared at her. It was a quotation from one of Vita's gardening columns, written ages ago for the *Observer,* when the White Garden was just an idea in the Nicolsons' brains. *The pale garden that I am now planting, under the first flakes of snow . . .*

"I've no idea," she replied. "I'm not often here at night. You've read about her, then?"

"For years. I grew up with Sissinghurst. I think I mentioned my grandfather was from Kent."

"Was he a gardener?"

"Professionally, you mean? Yes. A long time ago. I inherited his green thumb."

She held up her hands, which were already stained brown with dirt, and dusted them matter-of-factly on her corduroy jeans.

And for reasons she could not afterward explain, Imogen Cantwell felt a sudden frisson of fear — as though a serpent, in the form of this mild American woman, had suddenly slithered through Sissinghurst's garden.

CHAPTER TWO

Cranbrook sat a few miles down the A262 from Sissinghurst. It was famous for being the smallest town in Kent, for being unreachable by train, and for possessing a windmill — all of which Jo Bellamy learned from a town council flyer over breakfast the next morning. This was a solitary if splendid affair involving silver chafing dishes and broiled pale pink tomatoes, both of which Jo ignored in favor of more humble carbohydrates. *Posh,* Imogen Cantwell had called the George; but *hip* was more accurate — it was a place that cried out for French manicures and Manolo spikes. Jo possessed neither. She could not imagine Vita Sackville-West loping along the inn's half-timbered corridors, as she certainly once had — the Nicolsons set up camp at the George just after buying Sissinghurst in 1930, their newly acquired ruins being uninhabitable for several years. Jo wondered, inevitably, whether her bedroom (repainted a deep mandarin orange) had once been Vita's — then put the notion firmly out of her mind. Copying Vita's garden was one thing; copying her life was another.

Jo's habit of early rising had marooned her amidst the breakfast buffet at an hour when mere tourists were still snoozing. Without the council flyer or the landscape drawings nestled by her elbow, she might have lost herself in thought, and Jo was avoiding her inner life at the moment. Her cell phone was stationed on the table, yet she had deliberately silenced its ring. Everything about her gentle appearance suggested welcome and pliability, when in truth she was rigid with denial.

She pushed aside the china plate littered with the crumbs of her scone, and unfurled a sheaf of black-and-white CADD blueprints. *Westwind* was noted in careful print on the lower-left-hand side of each sheet; and beneath that, *Plan for Landscape Development, The Westlake Residence, East Hampton, New York.* Stamped on the right were the interlocked B and D of Bellamy Design's logo, the firm's Delaware address, and a dated notation with her initials. This was the fourth revision of her original drawings, printed only six days ago, after her tenth meeting with Graydon Westlake and his wife, Alicia — the woman Jo always referred to as her client, when in fact it was not the pretty, whipcord-thin blonde on the shady side of thirty who planned the gardens with Jo, but her husband: Graydon the enigmatic. Graydon, who could shave half an hour from his departure by helicopter in order to run his sensitive, long-fingered hands over the kitchen garden's walls, an idea of pear trees rising in his mind. Jo had watched those fingers caress the stone, had felt the hooded eyes fix on her bent head, and had shivered.

She would not think of Graydon.

He was past fifty. Alicia was his third wife. There were two children from an earlier marriage, already grown. People who knew such things referred to Graydon as a financier, which meant that he had inherited an investment firm founded by his father. As CEO of the privately held, multibillion-dollar international concern, he spent his time tending the fortunes of universities and pension funds, the hopeful college savings of middle-class people he would never meet. Without understanding an iota of his business, Jo recognized Gray's intelligence, his scrupulous concern for detail, his drive for perfection, his ruthlessness. The force of his personality at times was paralyzing. Alicia seemed to adore him — her well-tended hand hovering always a half-inch above his French-cuffed sleeve, as though for comfort or support — but Jo detected hypocrisy in that air of devotion. She suspected Gray saw it, too. This was one of their complicities: she and Gray, mutually recognizing the truth about Alicia. Didn't most betrayals begin with a sharing of some kind?

The house the Westlakes were building in the Hamptons was a Shingle-style sprawl covering more than twenty thousand square feet; and the six flat, farmland acres Jo was charged with turning into a corner of England were also expected to incorporate the aforementioned helipad, a four-thousand-square-foot guest cottage, a pool house designed as a rustic Parthenon, the pool itself, and a caretaker's quarters. Incidental to her plans were security cameras, decorative lighting, speaker systems for music; a ten-car garage set at a remove from the house but requiring visual and physical linkage with a series of paths, or perhaps, as Graydon had recently suggested, a Federal-style arbor draped with wisteria vines. . . .

He assumed wisteria would bloom, of

course. He knew nothing about the temperamental plant — what a fickle beast it was to establish, the amount of careful pruning required to coax it into flower, the possible decades before it looked as he expected. This was emblematic, Jo thought, of Graydon's entire approach to life. People all around him committed seppuku to achieve his heart's desires, and in reply he gave a charming lift of the lips, a flick of a wave, already on his way elsewhere. Jo's mouth pursed now, remembering what he'd said about wisteria: *But at Princeton it trailed over everything. All the dorms. The lecture halls. Nobody fussed about it —*

That was Gray, she thought: determined to re-create *This Side of Paradise* in his Long Island backyard.

The cell phone vibrated. The shudder in her hand turned to a pulse in the blood. She ought to send him directly into voice mail, but —

"Jo," he said, intimate in her ear. "Did I wake you?"

"Hardly." She heard the crack of adrenaline in her own voice, closed her eyes, and cursed herself. *Weak. Susceptible.* "I've already had breakfast. What can I do for you, Gray?"

"Tell me about the garden. I like to think

of you there."

It was uncanny how seductive her client could make those few words sound: *Tell me about the garden.* He seemed to know that the sight and smell of growing things were for her an aphrodisiac, an almost painful happiness she longed to share. He slipped right through her best defenses, because somehow he had glimpsed her soul all those weeks ago, when they had met in the rain for a hurried cup of coffee over the first draft of the plans, Alicia absent at the London auctions, Gray's time as always precious and stolen. *Lilium regale,* he'd said. *Rising white in the moonlight. We could drink wine in the garden under the stars, with the scent of lilies all around us —*

For that brief moment, his dream included her.

"Sissinghurst is bittersweet this time of year," she said now. "Drowsing into sleep. A few shafts of bloom amidst the withering of growth. Space clearing around the fallen places and the angular shape emerging: all the clipped boxwood, the pyramid beneath the roses. The White Garden fading to black."

He was silent a moment. "Is it raining?"

"It is."

"So there's mist in your hair."

"Cigarette smoke, actually — I'm in the hotel dining room." She drew an unsteady breath. "Gray — did you call for a reason?"

"I wanted to hear your voice," he said. "I'm in Rio de Janeiro. Tomorrow, Buenos Aires. After that — who knows? Touch something for me this morning, Jo — a last rose. A wet leaf."

He hung up before she could answer.

"Shit," she whispered into the silence.

"This is Terence," Imogen Cantwell said crisply. "He's a National Trust intern, in his final year of fieldwork. We've had him the better part of six months. I've made him responsible for deadheading the White Garden — it should have been done yesterday, but he pulled a few, Wednesday night, and was bloody well useless. He'll take you along now."

The Head Gardener was not exactly unfriendly as she stood before the Powys Wall, feet planted in much-abused Wellies; but she was as focused as Eisenhower off Utah Beach. Sissinghurst opened to paying visitors at eleven o'clock, and despite the rain, there would soon be hundreds of garden lovers strolling along the stone and grass paths, umbrellas vying for passage between the towering yews. A professional poacher like Jo was a nuisance today, and knew it.

"I printed a few files," Imogen added grudgingly, and thrust some damp pages at her. "Plant lists. They go back five years, as long as I've been Head. Terence will explain the notation."

Terence, who was probably Ter to his friends, was a squat, muscular youth with a lumpen face and a shock of bleached hair. He grinned cheerfully at Jo, pruners dangling from one hand and a tip bag from the other. "You're from the States, then?"

"Yes. Just outside Philadelphia."

He looked disappointed. "Ever been to L.A.?"

"Once."

"I reckon that's where I'll head, when this internship's done," he said as he led Jo through the drenched Rose Garden. "Reckon there's a film star who'd pay a good bit for real English gardening."

"Undoubtedly there is. But the climate's Mediterranean." Jo ran her eyes over Imogen Cantwell's lists as she walked, noting the familiar names of cala and lupine, *paeonia* and iris; the dates certain plants were divided or first put into the ground, with notes for revised schedules in the future; early bulbs and perennial bloomers, June elements, late summer show; fertilization schedules, losses due to frost or disease or poor performance. Sissinghurst was a huge outdoor arena for the entertainment of the masses, with no tolerance for plants that disappointed. Those that failed to live up to hope or reputation were swiftly uprooted and tossed on the compost pile. The White Garden showed evidence of these trials: any number of tested performers held their ground in Imogen's lists, but perhaps a fifth of the plants were regularly changed out due to poorly sustained bloom, or a tendency to disease, or an unacceptable yellowish cast to their creamy petals.

Jo stopped short in the midst of the Yew Walk, her brow furrowed. She could feel raw ambition almost crackling off these pages. And something else: a grim denial of all that was imperfect — of the force of nature itself. Was that Imogen Cantwell's goal? Or the National Trust's? Sissinghurst had hardly been perfect in its first four decades — the Nicolsons were family gardeners, working on ideas they tossed across the dinner table and jotted down in their daily letters. They were always searching for funds to throw at stone pavers and suppliers of bulbs. They were chronically short of help. Friends gave them cuttings of prized plants, sent hybrid offerings to Vita when her fame as a garden columnist put Sissinghurst on the map. But Jo had read those columns. The garden Vita's columns described was most beloved when it was most human — when the failures and mistakes cast the glorious triumphs into sharp relief.

"Question?" Terence called from the entrance to the White Garden.

"Yes," Jo replied, as her fingers tidied the errant lists. "What in God's name is *pulling,* and how did it make you useless?"

Terence smirked. "Pulling a pint. Or seven. I was hungover yesterday. Didn't come in to work at all. I'll start on the right-hand bit, and leave you a clear field on the left. Just shout if you've need."

Jo stood for an instant in the gap between the yew, staring out over the White Garden. Cosmos still flowered gamely in the October rain; *Artemisia aborescens* spilled wildly over stiff boxwood. These, Vita would have loved and understood. But a hidden forest of brushwood stakes, relentless trials, and a war against nature itself? That was uncannily like Gray Westlake. Jo had come here looking for a way to bring the White Garden home — but he'd wanted a public showplace, not an intimate wilderness.

He's going to get something else, she

thought with amusement. *Something unsettling. Unexpected. Beyond the bounds of his control.*

Perhaps they both were.

With a small sigh of exasperation, she forced Gray aside, dumped her shoulder bag on the White Garden's uneven brick walkway, and rummaged inside it for her digital camera.

CHAPTER THREE

The camera, a tiny Olympus resistant to both cold and wet, had been a gift from Jo's grandfather.

It was an uncharacteristic one, she thought as the lens hovered a few feet in front of the gray-green spikes of onopordum, the architecture of the thistles coming into prickly focus. Jock loved hand tools, not technology. He'd collected them for years, mostly Burgon & Ball forged in Sheffield, where the company had been making such things for three centuries. Jock's topiary shears alone were worth hanging as industrial art; and that's what he'd done with them, hooking them to pegboards in his tractor shed in the Delaware Valley. For a man who'd abandoned gardening as a profession years ago, the shed was painfully revealing — something between a trophy house and a mausoleum. Jock had left the tools — more than a hundred and fifty items — to Jo at his death, two months before.

His death. The camera wavered before a clump of euphorbia, long past blooming. Even in the privacy of her own mind, she still could not say *his suicide, his brutal and inexplicable hanging.*

August, and the peak of the summer season in the Delaware Valley. The riotous bloom of July dwindling now to the hot colors of dahlias and Echinacea and Black-Eyed Susans. She'd been supervising the destruction of a hoary juniper hedge at a historic home in Bucks County when she got the call from Dottie.

Her grandmother was composed; she delivered the news without weeping; but blank astonishment was behind every word.

I lived with the man for more than sixty years, and he couldn't just tell *me his plans?* Dottie demanded.

How did a person share that kind of thing, Jo wondered now as she withdrew a measuring tape from her bag and paced off the depth of the massive bed (eighteen feet). How did a man say to the woman he'd loved since the age of twenty, *I am going to walk out the kitchen door this morning as I always do around seven-thirty, only today I'm going to take a length of tractor chain and loop it over the beam in the garage?*

Nothing had prepared Dottie for the body swinging from the ceiling, the limpness of the blue hands. Nothing had prepared Jo. She'd left the junipers and the backhoe and the historic house under renovation, and did not return for two weeks.

They had asked each other why, of course. They had hours to talk after the funeral. Depression? Jo wondered. Dottie had seen no sign of it, although she wasn't the best at detecting those things. After six decades of marriage she and Jock kept themselves to themselves, they didn't probe each other's souls like young people did nowadays. They ate dinner in silence if their minds were heavy and left each other to sort things out. Perhaps she'd been at fault, there. But he'd never asked her for advice, he'd never seemed troubled. Getting older, of course . . . They both were. . . .

Jo called Jock's doctor and asked whether there'd been a diagnosis. Something out of the ordinary. A death sentence he couldn't face.

None, the doctor answered regretfully. He, too, felt obscurely responsible. *And in any case, your grandfather was no coward.*

No. Even that final tractor chain demanded courage; self-hanging was not the act of a fearful man.

She was haunted by him in dreams: perfectly ordinary visits, Jock in mid-conversation across the breakfast table, one of his old plaid shirts rolled to the elbows. She always asked why he had to leave. He smiled at her fondly, told her nothing. He'd killed himself the day after she told him about the biggest gardening coup of her young career: Gray and Alicia Westlake wanted a copy of the White Garden, and she, Jo, was going to Sissinghurst. . . .

For reasons she could not explain, Jo was struggling with guilt. As though *her news* had driven Jock to suicide.

Then, one morning in September — maybe three days after that intimate coffee with Gray, the two of them talking of lilies and moonlight — Dottie appeared in Jo's office holding a letter.

"I was going through your grandfather's things yesterday," she explained. "I should have done it before, but to tell you the truth I hadn't the heart for it."

She'd started in Jock's office — just a desk, really, with a stack of catalogs, some tidily paid bills. His Last Will and Testament, which she'd witnessed only six months before, secure in a drawer. She'd moved on to the tractor shed, avoiding the garage and its accusing beam. All the tools were in the tractor shed, Dottie explained, and the Will reminded her she'd need to have them valued. "He left them to you, of course — the hoes and clippers and what-not. Honestly, Jo, if you want it all carted away I'm happy to get rid of it. Don't worry about the Will, we know he must've been crazy in the end —"

"I want Grandpa's tools."

It was in the shed that Dottie noticed the envelope, sitting in a wheelbarrow, in plain sight, as though Jock meant to mail it and simply forgot in all the bustle of hanging himself. "*In the Event of My Death,* he'd written in the lower corner," she sputtered. "I mean, *really,* Jo —"

She'd expected a suicide note. Instead, what she got was a postcard from the past.

"It was one of those things they carried, in the war," Dottie told Jo, "— in case their bodies were found. The soldiers wanted something sent back, as a kind of farewell."

It was dated *Somewhere near Brindisi, September 1943.* And addressed to Jock's mother.

Dear Mum and Dad and young Kip, If you are reading this, it is because old Jerry

39

has done for me at last, never mind how, it's all the same in the end. I want you to know that I don't fear Death — that whatever happens, I will be all right, because it's a relief to think of lying in the long grass as much as I like, and no marching just because Captain tells me to. I have seen a lot of Death, starting with that lady back home, and I know that what is left behind is like stubble in the fields after harvest time, the ends of things that have been used up, with the best of 'em put back into the earth.

Jo glanced around at Vita's dying garden. The rain had thrown a sheet of ground fog between her camera and the last of the argyranthemums; the effect was unutterably lonely. *The ends of things that have been used up.* Is that how Jock viewed his life, in his last days? How could she have failed to notice such despair?

She stopped before a slim statue of a figure, somberly robed, more religious than classical. She glanced at her map of the White Garden; this must be the Little Virgin, the face almost obscured by the branches of a weeping pear tree. It was the sort of thing that could be adapted for the Westlake garden, with a modernist sculpture

— possibly even an abstract one — something that gestured toward the original without copying it slavishly. Jo positioned the Virgin in her viewfinder and took several shots, then noted the height and breadth of the weeping pear. Flowering quince or a tree-form wisteria might do just as well — there were several varieties available in the States.

The drizzle was turning to rain, so she slipped the camera back in its case and straightened over her bulging shoulder bag, aware that Terence had moved out of view on the far side of the box parterre. It was almost impossible to imagine the glory of this place on a sunny July day; a raw chill had seeped into the White Garden. She shivered.

I cannot go without telling you why I ran that day, Jock's letter had continued.

I lied about my age, Mum, and nearly killed you with it. I hope Kip never does the same. War comes soon enough by the front door without hustling it in at the back. But I could not bear what happened, nor explain it neither, and going for a soldier seemed best. If I am dead, I hope you will believe and honour my word: I never did nothing for the Lady but what she asked.

41

Before God, I tried to help her, though I only harmed in the end. I will see her huge eyes before me however long or short I may live, but my soul is easy: I was not a bad boy, Mum, only unlucky.

Hoping as I have not brought shame or worry upon you and all the home folk at Knole, and sending you my dearest love, even in death — I remain,

Jock Bellamy

Jo had stared at her grandfather's familiar writing, unwilling to hand the letter back to Dottie. There *must* be something more than this — some reason —

"Beneath the envelope," Dottie was saying, "he left a slip of paper. Probably torn off the pad he kept in his shirt pocket, you know the one . . ."

A three-by-five block of steno sheets, useful for jotting reminders. And lists. They both loved lists.

She took the scrap of paper from Dottie's hand and read: *Tell her pictures at Charleston.*

South Carolina? Jock had never been there in his life. Jo shook her head in frustration. "So who's this lady he wrote about?"

"No idea." Dottie sniffed.

"Oh, come on, Nana — you knew Jock

better than anybody alive!"

"I didn't know he'd kill himself that day!" She made it sound like an accusation.

"No one could have known."

"I *should* have."

There was no answer to this.

"But you two must have met around the time Jock wrote this letter," Jo attempted, as she folded the sheets and held them out to her grandmother. "In Italy."

"He never mentioned its existence," Dottie replied stiffly. "And he never mentioned *me*."

This, Jo thought, was part of the trouble: Dottie felt betrayed. Jock's suicide was insult enough, a wrenching-out of Dottie's heart, as inexplicable as it was ugly; but *this . . .* She was completely absent from the farewell he'd written, so long ago, to his parents. The unknown lady had taken his wife's place.

"He was in some sort of trouble, wasn't he?" Jo asked thoughtfully. "He talks about *running*. As though it were a matter for the law."

"He used to tell everybody he'd joined up young — only seventeen, that spring of 1941 — because he couldn't be tending roses when the fate of Britain was at stake. He never said he was wanted by the Law."

"But this sounds like . . ."

"He had no choice. I know. That's why I came."

Jo had stared at her grandmother that day in her office, sharply uneasy. She knew nothing whatever about Jock's war — only that he'd lost his entire family while serving in Italy, to a German bomb. It was all so long ago. It had nothing to do with the sad end in the garage. What did Dottie expect Jo to do?

"You could find out something," Dottie persisted. "In their records. While you're there in Kent. He mentions Knole, Jo. The great estate. That's where he grew up."

Vita Sackville-West had grown up at Knole, too. It was the ancestral home of the Dukes of Dorset, built before the reign of Henry VIII — a fifteenth-century house the size of a small village. Less than an hour from the garden in which Jo was now standing. But she hadn't found the courage, yet, to visit Knole. Or ask questions about an unknown woman's death, nearly seventy years before. She was afraid of what she might learn: That Jock hanged himself rather than face his granddaughter, after her trip to Kent.

"What if I learn the truth, Nana?" she'd asked gently. "And you don't like it?"

"Jock left this letter for a reason," Dottie insisted. "He's dead, for a reason. I want to know what it is, Jo. I want to know what it is."

CHAPTER FOUR

Friday's rain was a confirmed torrent by breakfast Saturday morning. The October world beyond the leaded windows was depressingly gray. Jo had slept badly. Little things bothered her: the gurgle of water in Cranbrook's gutters, the wet dripping from every Tudor eave. And so she allowed herself a third cup of coffee while she thought about Nana and Jock and death of various kinds. She took stock of her situation. She made lists.

Lists were a staple of Jo's life. They made her feel purposeful and competent, and they were usually written in red ink. Several were floating around her leather shoulder bag already — *Lilium regale or substitute white Casablancas?; paeonia Cheddar Delight; discuss staking, need for team of real gardeners not hired labor,* read one — but this morning's list was a compilation of unknowns.

46

She wrote: *1941?*

That was the year Jock had lied about his age and run away to war.

She wrote: *Police records, Sevenoaks?*

Knole House sat on the eastern edge of Sevenoaks, in the part of Kent known as the North Downs. Simply pulling up before the gates of Knole, however, would not guarantee Jo answers. Did anybody — serving class or lord — still live there? Or was the vast sprawl of Kentish stone in its thousand-acre deer park just a National Trust mausoleum? And why assume Jock's brush with the Lady had happened there?

She had no idea what her grandfather's life was like in 1941. He had said so little about his own childhood; it was as though only the present existed for Jock. Jo knew vague and impersonal things about England during the war: Luftwaffe bombing raids over Kent, hop fields burning, children sent away by train. Rations and petrol shortage, cooking pots hammered into airplane propellers. Was seventeen still considered school-age in time of war? Or had Jock been sent out to work while the men were fighting?

She wrote: *Ask Nana, family friends.*

Jo's eyes rested on the dripping iron hitching post beyond the breakfast-room window.

47

It was shaped like a horse's head, and might perhaps have been antique. Even this irritated her; a bit of Merrie Olde England intended for the tourist trade. She set down her red pen.

She ought to find Imogen Cantwell this morning and spend an hour in Sissinghurst's greenhouses, studying the biennials raised from cuttings and seed. She ought to discuss boxwood clones. Hedge-trimming schedules.

She ought to earn Gray's money.

Instead, she pushed back her chair and went to look for the concierge.

"Local archives?" he repeated, frowning. "Birth and death records? That sort of thing? You'll want the Centre for Kentish Studies. It's only a few miles up Tonbridge Road, in Maidstone."

When her phone vibrated a few seconds later, fresh with a call from Buenos Aires, she let Gray slip into voice mail.

We advise visitors to book a seat in advance to avoid disappointment.

Jo had found the careful British warning posted on the Centre's website after breakfast, and dutifully called ahead. There were rafts of people eager to troll through microfilm of seventeenth-century parish registers and polling data from 1869, or so she was told; particularly the Americans on holiday.

"Think they're related to the Queen," sniffed the staff member to Jo, "though most of 'em are Irish and Polish or whatnot."

She bought a County Archives Readers' Network ticket, and was given a plastic tag emblazoned with the number of her reserved seat. The Searchroom, as it was called, was like a researchers' holding pen. At the far end of the space were shelves of archive catalogs — a series of color-coded ring binders divided by subject: green for family and estate records; red for the court reports of the Quarter Sessions. There were also numerous card indexes for parishes, personal names, and miscellany going back ten centuries. *Eleven kilometres of data in our archive centre,* the website boasted; but most of those facts were inaccessible by computer. She would have to pinpoint the sources she needed to consult — write their catalog numbers on a slip of paper — offer this to an archivist — and wait a quarter of an hour for the volumes to be fetched. She had no idea where to start. She nearly called Nana then and there to announce defeat.

"Can I be of service?"

He was short and slim and mild-eyed; a dark-haired cipher of a man with a neat name tag pinned to his blue dress shirt. MR. TREVELYAN, it said. Such a self-effacing soul would never put ROGER or IAN or HAL on his breast. He would always be Mr. Trevelyan. This, to Jo, was reassuring: she had found authority in a sea of doubt.

"I'm researching my grandfather," she said. "He grew up somewhere near Knole House."

"When?" Mr. Trevelyan inquired.

"He was born in 1924. June sixteenth, actually."

"In Sevenoaks? Or on the estate itself?"

"I don't know. He's dead," she added, by way of explanation.

"Let's start with official records. Polling data, parish registry, that sort of thing." He led Jo toward the card catalogs. "And the name?"

She told him. While Mr. Trevelyan pulled drawers from cabinets, Jo debated whether to broach the subject of police records and an unknown woman's death nearly seventy years before, the sudden terrible divide that might have fallen between childhood and *going for a soldier.*

"Bellamy?" Mr. Trevelyan repeated. "That's a very old name. Norman in origin. *Belle Amie.*"

Jo smiled to herself. Jock was no aristocrat.

50

If the blood of the conquerors descended in her veins, it was surely from the wrong side of the blanket — a *belle amie,* a beautiful mistress with an illegitimate child.

"Here it is." The archivist's finger was poised over a catalog entry. "Quite straight-forward. We'll just fetch the parish records, shall we?"

From the parish records Jo learned enough to fill half an index card. The names of Jock's parents, Rose and Thomas Bellamy; the date of Jock's birth, which she already knew; that of his younger brother, Christopher, called Kip; and a street address in Sevenoaks: 17 Bells Lane. There was also a single date of death for Rose, Thomas, and Kip, in February 1944.

"That would be a bomb, of course," Mr. Trevelyan observed. "One hit Knole itself that month. Damaged a good bit of the building."

It was so bald, that date. So quiet, in the records of the parish registry. When what it really recorded was the end of Jock's known world. He had emigrated to America with Dottie after V-E Day.

"Thomas Bellamy's profession is noted as gardener," Trevelyan added. "Nine chances out of ten, he was employed at Knole House. The family gave the place into the

51

National Trust in 1946 — with a two-hundred-year lease on the private apartments and complete retention of the park — but in the first half of the century, Knole kept most of Sevenoaks in bread and butter. The garden is five hundred years old, and largish — a full mile of ragstone wall encloses it. They'd have needed a small army of gardeners, I should think. Shall we consult the estate records?"

It was here that Jo came into a kingdom.

The catalog of Knole's books was astonishingly vast and various: steward's accounts dating to the fifteenth century; gamekeepers' records of pheasants bagged and deer killed; workshop accounts of upholsterers and woodsmen and joiners and glaziers; tenants' accounts; harvest figures; housekeeping and stillroom books; lists of servants, the same local surnames appearing generation after generation. And records of the state visits of kings and queens: Henry VIII. Elizabeth I. James II. Edward VII.

She ignored all of these. Only one group of documents held any interest for her: Knole's garden archives.

She would have liked to waste an hour scanning the drawings from *Britannia Illustrata* in 1707, or the accounts of George London, royal gardener, who'd supplied fruit trees in 1698; or Thomas Badeslade's record of the bowling green's construction, or the third Duke's pineapple hothouse, or the Orangery that dated from the Regency period. But she had too little time. Another stranger was scheduled to take her numbered seat in less than forty minutes. She was forced to concentrate on the years between 1918 and 1939 — England's Long Weekend between two devastating wars — when Thomas Bellamy, gardener of 17 Bells Lane, had raised his sons.

Skimming the lines of the Head Gardener's book with her forefinger, Jo stumbled on April 1919.

Took on Harry Leeds, Joe Weston, Tom Bellamy as undergardeners with pay of fifteen shillings per week, Tom to receive eighteen, as he was trained up as a lad here before the war, and his brother Frank lost at Ypres.

No mention of Jock's father after that beyond the occasional reference to duties in the herbaceous beds or among the rhododendrons, until September of 1923:

Tom Bellamy raised to Hothouse Overseer, as he has proved himself a steady man enough, and has a child coming.

And finally, an entry from the spring of 1936 that gave Jo a strange shiver:

Hired Tom Bellamy's son as jobbing lad this day and set him to work weeding knot garden. A quiet boy enough and no nonsense, John by name but called Jock he bids fair to be strong and canny with his hands though not yet of age to leave school.

Tom Bellamy's name disappeared from the accounts after that, until September 1939:

War with Germany declared this day and the Staff can talk of nothing else than soldiering. Tom Bellamy to join up.

No word of Jock.

Jo's fingers fluttered nervously over the final days of 1939, and on into the spring of 1940. *Tom Bellamy refused the service due to dicky heart.* Knole's garden ranks dropped by two-thirds; only the unfit, the old, and the young remained to work the beds and maintain the plantings. Copper sulfate for the roses was impossible to find, due to the demands of munitions factories; the kitchen garden was all anybody cared about now, for the production of desperately needed food.

And then, suddenly, something unexpected:

Hired as jobbing lad this day Tom Bellamy's son Christopher, called Kip. Jock Bellamy sent over to Mrs. Nicolson, Miss Vita as was, due to shortage of men at Sissinghurst.

Sissinghurst. Her grandfather had once bent and strained over the very beds she'd photographed in recent days — and she hadn't known.

Was it possible that *Vita* was the Lady? But no — Jock had distinctly written about the woman's death. And Vita had survived the war by several decades.

Jo sank back against the unforgiving Searchroom chair, baffled. It made sense that Lady Nicolson, desperate for garden help, would look for it at Knole — Vita made a habit of borrowing from her childhood home. Furniture, pictures, garden urns — and now a teenage boy who *bid fair to be strong and canny with his hands.*

Jo skimmed ahead, hoping against hope for something more — but the Head Gardener's account ended abruptly in June 1941 with the words: *Called up for service this day, and will report for duty tomorrow at dawn.* Five years of silence were contained in the single page separating this entry from the next — which was dated September 1946, and written in a stranger's hand. *Knole House to be given into the National Trust.*

Jo went in search of Mr. Trevelyan.

"Do you keep anything about the Sissinghurst Castle Garden in this archive? From the war years, I mean?"

He straightened from the pile of books he'd been tidying. "No. Particularly *not* the garden. Sissinghurst passed to the Trust in the late sixties, you know — and the Head Gardeners employed by the Nicolsons at the time were retained for decades after. They'd have kept their own records. Probably passed them on to their successors, whoever they are. You might check with the National Trust."

Jo thanked him, and turned in her numbered seat tag. She felt a pang of guilt. She should have kept to her proper job that morning — should indeed have earned Gray's money. The answers were with Imogen Cantwell, at Sissinghurst.

"We'd given you up," the Head Gardener called genially through the open office door.

56

"Thought you'd had a late lie-in and spa treatment at the George."

Imogen was bent over her computer, the kind of work she detested, but the obvious task for a day of steady rain. Let Ter and the others slog around in their Wellies while she tended to the business of the Castle gift shop: stocking orders for tea towels and gardening books and potpourri that captured the scent of Vita's musk roses. A few plants associated with Sissinghurst were sold there as well — stout rosemary shrubs and viola. All of this fell under Imogen Cantwell's purview. She worked incessantly. She had no family, only a trio of indifferent cats she loved with pathetic ferocity.

"I suppose it's the jet lag," the American said vaguely.

Jo Bellamy did look strained for a person who'd slept late. Her skin was pallid, and the hollows of her eyes almost bruised. But something — a barely discernible crackle of excitement — churned beneath the surface, Imogen decided. It was evident in the lower lip she worried surreptitiously with her teeth, in the flutter of her restless hands.

Imogen's eyes slid to the wall clock hanging near the room's sole window: nearly half-past two. "Care for a cuppa?" she suggested, and closed her file.

While they waited for the electric kettle to sing, she found mugs and Jo puttered about the small space, pulling books off shelves distractedly, then shoving them back. "You got on with Terence, I gather?" Imogen said. "Went over all those plant lists I gave you?"

"Yes. Thank you."

Imogen had expected rather more; Ter reported that the American was put off by the discipline of the bedding trials. Had said something about the value of *propagating disorder rather than perfection.* Imogen had muttered to herself when she heard this; Jo sodding Bellamy didn't need to justify *her* job to the National Trust, thank you very much, she wasn't charged with bringing immortality to an aging icon.

The kettle sang.

Imogen poured, and handed a mug to Jo.

"I've been thinking about the war years," the American said.

"The war years? You mean — the Second World War?"

"Exactly. What was it like here then?"

Imogen rested her broad bottom against the edge of her desk, puzzled. "I don't know. Bombs, I think. Kent was a highway for the Luftwaffe, straight across the Channel from Paris. What part of the war do you mean, exactly?"

Jo shrugged. "I know the Nicolsons stayed here for most of it. Or Vita did. Harold was up in London, weekdays. I've read the biographies."

"Right," Imogen said briskly. "But you're interested in the garden. Not the family."

"True." Jo met her gaze directly. "And the family made the garden. The war should have killed it. How did they manage, with everybody fighting the Germans, and no supplies or anything, and air raids every other minute?"

"I suppose a lot was . . . put on hold." Imogen took a gulp of tea. "Your own bit's an example of that. Vita came up with the idea for the White Garden during the war. But it wasn't possible to actually *make* the thing for years after. Like you say — no labor, no plants, no money. They were more interested in begging petrol than peonies in those years."

"Are there any records? From the gardeners — if there were any — who tended Sissinghurst then?"

Imogen frowned; there was a strange glitter to Jo Bellamy's eyes. *The woman's on something,* she thought. *She's barmy.* "I can't see why it matters! The White Garden didn't exist."

"I just need to know." Jo set down her

mug and folded her arms protectively across her chest. "Okay, it has nothing to do with why I'm here. But my grandfather was from Kent — he was in the war. . . . I've started to wonder what *happened* here."

Imogen sighed, and rubbed the back of her neck with one hand.

"I'm two Heads removed from Pam and Sibylle, who made Sissinghurst what it is. The Mädchen, Vita called them. They spent nearly forty years here after Jack Vass — the only other real gardener Sissinghurst ever had. He started during the war, then joined up and returned to Sissinghurst when the fighting was over. Vass was quite a local sensation — he'd worked at Cliveden before us, and escaped from a German POW camp or something — but he went Communist, and Vita was scared. So she fired him."

"There are no records from those years?" Something in Jo had flickered and gone out as Imogen was talking.

"Not much." She straightened, intrigued despite her growing mistrust. "Look — it's raining. I've done all I can do here. Why don't we have a rummage through the stores?"

Imogen led Jo through the rain to the brick-walled nursery west of the Rose Garden, where sheds and glasshouses and cold frames and plunge beds were scattered with a haphazard air, as if they had sprung up over successive decades, as indeed they had. Jo had toured the area previously, and she recognized that the crux of Sissinghurst's success was the range of horticultural techniques Imogen commanded beneath the low-slung roofs of the various sheds. The magnificence of the carefully tended beds — all that most visitors saw of the garden — was inconceivable without the regimented cycles of propagation, potting, cold frame, and division that went on, with only the briefest of pauses in spring planting season, throughout the year.

"This used to be Harold and Vita's kitchen garden," Imogen tossed over her shoulder as she bypassed the Cambridge glasshouse and made for a small tool shed. "Dead useful during the war, of course, but neglected once the two of them passed on. Here we are — mind your head — this is a sad excuse for a lumber room, but we've been forced to make do."

It was a ramshackle wooden building, airless and poorly lit, with a strong suggestion of spiders and other unmentionables lurking in the corners. A wall of boxes, staking materials, and pruning ladders rose before them, cheek-by-jowl with hedge-trimming templates and folded hessian squares. A strong smell of dirt and damp wafted to the nose. Imogen cursed inwardly; surely the place was swept when the boxes were shifted from the old cow barn? But who would expect cleanliness in a tool shed, after all? Not even an American could be so daft.

"This isn't the *working* tool shed, you understand," she told Jo. "Just a place for overflow. Now that The Family have gone all gaga over organic farming we've been forced to bid for space."

"Wasn't there always a farm?"

"Well, yes," Imogen said, "but it was nothing to do with the Trust. The fields were leased, time out of mind, to the same handful of families. Just lately the whole thing's shifted — come under the aegis of the Trust — and the new people snatched up the old outbuildings we'd come to think of as ours. The cow barn, for instance."

Jo glanced around the shed, eyes narrowed against the dusk. "Didn't Vita keep cows?"

"She kept any number of things that couldn't be sustained." Imogen's tone was grudging. "Sheep. Hop fields. The Trust have seen their way clear to pigs."

"You're not enthusiastic."

"Pigs, I ask you! Did they give any *thought*

to how all this clutter *looks* from the garden? Much less smells? Sissinghurst is a cultural gem! With the odor of cow dung wafting over the Rose Garden!"

"I take it the project is recent?"

Imogen glowered with resentment. "Oh, it's *new* all right. That's why everybody's so keen! We're a test case for the National bloody Trust. We're to prove whether *an integrated landscape in balance between cultivation and pleasure can be a self-sustaining prospect.* And without spraying, no less. There was even a BBC special on the telly, waxing lyric about Vita's feeling for the land, when she was the first person to crow about the pleasures of killing weeds with a healthy tot of DDT. Camera crews trudging through the muck down by Hammer Brook and swooning over the frog spawn. Try juggling all *that* internal politics with hundreds of thousands of visitors each year, and see where it puts you."

"Thigh-high in manure," Jo said, with pardonable amusement. "But you're not responsible for the farm?"

"No," Imogen admitted. "I've nothing to do with it, really. There's a separate head, separate staff, separate . . . *world,* really . . . it's just —" She paused, searching for the right words. "I get the concept. I *do.* Grow the food here that we sell to the people who visit. But the visitors come *because of the garden.* Not the pigs. You know what I mean? I just hope the Trust don't lose sight of that."

"It's not like they value the garden less because they've undertaken organic farming, is it?" Jo asked mildly. "Doesn't the farm just add to the whole picture?"

"At some cost," Imogen retorted tartly. "You understand that Trust houses are forced to support themselves? That we're not all the recipients of boundless government largesse? Here at Sissinghurst we've a fixed pool of income — mainly derived from ticket sales to the garden — that's expected to pay all our salaries *and* the Castle maintenance *and* all the expense of keeping the horticultural show going — and we've been lucky to earn a *surplus* over the years. What if the hedges suddenly die or all the glasshouses fall in? Now it's my funds that're being tapped for the *farm* project. I wish The Family had never come up with the idea. You don't have to deal with resident families at your historic houses in the States, do you?"

"Not at all."

"Yes, well — it's a peculiarly English privilege to hand your house over to the

Inland Revenue as satisfaction against taxes, and live there to the nth generation regardless. But we didn't come here to talk about my job — it was the old books you were wanting. We've crates and crates of them here."

She tugged at a chain and a single bulb blossomed into yellowish light. "Pam and Sibylle — the Mädchen — inherited the gardener's books when they came, and kept scrupulous records themselves. I've never had time to go through the lot — though I've *wanted* to, of course. You might find something from the war."

Together they lifted a box at random. Its flaps were taped shut, and neatly penned in black was a date: *1963–65.* "Too late," Imogen murmured, and they retrieved a second one. *1979–81.* A third: *1985–87.* A fourth: *1991–93.*

"When did Pam and Sibylle arrive at Sissinghurst?"

"Nineteen fifty-nine," Imogen answered tersely. "People like to say Vita made the garden, and that's technically true; but those of us who work here know that without Pam and Sibylle, it wouldn't exist. Not in its present form. Ah — this may offer something."

The box was smaller, older, shabbier than

the rest; a box made not of paper, but of wood. A crate, in fact, reinforced at the corners with rusted strips of metal and a lid that had warped from age and weather. A paper label was affixed to its surface with peeling tape; the black ink was blurred. *Miscellaneous.*

Jo knelt on the dirty floor and pried at the lid with her fingernails. It splintered under her hands.

Inside was a heap of what looked like notebooks, some of them bound in leather that was parched and crumbling. She lifted one into the light and carefully turned the pages.

"Vita's garden diary, from 1938."

"Really?" Imogen was suddenly interested. "That should be properly locked away. Most of her originals are kept in archival conditions. I wonder if The Family know?"

"You'd better take it."

"Care to look through it first?"

Jo shook her head. "I'm interested in 1940 and after."

"Vass came over from Cliveden in '40." Imogen flipped through the garden book idly. "Before that, they employed an assortment of locals. That would be why Vita wrote this — she was very much in charge of the garden in 1938."

"Here's something." Jo withdrew a slim little notebook with a bound edge — the sort of copybook a schoolboy might use. Someone had tied string around it, like a parcel. A neat label was affixed to the string.

"Jack's Book," Imogen read aloud. "That would be Vass, then."

"No," Jo replied. Her voice was almost a whisper. "It says *Jock,* not Jack."

Imogen stared at her. Before she could speak, Jo had slipped the string from the slight volume.

"What're you doing?"

Jo held up an open page for inspection: cloudy furls of ink, the paper yellowed with age. "Is that Vita's writing?"

Notes on the Making of a White Garden, it said. And there was a date — *29 March 1941.*

"No." Imogen crouched down to have a better look. "It's not. Don't think it's Harold's either, although I'd have to check. Probably Jack Vass, like I said. Distinctive handwriting, anyway — not just the copperplate people learnt in those days. Is it signed?"

Jo flipped through the pages. There looked to be at least fifty, close-written in the same furled and tentative script: much crossing out and editing of certain lines, a leaf torn straight from the binding here and there.

And every few pages, another date.

"A little over a week," Jo mused, "in the spring of 1941. Not a garden book, but something else. A *diary?*"

Imogen was suddenly conscious of the passage of time; of the darkness beginning to fall beyond the door of the shed; of the staff who'd be finishing elsewhere in the garden, and looking for her.

"Take it with you," she urged. "Have a go tonight, back at the George. You can return it in the morning."

"Thanks," Jo said — and slipped swiftly toward the door, as though afraid Imogen would change her mind. An odd woman, Imogen thought again; if she wasn't on something, she ought to be.

CHAPTER FIVE

29 March 1941
Sissinghurst

NOTES ON THE MAKING OF A WHITE GARDEN

When a body dies the ghost it is said sometimes haunts us. But when a book is read, and shut up and put away, what happens to that ghost? The life we have known solely through words, may yet haunt the mind; it jumbles with our days, becomes something else entirely, unrecognisable.

It would be an achievement, she thought, to be unrecognisable.

It began as the desire for escape — from her husband and the smears of lead on his fingers. From the boiled cabbage smell of the kitchen. From the perpetual fear of the creeping water spreading like infantry across the meadows, creeping up to the house under cover of night. The ruin of the smashed dykes, the water no one could contain. She had

69

never felt safe when the water was rising.

Escape, then, from the dead pages and winter. Put on the old furs, limp as stoats piled carelessly by the gamekeeper's back door — her husband was notoriously mean with his money, he never allowed her to buy anything new, she had to beg for her fare to London sometimes. For weeks, now, in anticipation of freedom, she had been careful with her shillings and pence; she had gone the length of selling ration tickets in the village.

Pull on the stout Wellingtons, smelling of rubber tyres, of warfare and aeroplanes. Take up the walking stick; you might hit him if he comes after you. Hurry, hurry, he's working still before lunch, Hurry up it's time, leave the note with your shaking fingers he will look first above the mantel. I don't think two people could have been happier than we have been. . . . Run from the hanks of wool, sewage-coloured, in the knitting basket beside the chair —

The writing broke off. Or trailed away, perhaps, was more accurate. The whole passage was difficult to read — Jo had to study each word, search for context, and still the writing made no sense. She had expected something forthright, something about Sissinghurst and Jock that would explain her grandfather's suicide.

Carefully, she set the old copybook on her knees and turned a yellowed page. She had bolted her dinner in the George's bar and retreated immediately to her room so that she could open this book. It had seemed wrong, somehow, to leaf through it as she ate her meat pie and the locals pulled their pints. But now, propped up against the pillows, she felt the thin wedge of disappointment. What *was* all this? Should she skip ahead — look for the word *Jock* again, somewhere in the middle?

If it had not been for the bird singing, she might have gone into the water that day. She had been looking for stones to weight her pockets, something heavy, she might have slid them into her Wellingtons. What was it? A thrush? Nondescript, English, like the flooded meadows. Brown as dyke water. Life! it sang. She could not quite meet its sharp black eye. Had the bird flown, leaving her to Fate with an indifferent wing, she would have set her foot upon the muddy bank and closed her eyes.

The bird did not fly.

Life! it sang. Vita!

She gave herself up to the pure liquid sound, so different from the metal drone of aeroplane engines. A great peace descended. It filled up the meadows like clear water. She did not hear the warring voices, accusing, arguing. She did not smell the smears of lead on his fingers. Her sagging flesh. The hopeless despair, heavy as coffins.

Yes, she thought. I shall go to Vita.

And she tumbled the stones from her pocket.

In her bedroom at the George, Jo Bellamy held the fragile notebook directly under the circle of her bedside lamp. The faded chocolate ink — had she read it clearly? The name was certainly Vita. Written with a sharp stab in the initial *V*, the *T* rakishly crossed. The book, and its writer, had found their way to Sissinghurst; and not for the first time, it seemed.

Jo smoothed the crinkled page.

Haste, haste, to the village station. Trudge through the muddy meadows, the path submerged. Tempting, the river always tempting — Swing your stick the bird has flown. Cowering near a platform pillar, hat pulled low. This is no time to smile at the station master, he cares not a snap for your kindness, the entire village thinks you mad. He will read the note when you fail to appear for luncheon. He will come hunting. Lapinova in the snare.

To London, first. The ruins of Mecklenburgh Square. I should like to touch the stones. An ordinary death, a death like anyone else's, it might have been an accident, there was nothing we could do for the lady, sir, she was blown to bits packing books in the cellar —

The Lady.

The simple words pulled Jo's mind from the text and back to Jock: what was it he had written in his wartime letter? Something about the poor lady's huge eyes, how he'd tried to help her, but had only made things worse. "Lady" was a common-enough word; the two references might have nothing to do with each other. But she needed to reread Jock's letter; it was tucked into her suitcase.

The train pulls in with a failing sigh. She mounts the steps of the second-class carriage. The station master is busy with an Important Person, a man for Westminster, all black leather cases, he sees nothing of her treacherous escape. She is mad in any case, the whole town knows. The mad are so difficult except when they write. She takes her seat in the compartment, a seat near the window, her gaze fixed on the countryside. If the bomb fell now and took the train no one could blame her. The station falls back, the speed mounts like a horse between her thighs. He has not looked for her. He has not run screaming behind the train, his right arm raised.

Another ghost, shut up and shelved . . .

"But a ghost from a book?" Jo murmured, frowning. "Or the ghost of someone real?"

She had no idea. The fragments of strange script swirling across the fragile pages might be an attempt at fiction. Or they might be an account of something else. A woman who felt hunted to the point of drowning herself; a woman who escaped in fear. To Sissinghurst?

She flipped to the back of the notebook and felt her stomach plummet.

A chunk of paper had been torn from the spine, wrenched out, it appeared, by a dull knife or a vicious hand. Scrawled on the inside of the back cover were the words *Apostles Screed.* But that was wrong; surely the term was *Apostles Creed?*

The story she'd only just started, had no ending.

The cell phone lying under the circle of light shuddered visibly, skittered on the tabletop, demanded Jo's attention.

"Good evening, Mr. Westlake," she said, with deliberate lightness. As though the formal address could recast their relationship. As though it were still possible to be just a gardener and her potentate.

"It's morning where I am. Where are you?"

"In my room."

"Then I'm not distracting you from work. Good." He paused. "What would you do, Jo, if I showed up on your doorstep?"

"You mean . . . here?" She sat up straighter against the pillows, reached unconsciously to tidy her hair, as though he could see her. "In Kent?"

"Or London. Or the middle of the Atlantic, if you happened to be there."

"Is Alicia flying over for another auction?"

"Alicia's at Canyon Ranch. For the next ten days."

Jo gripped the phone spasmodically. There were several possible meanings behind the careful words. "But you're in Argentina."

"For the next few hours. Then . . . who knows?"

She could almost see him, in that half-remembered, half-imagined way the mind supplies: a wing of dark hair, peppered silver; white cuffs rolled back to reveal his forearms, tanned from sailing. But no — it was morning in Buenos Aires. He'd have his jacket on. A tie, Windsor-knotted. The cell phone resting against his crisp collar . . .

"You want to see the garden?" She was stalling, and knew it.

"I want to see you."

Gray was extremely good at dropping sentences like bombs. Assessing the damage.

"What are you saying?"

He laughed.

That quickly, she could see the quirk of the lips, the amusement reserved for himself alone. The essential unreachability of the man.

"You think I know? What *am* I saying? That if I rang your English bell —"

"— You wonder whether I'd . . . open the door?"

"Exactly."

Jo's gaze drifted over the half-timbered walls, the deep orange of the plaster. It was not a restful room, this hip outpost at the George. Her mind was full of an unknown woman, a hunted creature gone to ground. The impulse to tell Gray what she'd been doing — the research, the notebook she'd found in a dusty cupboard, her grandfather's suicide — was strong. But she couldn't. The world of water and singing birds, train rides to nowhere, had nothing to do with Gray. They'd never talked about her, *Jo.* She'd never told him anything real. They didn't know each other at all. They shared a spark — a sexual frisson of recognition, completely wordless. Gray liked it that way.

Did she?

If she let him in, when he knocked at her door?

Sex. Entanglement. Deception.

And all the possibility of Gray's world. Power. Privilege. Being wanted —

What was she afraid of? *Walking in too deep. The water closing over my head —*

"Jo," he whispered. "Where am I flying tomorrow?"

"Let me sleep on it," she said.

CHAPTER SIX

On Sundays, the people who made the garden their church would wander through Sissinghurst's gates and spend the morning in communion with nature. Imogen Cantwell understood the impulse — the essential piety of the place, particularly on a morning like this, when the rain was done and the October world glowed with color. Her feelings were bittersweet: Sissinghurst was open to the public only another week, and then the massive show she had been sustaining for half a year would be over. Between November and March the castle and its grounds slumbered in winter cold, a private kingdom restored to The Family.

Imogen put in four hours of labor before the opening at eleven o'clock. Three of her staff were set to trimming the massive Irish yews that flanked the Top Courtyard paving; two others were busy at the Powys Wall in the Rose Garden, where the crowning glory of the curving brick, five Perle d'Azur clematis vines, were ruthlessly cut back in preparation for winter. Imogen herself ventured over to Delos, a disconcerting bit of ground west of the White Garden. It had never come together to Imogen's satisfaction, in Vita's day or hers. Vita had thought of it as an Attic Ruin, a place where saxifrages and aubrietias ran wild among massive fragments of masonry, like a windswept terrace on a Greek isle; but most of the rock bits had been carted off by the Nicolson boys in their youth, and the original maze of wandering paths had been tidied over the decades. It was an outer wing of the garden, frequented most often by people who loved Sissinghurst well and had long since surfeited on the stagier parts; these were the sort of visitors who were sometimes discovered long after closing, absorbed in a book amidst Delos's teal-blue bromeliads. This morning, Imogen found Jo Bellamy there.

The American was standing stock-still in the middle of the curving brick path that bisected the Aegean wilderness, and a book did indeed droop from her hands. Oast houses loomed behind her, but there were no hops any longer at Sissinghurst, to scent the air with beer. Jo was studying the rear of the White Garden, or what could be glimpsed of it through a gap in the hedge; taking notes, Imogen surmised. She ought to be nearly finished poaching on other people's grounds.

"Hullo," Imogen called as she swung into view from the Top Courtyard. "Conjuring the Ghost of Gardens Past, are we?"

The American started slightly. "How did you know?"

"You've gone all unfocused about the eyes. Rather like the psychic my batty sister-in-law consults about her children's future. Are you planning to stay on through Visitor Hours? See how the garden bears up under the strain of all those dragging feet?"

Jo smiled faintly. "I've been wondering about that. The grass paths. They must get worn down."

"Special blend of seed," Imogen confided, "and strenuous mowing schedules. We only cut midweek, during Closed Days — gives the turf time to regroup before the weekend onslaught. But you won't have to worry about that. Yours is a private client. A game preserve."

"Yes," Jo murmured.

"Today's almost the last of it, you know." Imogen stabbed the end of her grubbing hoe into a hillock of hellebores. "We shut down next weekend until mid-March, barring the odd festive note at Christmas. I must say I'm looking forward to the peace and quiet — time to concentrate on the *real* business of gardening. Get into the greenhouses and the cold frames. *Propagate.* What about you? Heading back to the States?"

"Next Sunday." Jo stepped toward her. "Can I ask you something, Imogen?"

"Course."

"Did Vita's friends stay here at the castle? For weeks at a time?"

Jo's eyes had gone from unfocused to probing. Imogen wrinkled her brow and glanced away. "Lord! I don't know. She had scads of friends, I should think. Vita was known for collecting people — but you'll have read that, in the biographies."

"Is there any way to find out? — Who might have been here during a particular time frame, I mean?"

"Jo," Imogen said with a sigh, "she died in 1962. Why do you want to know? It has nothing whatsoever to do with the White Garden, surely?"

By way of answer, Jo held out the book she'd been reading. Imogen saw that it was the slim notebook they'd unearthed from the tool shed the day before. "It has no ending."

"Vass's book?"

"Not Vass. Someone else. A woman. Read this section," Jo urged. "I want to know what you think. Whether I'm out of my mind or . . . just *read* it. Please."

29 March 1941
Sissinghurst

London, as it happens, was a mistake.

Big Ben was striking as she stepped into the street. Something solemn in the deliberate swing of the strokes; the murmur of wheels; the shuffle of footsteps. There is much more to be said about us than that we walk the streets of Westminster; but she had loved London in the old days, loved it far more than walking in the country. Her London was gone as brutally as childhood —

Mecklenburgh Square, a jumble of brick and Portland cement. Book bindings scattered like dead leaves. Somebody's old pot resting on a broken pediment. One pigskin glove, lavender-coloured. The air-raid klaxon. The shouts of men in pompous uniforms. Whistles! The granite bulk of Queen Victoria, sandbagged in her chair. The klaxon sounding again and the breathless descent of crowds, flowing like rats into the Underground. She hugged her elbows to her chest as the earth shook around her.

"It was the same with me," Vita said later, when they were tucked up in the sitting room. "There was a filthy run last autumn, the whole world coming to an end and Hadji gone in London. I lay under the bed with the dogs until the bombs stopped falling. Shook for days afterwards. You oughtn't to have gone, truly. One only thinks one can go back. But it is impossible, isn't it? We go only forward."

We go only forward.

The words made her shiver again, now that she was alone in the delicious feather bed, the curtains drawn round. Ben's bedroom, it was, and determinedly mannish; he was attached to the Gunners at Rochester, while Nigel had gone into the Grenadier Guards. Vita worried constantly despite her brisk talk of her brave boys, sound as a bell, doing their bit. She grew anxious by week-end for Harold's arrival, although some Fridays he never got away from the Ministry at all. Aloof as Vita always was, careless of the people she desperately loved — unkind to them even — she'd opened her arms wide for this unexpected visit. Sent a boy to Staplehurst when she got the wire — a lad named Jock, peering through the dusk for this old woman.

He took my stick — I had no bag, it was an embarrassment to me, something that ought to require explanation — but the boy asked for none. Helped me up into Vita's pony trap, the petrol or perhaps the sumptuous car too precious to trust to a schoolboy. Became my saviour, though he can't have known it. A simple boy, dark and serious, with sensitive hands managing the reins.

Vita was quite alone. Gave me sherry, then more of it. Patted the dogs and fed the fire while she let down the blackout shades. "Now then," she said. "What's it all about?" Both of us warm, free of care, snug as Ali Baba in his cave. I took still more sherry. "Life," I said. "Singing life."

"So I gathered, from your wire."

I telegraphed from London. Wrote of the treacherous river, the persistent bird. No time to wait for Vita's answer; the train was leaving. But she had not failed me. The boy, Jock, standing in the station's gloom.

"Now then," she said again, and sat at my feet.

How old we both are! All those years ago, when I first loved her, Vita scared me a little with her riches. Young and ripe as a sheaf of corn. Or a bunch of grapes — that was how I thought of her — the aristocratic mouth, the heavy breasts, the fat pearls she looped about her neck. Her need for love, her pursuit of it despite her children and the demands of public life. Her lordship of the manor. She was like a goddess in those days, Junoesque, heavy and omnipotent with lightning at her command. And now? As spare and wizened as an old strip of saddle leather.

"It was the lead poisoning," she says with her usual carelessness. A bout of illness several years back, something to do with lead in the cider-press; I remember it now. Vita propped up in bed, surrounded by gardening catalogues. Illness stripped the flesh from her bones. Her cheeks are riven with vertical lines, her fingers crabbed from digging. I know the truth: we have both of us been worn down to bones. The loss of too much love, the loss of our singing lives.

"What do you mean to do," she asked me quietly, "now you've really left him?"

"Live," I said.

Imogen Cantwell looked up from the pages into Jo's anxious face. "Devilish hard to read, isn't it? She could have tried for neater handwriting. But I thought it was a garden book — a diary of some sort."

"So did I."

"Why would Vass have kept this?"

"He didn't." Jo reached for the notebook as though she couldn't help herself, couldn't leave it in Imogen's hands a moment longer. "The boy she writes about — Jock — that was my grandfather's name. He would have been seventeen. Sent over from Knole, where he grew up, to work here during the war."

"Ah." Imogen leaned on the handle of her grubbing hoe and studied Jo frankly. "A personal interest, is it? That's why you're so keen to see our records from the forties. It's not about the White Garden at all."

"It may be. Remember the title of this."

"Title?" Imogen frowned. *Notes on the Making of a White Garden.* "You think it's . . . some sort of fiction? But the writer mentions Vita. That's real enough."

"Yes. And she's careful never to mention her *own* name at all. Who would have been close enough to Vita Sackville-West in 1941 to arrive at Sissinghurst on the strength of a telegram, and be immediately welcome?"

"A lover, you mean? Vita took them in scores. Mostly women, though the odd man does come up."

Jo turned the book in her hands. "Only one of them could write like this."

Imogen stared at her, thinking. Like everybody who'd made Sissinghurst their world, she'd learned a lot about The Family along the way. It was impossible to sustain Vita's garden without knowing about Vita herself. She was everywhere: in the roses, the heavy Bagatelle vases that dotted the landscape, the looming shadow of the tower. Imogen had read the biographies. Lord, she'd even read Vita's poetry, which almost nobody bothered with now. What was Jo saying? A lover of Vita's, who'd had the ability to *write?*

"We should tell The Family," she decided. "This might be valuable. If it really *is* . . ."

". . . a lost manuscript of Virginia Woolf's?" Jo finished.

The two women stared at each other in silence. The American's eyes had gone unfocused again, Imogen noticed, and her own mind was racing. *Virginia Woolf.* Vita's friend and correspondent for two decades. Vita's lover, until she moved on to everybody else. A manuscript of Virginia Woolf's, however partial, abandoned in the tool shed with the mice and spiders? Which reminded her —

"So it's not *Jack's Book* written on the notebook label," she attempted, "but *Jock?*"

"I think so."

"How did a gardener's lad get his hands on this?" Imogen demanded. "Oh, Jo. It *can't* be a Virginia Woolf —"

"Imogen," she said hurriedly, gripping the notebook, "I know you've got to tell The Family. I know it's terribly important. I know you owe me nothing — you've already done me several favors, and I'm very grateful. But if you could manage just *one more thing* — if you could give me twenty-four hours, to finish what's here and learn what I can about my grandfather — it would mean everything. Everything," she repeated.

Imogen glanced over Jo's head, toward the oast houses. *Notes on the Making of a White Garden.* Which hadn't existed when this journal was written. What in all that was holy did it mean? And why should she do anything for Jo Bellamy, who kept more to herself than she was willing to share? If it *was* a lost Woolf manuscript . . . and she, Imogen, was credited with the find . . . the publicity would be enormous. For Sissinghurst. For the gardener.

"Can't you ask him? Your grandfather, I mean?"

"He's dead. We found him hanged in the garage. The morning after he learned I was coming here."

"Bloody for you."

"I can't shake the thought that I'm somehow responsible. That the news of this trip triggered his death. Do you see why I *have to know?*"

Imogen shivered suddenly in the October sun; the American's expression was too intense, too painful to bear.

"Twenty-four hours," she relented. "No more. But then you bring that book back, understood? I'm jolly well not going to lose my place over you, Jo Bellamy."

CHAPTER SEVEN

Peter Llewellyn was halfway through his *pain au chocolat* that morning when she walked into the café.

He was late for the Group Meeting. He should have forgone his breakfast entirely; but he had no desire to listen to his Director, Marcus Symonds-Jones, summarize the results of a recent sale. He liked eating his *pain au chocolat* at his usual table in the house café, with a pot of Assam; and why provide Marcus with another opportunity to demonstrate Enlightened Management? Marcus was one of the new breed of directors at Sotheby's UK; he had suffered through a four-day training course in New York last summer, and consequently assured his subordinates that they were All On One Team, Although Competition Among Equals was Quite in Order. Marcus had perfect teeth, which Peter found suspect. He hewed to an extreme of Savile Row tailoring, but affected a proletarian accent. Peter judged him false from shell to core. Marcus was a rousing success at Sotheby's, however; and the slight suspicion that he, Peter, was simply jealous of Marcus's ease, made him vaguely uncomfortable, as when he'd once disturbed a fellow seventh-former wanking off in a neighboring stall. Peter averted his eyes from Marcus when the two came into contact; the Results meeting would be sheer torture, Peter twiddling a pencil between his thumbs as Marcus spoke roundly of Better Than Projected Earnings. Far wiser to finish his breakfast and get on with the appraisal of the Broadwell collection.

Later he grew accustomed to the tentative expression Jo Bellamy wore whenever she was far from a garden; but that morning, as she hesitated in the café doorway, Peter took in the corduroy jeans, the mud-spattered Merrells, and the tied-back hair and concluded that an American tourist had lost her way between the Oxford Street tube station and Thomas Pink's on Jermyn. Sotheby's clients tended to dress for New Bond Street; they were careful to betray their ability to meet their financial obligations, before they breached the doors of the auction house. Whereas this woman's appearance suggested she was in search of cab fare home.

As Peter sank his teeth into his final bite of *pain au chocolat,* however, the stranger met his eyes and smiled. His throat constricted from sheer surprise, and he gagged. Spluttering, he half rose from his table as she hurried toward him.

"Mr. Llewellyn? Are you okay?"

"Fine," Peter gasped, peering at her through his glasses. "But I'm afraid I don't . . . that is, I'm not sure —"

"They told me I'd find you here," she said. "Table in the corner, pastry and tea, blond hair and glasses. I'm Jo Bellamy. Would you have a moment to talk?"

Peter cleared his throat, released the death grip he'd fastened on his napkin, and gestured toward the opposite seat. "Do sit down. Cissy sent you, I suppose?"

"Cissy?"

"Department coordinator." He sketched vaguely at his necktie. "Pearls. Twin set."

"How did you know?"

"The rest of the Department will be in a meeting. I'm playing truant."

"I see." She smiled again as she pulled out her chair, and absurdly, Peter's heart raced. He ought to have drawn the chair *for* her. But perhaps Americans ignored such things. And he was too late, in any case.

"How may I help, Miss . . . ?"

"Bellamy." She slid a large leather shoulder bag to the floor. "I don't really know. I've never done this before. I'm not . . . good at things like auction houses." She glanced around the café apprehensively, as though an alarm might go off; the tentative look was back again.

"You're at a breakfast table, not a preview," he said dryly.

"Right." She drew a breath. "I found something. Something that might be important. Only I don't know. And it's not even mine. In fact, I stole it."

Peter's eyebrows soared. It was not unknown for the more audacious of fences to approach the house with suspect goods; it was not unknown for fakes — art, jewelry, anything of value — to be passed off as original. But such tactics were rarely shouted out loud.

"Sorry?" he said.

"I'm not explaining this right." She blushed and slid a hand over her hair, as though it helped her to think. "Cissy said you were a Manuscript Expert."

"That's a job title here," Peter explained. "It means I sell rare books. In your country, they'd probably call us Specialists."

"Fine." She dismissed job titles. "But can you figure out the identity of an author from just the handwriting? If the manuscript's unsigned, I mean? And how would we *do* that? — Identify it as Virginia Woolf's, say? — Or rule her out entirely?"

"Hang on." Peter raised his thin hands above the table. "What in bloody hell are you on about?"

"This," she replied, and withdrew a shabby notebook from her bag.

Peter did not immediately take it. *Woolf. She had said Virginia Woolf.*

"We could, in time, do all manner of things," he said cautiously. "But what exactly are you *requesting*? A valuation? Manuscript analysis? Sale to the highest bidder?"

"Not that," she said, alarmed. "I told you — this isn't even mine."

"Then any request for service should properly come from the owner. We'd require certain information, obviously, before we could entertain —"

"But I don't *have* information. That's why I'm here. I've got to find out if it was *her*. And I'm running out of time —"

Peter sat back in his café chair and glared at her. "Miss Bellamy, you're not making a good deal of sense."

94

"I found this notebook at Sissinghurst," she said wearily. "And I think it was written by Virginia Woolf."

She set the shabby volume on the white tablecloth between them.

Peter opened his mouth, closed it again. He adjusted his glasses. Then he skimmed the notebook cover with his fingers as lightly as though it were the face of a child.

"One doesn't just *find* things in National Trust houses," he told her quietly. "Not after they've been open to the public for forty years."

"It was in a tool shed with some stuff of the gardeners."

"So?"

"The gardeners' books weren't turned over to the Trust per se. They were passed down. To the current head."

Peter frowned at her suddenly. "To whom *does* this belong? The gardener? The Nicolson family?"

"It should belong to whoever wrote it, right? Or if . . . she's dead . . . then, to whomever she gave the book . . ."

"Are you *attached* to Sissinghurst in an official capacity, Miss Bellamy?"

"Not at all." There it was — the smile, impish and uncontrolled — and the worry drained immediately from her face. "I'm a gardener myself. But visiting, from the States. I should never have seen this."

"Then why —"

"It's a long story. Please." She pushed the notebook toward him. "Could you just . . . *look* at it?"

He did not immediately answer her. Lifting his glasses slightly from the bridge of his nose, he peered intently at the binding. Cheap, medium-brown cotton over boards, the leaves glued rather than sewn. Size, roughly five inches by eight. A school copybook, perhaps of the last century. He lifted the cover, searching for a manufacturer's imprint: *Gould & Tennyson, Liverpool.* He had been avoiding the handwriting itself, on the title page, from fear of disappointment —

Notes on the Making of a White Garden.

It might just be Woolf's, at first glance: the looping, hurried script, certain of the letters elided. It would have to be studied, of course. Compared with known samples. Analyzed —

He glanced at Jo Bellamy, who was looking from the notebook to his face with the eagerness of a puppy.

"Why Woolf?" he demanded. "Merely because she knew Lady Nicolson?"

"Because of the writing," the American replied.

Peter snorted. "Are you going to tell me it's haunting and lyrical?"

She shook her head. "It's . . . insane, actually. Very difficult to understand, in places. I'm not even sure if it's fiction or a diary."

"Rather like most of Virginia Woolf, now that you mention it."

"Exactly!"

They grinned at each other; then Peter's smile faded.

Marcus Symonds-Jones was looming in all his sartorial glory in the café doorway. He wore his most sympathetic and sensitive look, the one reserved for particularly splendid clients; beside him stood Julian Browne, solicitor for the Broadwell family. Whose priceless collection of bound volumes Peter was supposed to be cataloging.

"Look," he told the American as he rose hurriedly, "can you leave this with me for a bit? I'm afraid I've got several pressing engagements this morning, and it won't be possible to —"

"What do you mean by 'a bit'?" she countered. "I've only got a few hours. I'm returning to Kent this afternoon."

"Fine." Peter's napkin drifted to the floor beside his chair; out of the corner of his eye, he could just make out Marcus and the Broadwell nightmare being led to a table at the far end of the room. The doorway was cleared for escape. "You've a mobile number, yes? You'll leave it with Cissy? Know some shops to look into? The V&A, perhaps? Or — you're a gardener! There's always Kew!"

He was nearly out of the café by this time, notebook clutched in his hand; Jo Bellamy looked bewildered, the beginning of alarm on her face. He read the signs — she ought to have got a receipt, what if he absconded with her treasure, which wasn't even *hers* — but it was too late to reassure her; she would just have to take Peter Llewellyn, Manuscript Expert, and the hallowed Sotheby's firm on faith. She would have to wait for his call.

He ducked into the loo conveniently positioned just off the café corridor, and with relief closed a stall door behind him. That made twice in one morning he'd avoided Symonds-Jones. His need for flight — the revulsion driving him from every room his Department Head entered — could hardly be healthy. But he'd experienced a sudden horror at the thought of Symonds-Jones fingering Jo Bellamy's notebook. Symonds-Jones's uncouth vowels pronouncing the elegant little title. Symonds-Jones drawing Jo Bellamy's impish smile. *Absurd.* How had things come to such a pass?

A square of milk glass set into the ceiling — an old-fashioned skylight — cast a grayish halo over Peter's stall. He stared up into the glow, wondering if he'd gone slightly off the rails during the past few months. It was due to the place, he reckoned. The expectations. The persistent sense of inner failure. And Margaux's leaving hadn't helped. He would *not* think of Margaux, the annoying cow. . . . He hadn't been born for this — for the title of Expert. Passing judgment on other people's passions, other people's sins, their hoardings and jealousies and impossible dreams. He would have to get out before he was much older.

But first: the Broadwell collection.

He slipped the old brown notebook into his breast pocket, flushed the loo for the sake of appearances, and prepared to brave the corridor once more.

Jo Bellamy was already trying on women's dress shirts at Thomas Pink's, Jermyn Street. They looked, she thought, like the sort of thing Gray Westlake would wear. But not his wife. Perhaps his mistress . . .

Mistress. What a hideous word.

She was holding a lavender stripe under her chin when her cell phone rang.

CHAPTER EIGHT

"Are you in the garden?" Gray asked.

Jo nearly dropped the phone. Although barely half an hour had passed since leaving Sotheby's, she had expected the voice to be Peter Llewellyn's.

"No," she said abruptly. "I'm at Thomas Pink's. It's a store."

"I know. So you're in London?"

"Just for the morning. I took the train up."

"You must've guessed I'd be here."

The lavender-striped shirt slipped from Jo's hands. Clumsily, she bent to retrieve it. "Gray, you *didn't*."

"I did. Want me to send a car for you?"

"No! I mean — where are you, exactly?" She shoved the slim wooden hanger back onto a rack, aware that she sounded distracted — unwelcoming —— actually put out about this delightful surprise. "It's just that I'm shocked. I never thought you'd really —"

"I'm at the Connaught," he interrupted, that faint ripple of amusement in his dark voice. "Don't move. I'll find you."

She stood there for an instant in the middle of Thomas Pink's. Panic washed over her. *Gray. In London. Which meant* —

He had flown in from Buenos Aires to see her.

For one wild instant, she wished the call *had* been from Peter Llewellyn. But that was nonsense. She closed her cell phone with a snap and went out into the street to wait for the car.

It was a black Bentley. Presumably the Connaught owned it, and lent it to people like Gray when they had to fetch their mistresses from London shops. A chauffeur stood by the open rear door; he was better dressed, Jo reflected, than she was.

"Look at you!"

Gray swarmed out of the backseat. His hand was at her elbow, his lips brushed her cheek. A current of energy ran up her arm. He looked so good — so alive and intensely exciting — when he ought to have been dead tired. How long was the flight from B.A., anyway? But she was forgetting. He owned a jet. One of those things with plush seating and Porthault sheets. He might as well have been sleeping in his own bed at home.

With Alicia, said a voice in her mind.

A slight pressure in the small of her back; he was sweeping her toward the car. It was inexorable. It was unnecessary for her to make a decision; everything had been determined for her. That's how life with Gray was.

Her cell phone vibrated gently in her hip pocket.

She ignored it, and got into the car.

"So why did you leave your castle?" he demanded, once the butler had poured them each a drink and left them alone in the suite. It might have housed ten; Gray had taken it indefinitely. It was possible he'd be there for a week; possible he'd leave tomorrow. Jo sensed that his decision depended upon her.

"Do you really want to know?"

"I don't ask idle questions."

That was true. It was one reason he haunted her — words were rarely wasted around Gray. But they had talked only of gardens for so long; talked of possible paradises, their words a foil for deeper things. They had been groping toward each other, Jo realized, in all those months of planning walls and beds and flowers for different seasons — walking the Long Island acres in the rain, they had been imagining an Eden, their own private landscape. Talking about her grandfather, now — that was different. Jock was reality. How would Gray regard a man who'd fixed tractors for a living?

"I found an unsigned notebook I think was written by Virginia Woolf," she told him. "I brought it to London to be analyzed."

"That's bizarre." He took a sip of wine, studied her over the rim of the glass. "People don't just find lost Woolfs. She's a known quantity. Was it in an antiques shop?"

"A tool shed at Sissinghurst."

"That's even weirder. And you think it's a Woolf because . . . ?"

"Because I'm a hopeless romantic," she replied unexpectedly.

Gray set down his glass. He leaned toward her, his arm reaching along the back of the sofa to caress her shoulder. "Liar. You've never worn pink in your life."

"What's that got to do with it?"

"You wear brown and green and deep russet red," he went on, ignoring her question. "You know where snakes live, and lichen grows. You're a mushroom hunter and a witch of possibility. You make things bloom,

Jo. You're utterly without shit or pretense and *that* is why I'm falling in love with you."

"Gray — you're not —"

"I am," he said. No laughter in his face now; no heavy-lidded desire. Only something like pain; and that, Jo thought, was terrifying. She did not want to cause Gray pain.

"Don't," he suggested, as she looked at him confusedly, "mention Alicia." And then he pulled her close and kissed her.

It was inevitable, Jo thought, from the moment she'd taken Gray's call in the middle of shopping; or perhaps it had been inevitable from the day they'd had coffee alone together, and she'd found him finishing her thoughts before she'd spoken them. As his mouth searched hers in the London suite, she could see the next few hours unroll like a predictable pageant: the intensity of lovemaking (his breathing was already faster as his hand slid over her shoulder), the dining table wheeled into the disheveled room by the discreet and wooden waiters; the champagne, the bathrobes, the steaming tub for two. It would be shocking and exhilarating and more dangerous than anything she'd ever done. And then she would awake the next morning and know that she had destroyed something important — not Gray's

105

marriage, that was his own problem — but something harder to describe. Her self-possession?

What happened to business owners who slept with their clients? What was more important — Bellamy Design, or Gray Westlake?

His fingers tugged at the elastic gripping her hair, loosened her neat ponytail, sent brown strands cascading over her shoulders. For an instant, his eyes studied her, and Jo felt a surge flow upward from her heart: half fear, half desire. Then her lips quirked suddenly in a smile. She couldn't help it.

"Do you always seduce your hired help, Gray?"

"What?"

"Is it noblesse oblige?" she mused. "Something rooted in your earliest ancestors — boinking the serving girl on the back staircase?"

"Jo, *don't,*" he said quietly. "You've never been hired help. You're my true north."

But she *had* begun to question herself, and there were too many interesting answers for a mindless plunge into passion. "Gray," she said briskly, "I'd like some time to think."

"Shit."

He let her go, his face a mix of puzzlement and frustration. Very few women, Jo imagined, were immune to the sort of triple-barreled assault Gray Westlake could bring: All that charm. All that power. All that *money.* She knew she was foolish. She'd probably lose Gray as a client anyway — so why not lose her heart?

Her cell phone vibrated again.

She reached for it, hair sliding into her eyes. Her blouse had come undone and her shoes were scattered. She discovered she was impatient with it all.

"Miss Bellamy?" said a cautious British voice in her ear. "Peter Llewellyn here. I've finished with your notebook."

She glanced at Gray; he was raking his fingers through his dark hair, that look of pain in his eyes again.

"I'll be right there," she said.

CHAPTER NINE

29 March 1941
Sissinghurst
We walked in the garden after dinner, quite late, the Priest's House lowering behind us, no flicker of fire or golden lamp escaping its heavy blackout shades. Vita still talks of bombing runs. She has no idea why I've ceased to fear the Germans.

"Do you see him?" she whispered. She was wrapped up in her sables, her nose emerging from the sumptuous collar like a ship's prow. "He" was a member of the Home Guard, posted nightly in the height of her tower. A spotter. A lookout for the sudden flower of parachutes over the hop fields; for Nazi troop planes vomiting men. How perfect, I thought, as I squinted up at Mr. Home Guard, the band on his arm, the inverted pie-plate of his hat. How perfect that Vita's tower should have its sentry posted once more. The tower and Orlando have been waiting for the enemy all these long years since Elizabeth; waiting for conquest, and night watches, and the Defence of the Realm.

There was no one posted in Sussex that night last November. No one but the dog to sound the alarm when the white silk flowered overhead.

Vita wanted to smoke; I could see the fingers of her right hand twitching where they grasped her left elbow. But she was no fool. Not for worlds would she allow the glowing fag to summon the Luftwaffe.

"There were incendiary bombs in the neighbouring field," she whispered. "Machine gun bullets down by Hadji's lake. Long Barn was hit, did you know that? All those children —"

They have sent the children out of London to havens like Long Barn. The place I loved her first, and best. Bombed, like all the best houses — Tavistock Square, Mecklenburgh.

Here is a partial list of the things Vita needs for survival: *Boots. Breeches. Jerseys. Shirts. Stockings. Sables.*

How like her to put the boots and breeches well before the furs. If the Germans land, she is under orders to load everything into her Buick and get out of Kent. But these are Harold's orders, who is still marooned in London. What else should she take? A Thermos, of course. Hot water bottles. Cigarettes

109

and lighters and matches. Harold's books. Her manuscript of *Grand Canyon.* Her bedroom slippers and a wooden statue of a saint she calls Barbara.

And then there is her bare bodkin, the poison Harold found somewhere. She will kill herself if Mr. Home Guard fails her, and the Germans reach Sissinghurst unannounced.

I am struck, as she talks, by the efficiency of her plans: Orlando at bay. She recruits for the Women's Land Army. She stockpiles straw to make beds for refugees. She agrees to serve as Ambulance Driver for the surrounding countryside, in the aforementioned Buick, which will naturally preclude loading it with sables and turning west. She will never leave Sissinghurst, which makes her resort to the bare bodkin all the more likely. Her lists — the act of making them — are all the salvation she needs.

Whereas I abandoned my life, my clamorous, inchoate mind, without the slightest useful provision. The river, my poison. Stones in my pockets instead of a torch. My furs on my back. I fled the way a child runs from home, expecting to be retrieved and scolded at any moment.

Only Vita never scolds.

She coddles me like a schoolgirl. Murmurs incantations as we stand in the inky garden.

She is talking, I realise, of what she cannot save: this place, the future. Those things she cannot list. This watchtower under the clouded night, the garden she dreamt from the ruins. She will never abandon Sissinghurst, even at the point of the sword. Her survival depends, in the end, on the Germans giving up.

"I wish you could see the tips of the daffodils poking through the soil," she murmured. "I bought scads of them at auction last fall. Also a magnolia, quite a lovely thing, but very slow growing. Hadji says I'm foolish. The whole place could be a ruin in weeks. But I must plant, don't you see? I must continue to believe that things will grow. Spring comes, regardless of the Luftwaffe. Or whether I live or die."

"The earth takes in our bones — and gives back the magnolia."

We picked our way through the beds near the Priest's House, where she and Harold take their meals. Roses, of course, everywhere — a nightmarish landscape in this season and the dark. Stiff, brutal canes like barbed wire. Leafless. I thought of trenches. The dead. Earth torn by shrapnel. Thorns. Crucifixions —

"No light," I said, my words thick. Panic in my throat. The man falling through darkness.

"Hadji painted all our torches blue last

autumn, when we cared about the blackout. So now I dispense with light altogether. Like a cat. And I've walked this path from dinner to bed countless times in the dark. Look!"

She seized my wrist and held me there. I lifted my gaze from the trenches and the sick barbs of stillborn roses, and saw it.

The great ghostly barn owl, drifting overhead. White as a wraith, silent as Nemesis.

"Isn't he *gorgeous,*" Vita whispered.

The Home Guard had missed this pair of wings. We kept the visitation to ourselves. And absurdly, I felt my heart lift. Sweeping through the air — Life! Life! Life! — impervious to despair. Its pale shade a taunt to the Luftwaffe.

"It glows," I said.

"Doesn't it just!"

I glanced around. "You should have white flowers here. Nothing else. They'd rise in the dark like fairy lamps, lighting your way to bed."

"*Lilium regale,*" she said. "Hadji loves them. Only not here — I thought perhaps in the Lion's Pond. Vass drained it."

"The Lion's Pond gets no sun."

Her eyes narrowed. "That's what Hadji said! Have you been writing to my husband?"

Harold and I, in mutual sympathy? No. He is a man, after all, and their instinct is mastery —

"White clematis. White lavender, white aga-panthus, white double-primroses. White anemones . . ."

Lists, again. How they comfort her.

I wanted to tell her she would never do it, with this constant maddening threat of war. She could not buy plants or the petrol to fetch them or the labour to thrust them into the earth, but the idea of all this whiteness was vital to her — a cleansing impulse, a need for clarity. Light in the darkness. How obvious it seems, how clumsy, how necessary.

"Is Vass still here?"

She shook her head. "Called up and gone the next day. But I have a boy — a good, sensible, Knole-bred boy, sent over for the duration. You met him yesterday."

The tall, silent one standing with his cap in his hands at the Staplehurst station. "Jock?"

"My faithful terrier. He worries about me, did you know?"

"He'll be off to war one day, too."

"Not if I can prevent it." Her voice was tight with suppressed anger. Fear for her own boys. Ben flying low over batteries, skirting the radar. The horrible deaths we witnessed in the last war. Trenches. Barbed wire. The trenches are flooded and our feet are rotting. How the water calls to me with babbling Death —

"His hands are too fine," Vita said. "There's suffering in them."

In all our hands.

We did not speak until we reached the South Cottage.

CHAPTER TEN

Peter Llewellyn stood waiting outside the auction-house entrance. The change in his expression when Jo pulled up in the borrowed Bentley — there were mini Connaught flags flying from the headlamps, as though she were a Head of State — was comical to behold.

"Shall we take tea?" he asked once the chauffeur had evicted her to the paving and resumed his privileged post behind the wheel.

"Sure. I could use a little caffeine. I'm not used to wine in the middle of the day."

"That's rather reassuring, in the circumstances. That you *aren't* a habitual drinker, I mean. Walk or taxi?"

She'd expected Sotheby's café again. "Let's walk."

They set off down New Bond Street, Jo conscious of a sudden shyness. It had been an unsettling day. And there was all of

London around her — this extraordinary city — the strangeness of the man beside her, kind as he was; the unexpectedness of Gray, waiting for her in an empty hotel suite.

"Do you like macaroons?" Llewellyn asked unexpectedly.

"Very much."

"Smashing. We'll have lots, shall we?"

She smiled, then noticed how he ducked his head as though from a physical blow; Americans, she recalled, were accused of smiling too much. She would have to curb her impulse in the future.

"You mentioned you were done with my notebook," she ventured.

"I did." He walked swiftly, with his blond head slightly bowed; a slim figure, unconsciously graceful. He might almost have been striding along alone — except that she was aware of him almost imperceptibly shepherding her through the crowd. "Miss Bellamy, would you describe yourself as a person of *integrity?*"

"Does my tea depend on it?"

He grimaced. "I'm feeling rather as though I've gone out on a limb. I don't suppose you understand me."

"You want to know if I'm honest." She tried to think objectively. "I have a great deal of integrity about my work — getting it right, for myself and the people who hire me. I would *like* to think I treat the people I love with honesty. But . . ." She hesitated, aware of conflict in her soul, Gray hovering over her. "I'm not perfect. I make mistakes. All the time."

"Which is in itself the most honest thing you could say. Thank you."

They dashed through traffic in Piccadilly and then into the Burlington Arcade. He was leading her to a place called Ladurée, a bright shining birdcage of a room filled with pastel-colored French pastries, melt-in-the-mouth macaroons for which Paris was famous.

"Opened recently," Llewellyn murmured. "We're not too sure about it. Londoners, I mean. Suspicious of anything too French. I got over that, myself, years ago."

They chose a plateful of exotic flavors from the rows of coat-button–size confections and sat down at a tiny table, their knees almost touching, to wait for a pot of tea. When it came, Jo closed her eyes and allowed the bergamot fragrance of Earl Grey to drift to her nostrils. "I should bring some of this home to my grandmother. She loves British tea."

"*Masterpiece Theatre* fan?"

"Military nurse. She was stationed here

for years during the war. Never got over it."

"Ah!" His expression, which had been curiously concentrated when he looked at Jo, suddenly relaxed. "That's all right, then. I suppose she gave you this?"

He had drawn the notebook out of his coat pocket and held it before her like a flag.

"Nana? How could she? I found it at Sissinghurst!"

"So you said." Llewellyn lifted the teapot carefully and refilled his cup. "Only, you see, it doesn't work. I wish it did, because you've said you're honest and I like you, Miss Bellamy. I'd hoped we could deal frankly with one another."

Jo felt her face suffuse with heat. Carefully, she set down her half-finished macaroon and wiped her fingers on her napkin. "I don't lie, Mr. Llewellyn. What about the notebook *doesn't work?*"

"It doesn't square with the evidence, I'm afraid. The historic record of Woolf's life." He took a sip of tea. "Whoever wrote this went to a great deal of trouble — the notebook itself is authentically of the period, the ink is probably prewar, although we'd have to verify that chemically; the language is similar to the sort of stuff Woolf wrote to be *just* plausible —"

"Then why —"

"Indeed, certain phrases and passages might almost have been lifted straight from her work — and probably were," he added hurriedly. "Then there's the references to Lady Nicolson and her family, their shared past, Woolf's novel *Orlando,* which is dedicated to Vita — and so on and so forth."

"So what's —"

"It's clearly a forgery, I'm afraid."

"Why?"

"You honestly don't know? You never noticed?"

Jo frowned.

"Open to the first page, Miss Bellamy, and read out the date."

She did as she was told.

"Twenty-nine March 1941," she read, *"Sissinghurst.* What's so wrong about that?"

Llewellyn leaned across the table. His gray eyes were studying her with something like pity. He had not touched his macaroons.

"Do you know when Virginia Woolf drowned herself in the River Ouse?"

Jo shook her head.

"The day *before* your notebook starts — March twenty-eight, 1941."

Chapter Eleven

30 March 1941
Sissinghurst

She woke me this morning with such an expression of worry that at first I thought I had offended her, from staying abed so late into the morning. I had been drowning in sleep for hours — down, down, into the depths of this feather bed, its curtains pulled close, like a Tudor princess sacrificed to policy — never in recent memory have I slept so sound. The voices in my head banished sleep, a constant argument overheard on the Tube, a BBC broadcast perpetually in the background, an intimate whisper of invective and abuse. I could not write for their clamour in my ears —

"He has written to me," she said. "There — you may see the letter. It's quite dreadful, darling."

I knew the hand. I did not have to take it to see who it was — why my Vita was agitated so dreadfully. L. is a terrible scold. With the

best intentions in the world — the preservation of genius — he will drive one to the edge
of insanity, and observe as one falls over.
Waiting with his net. Waiting with his snare.

I am never so much L.'s own, as when I am
mad.

It is the kind of mastery he craves; all our
friends, cooing with sympathy: *You have
preserved for the world her genius what would
she have done without you we should never
have known Mrs. Dalloway and To The Light-
house!* And I, dutiful child, nod swiftly and say
to them all: I have been so very happy with L.
So good to me, always.

"I won't read it," I said, thrusting back the
covers. I fancied I saw him folded up quietly
in a corner of the room, thin knees tucked in,
watching me. He was smiling; there was intent
behind his eyes, some devilment. "I shall
simply pack my things and go. You won't
betray me?"

"Darling, you don't understand." Vita sank
down onto the bed, the letter slack in her
fingers. "He has told everyone you're dead.
That you killed yourself. He intends to send
the information to *The Times.* Apparently
they're dragging for your body, back at Rodmell . . ."

My body.

The chuckling brown water, inviting me.

121

Seducing me. Dragging at my thighs. And but for the bird singing *Vita!* I might have plunged in.

"What did you write," she said, "in that letter you left him?"

"Merely that I could not go on. That I felt I was going mad again. That he would be better without me — able to work. That no one had been kinder."

Vita snorted. "He took it as Farewell — when you simply meant farewell. How you've made him wretched, darling. Should you like me to telephone from the village?"

"So you see," Peter Llewellyn was saying apologetically, "it's quite impossible. She was drowned the day *before* the journal begins."

"All right," Jo admitted, "I never focused on the dates. I didn't buy a biography of Woolf in a bookstore and check when she killed herself. It never occurred to me. My interest in this is secondary —"

"What *is* your interest, Miss Bellamy?"

It was a way of asking the question he'd been avoiding, Jo realized: *Are you a crook, Miss Bellamy? Are you attempting a massive literary fraud and hoping to use me as your dupe?*

It was kind of Llewellyn, she thought with

a rush of gratitude, not to have said all that outright. His tact impressed her as fundamentally decent, as optimistic regarding the goodness of other people — knowing what he did about the dates, he could so easily have thrown the notebook in her face on the paving outside Sotheby's. Instead, he had invited her to tea.

"My interest is . . . much more personal," she stammered. "I don't really want to go into it. But I promise you it has nothing to do with making money or anything like that. It's . . . a family issue."

"A family issue."

She could tell from his careful expression that he didn't believe her. "Look, Mr. Llewellyn — maybe Virginia Woolf didn't write this notebook. Maybe she really *did* drown the day before it begins. But what if she didn't go into the water on March twenty-eight? What if she just walked to the local train station and skipped town instead?"

He smiled faintly. "But her body was pulled out of the River Ouse, Miss Bellamy. It's one of those unavoidable facts. She tried to kill herself as early as 1913 and she'd been thinking about drowning for a while before she did it — her suicide note was dated several days *prior* to the twenty-eighth.

She even did a test drop, apparently, and came home soaked to the skin. Leonard wasn't noticing."

"Leonard?"

"The husband. Leonard Woolf. One of the great literary minds of Bloomsbury — all but overshadowed by his wife."

"You don't like her, do you?" Jo said suddenly.

Llewellyn's eyes slid away from hers; he looked uncomfortable. "I was forced to eat, drink, and sleep Virginia Woolf for a time, and it rather soured me on her worldview. One becomes impatient. With all the dramatizing. With the idea that writing is akin to madness. Or, perhaps, that being female is a constant state of persecution —" He halted, as though entangled in impossible thoughts. "Sorry."

"There's something fierce about this book," Jo said. "Something fearless, too — as though she knew death was coming for her, and was determined to outrun it."

"But Virginia Woolf didn't *write* that book." He pointed it out gently.

Jo sat back and stared at Peter Llewellyn. She was not going to move him. He was the Expert, after all; and he had made up his mind, drawing on a wealth of knowledge and expertise of which she could have only the barest idea. And with that recognition, she felt like a foolish child. She was embarrassed — by how naively credulous she had been, how much time she had wasted.

She set her neatly folded napkin at her place, along with a ten-pound note, and rose from the table.

"Miss Bellamy!"

"Yes?"

He was holding out her money. "Don't insult me, please."

"Consider it a fee for your appraisal."

"Now I *am* insulted." He thrust back his chair, walked around the table, and took the notebook from her hands. Opening the cover, he tucked the ten-pound note inside, and returned the book gravely.

Jo held out her hand. "Thank you for your time. I'm sorry it was worthless. The notebook, I mean."

"Pleasure," Llewellyn said.

She wove swiftly away from him, past the delicate little tables, and pushed through Ladurée's door, almost blinded now by unexpected tears. What was wrong with her? Jet lag? Gray and his assumptions in that suite at the Connaught?

No — it was bottomless disappointment.

She had snatched at the shabby little book as though it were a talisman, a gift from beyond the grave that might unlock the secrets her grandfather had refused to tell. Jock's notebook had given Jo hope: that there was a *reason* for the suicide she found so inexplicable. When in fact it was just another symbol of all she did not know. And her hope had been squandered. She spent so much time copying other people's work, it seemed, that she couldn't tell the difference between real and fake anymore. She wasn't equipped for the mission Nana had given her; she'd be lucky if she could manage to rip off the White Garden during her last few days in England, and get home with her landscape business intact.

Oh, God, she thought, missing her grandfather acutely. *If only I could talk to Jock. My worst mistakes were never this stupid, when he was there to comfort me.*

She'd come out of the Burlington Arcade onto Jermyn Street, instead of Piccadilly, and for an instant she was confused; but any taxi could get her back to Gray's hotel. She had only to flag one of the lumbering black cars and be safe. Except that she didn't want to see Gray right now. Not with this sharp bone of disappointment lodged in her throat. She couldn't begin to tell him what the notebook meant to her; she couldn't pretend, either, that it meant nothing at all.

I should just fly home, she thought despondently, *and accept that I'll never know why Jock gave up on life.*

A glimpse of green in the distance beckoned — a park. At the moment, all Jo wanted was a broad path under the shade of trees; the smell of damp earth; a few pigeons; possibly the sound of water. She had always gone to ground in gardens when her heart was aching.

And so it was on a bench in Green Park that Peter Llewellyn found her a few minutes later, absorbed in rereading the anonymous notebook.

"Miss Bellamy."

"What are you doing here?" she asked.

"You looked quite sad when you left the tea shop." He sat down beside her. "It's the family issue, isn't it? I wanted to be sure you were all right."

She hesitated, and then thought, *Why not?* There was something comforting about Peter Llewellyn — something akin to a Father Confessor. "How much of this have you read?"

"I skimmed a bit. Out of curiosity."

"Did you notice the name Jock?"

"The gardener's lad?"

"He was my grandfather."

Llewellyn whistled softly.

"When I found this book, there was a tag tied around it with string. Written on the tag was *Jock's Book*."

She told him then about the suicide two months before, and the war letter Nana had found. "I don't know how this book came to have his name on it, or why he left it at Sissinghurst," she concluded. "I will never know why Jock killed himself. But for a few days, I believed this book might be a clue. Can you understand that learning it's fake is like learning Jock's dead, all over again?"

"Absolutely," he replied. "You're coming to terms with a dead end. Which should lead you to the next turning in the maze, shouldn't it?"

She studied him dubiously. "What are you trying to say?"

"At a glance, the notebook itself — paper, binding, and ink — is quite possibly of the Second World War period. Could your grandfather — this Jock — have written it?"

Jo shook her head. "It's not his handwriting. Or, for that matter, his level of sophistication. I don't see him casting himself as a character in a book about Virginia Woolf and Vita Sackville-West, much less writing it. At seventeen, he wouldn't have known enough about their relationship or history."

"Very well. Did anybody at Sissinghurst — someone familiar with the place, mind — shove you in the right direction? To stumble over this book, I mean?"

"Imogen," Jo said suddenly. "The Head Gardener. But she knew nothing about my grandfather —"

"You never mentioned him?"

Of course she had. They'd talked specifically about Jock and the war. Even in her initial letter, Jo had referred to her grandfather as a Kentishman. Was it beyond the realm of possibility that Imogen had researched the name before Jo even arrived? Had she found a Bellamy who'd been at Sissinghurst, and constructed the whole packet of lies for her to find?

"But *why?*" Jo demanded. "Why would she bother? She doesn't know me. It doesn't make sense."

Llewellyn smiled faintly. "Are you aware that the National Trust is in financial straits? Too many great houses, too many gardens, not enough funds to keep them staggering along? Perhaps your Imogen has a mania about Sissinghurst — or keeping her job."

"She did say she was worried about the Trust's priorities," Jo said. "Funding issues. She seemed to think that the garden at Sissinghurst was suddenly eclipsed by some project with the farms."

"Perhaps this woman thought a remarkable find — the sale of your notebook for millions — would put the White Garden in the headlines," Peter suggested. "For plausibility, she used a complete stranger as errand girl."

Jo considered Imogen Cantwell's potential for dark conspiracy, and failed utterly to believe it. "But what about the letter my grandfather left behind? Or his references to the Lady?"

"Coincidence?"

She bristled. "Coincidence! Across six decades and two continents? Surely there must be a better explanation, Mr. Llewellyn."

"And you can't help believing that it's the one you started with."

"Despite the excellent advice of my Book Expert."

"You honestly think that Virginia Woolf left her home and her husband of thirty-odd years, hared off to Sissinghurst, and mooned about her marriage in the midst of the Blackout? — Where she simultaneously met your grandfather as a lad and came up with the idea for the White Garden? — Before jumping into the Ouse, regardless?"

"Maybe she was pushed."

Peter Llewellyn laughed. It was an unexpected sound; and it betrayed to Jo that he was less certain than he seemed. "You have the oddest way of stumbling over bombshells, Miss Bellamy. You did the same thing in the tea shop, you know. And I confess you set me to thinking."

Jo felt a flutter of hope, and repressed it. "About what?"

"Your notion that Virginia might have walked to the train station instead of ending it all on the twenty-eighth of March."

"You said she'd been trying to drown herself for days, thank you very much."

"But that's irrelevant, in the end." Llewellyn stabbed distractedly at his glasses. "What counts are the days *after* the twenty-eighth, not the days before. And nobody can say absolutely *where* she was afterwards."

"I don't understand."

"It took weeks for Virginia's body to surface in the Ouse, you see," Llewellyn continued. "It's believed she fetched up against a bridge rampart and was pinned below the water. For nearly a month, as I recollect. Well into April, in any case."

Jo's heart accelerated. "So if they didn't find her body the day she left home, she might have gone into the Ouse at any time."

"Exactly. She might have taken your

cherished train after all. And landed in Kent, where she met your grandfather." There was an unwilling note of excitement in the Book Expert's voice.

"Did anyone at Sotheby's study this handwriting?" Jo demanded. "— Somebody who could say definitely whether it's Woolf's?"

Llewellyn took the notebook from Jo's hand. He peered at the soiled brown cover.

"You can't imagine what this process is like, can you? I'd have to formally accept the manuscript with all sorts of papers you'd be required to fill out, proving your ownership of the article in question and your right to request such an analysis. Only you and I both know you *don't* own the article in question. The notebook would be entered in our computers. Submitted with forms to the correct departments. *It would be catalogued and known.* Then Marcus Symonds-bloody-Jones would be all over it. Ringing up his friends in the press, contacting private collectors — universities and libraries all over the world . . ."

"Who is Marcus Simmon-Jones?"

"Symonds," he corrected. "A perfectly loathsome individual who orders my life and half of Sotheby's. The point, Miss Bellamy, is that if your notebook's *in the system,* it automatically moves *right out of your control,* do you understand?"

"Which means?"

"That if this notebook is indeed what you think — if Woolf wrote it when she was believed to be dead — if she was alive after she left Leonard and came to her end in a different manner than history records — if this journal is *not a fake,* as I admit I'm beginning to wonder —"

"Why?"

He halted in mid-speech and studied her.

"Because you're so damnably plausible," he said at last. "Nobody invents a suicidal Kentish grandpa. Because I *want* to believe you're as honest as you seem. Which is the very worst reason to doubt my judgment that I can think of. It's pathetically subjective. And a Book Expert ought to be *objective,* always —"

"Thank you."

He nodded brusquely. "As I say — if any of this is remotely true, then you have the find of the century on your hands."

"We," she corrected, springing to her feet. "*We* have the find of the century. And you don't want to lose control of that?"

"Do you?"

"Not until I know what part Jock played in all of it," she answered decisively.

"And if the truth is something you don't want to hear? — the truth about your grandfather, I mean?"

"It can't be worse than what he's already done. I'll deal with whatever comes."

"Very well." Llewellyn rose from the park bench and held out the notebook. "If you go back to Kent, you might as well advertise this little item stark naked in Piccadilly Circus. The Family at Sissinghurst will pursue this themselves."

He was right. He was absolutely right. The book wasn't hers. She had no right to it. But she couldn't just . . .

"I can't just steal this!"

He glanced at her sidelong as he sauntered back toward the Green Park gate. "I thought somebody'd lent it to you."

Twenty-four hours, Imogen had said. *No more. I'm jolly well not going to lose my place over you.* Imogen would be furious if Jo failed to appear, notebook in hand. She'd wonder. Become suspicious. But should Jo trust Imogen? What if the Head Gardener *had* deliberately used her?

"The notebook was lent to me — but only in a manner of speaking."

"Good. That's settled, then. I've a car in Sotheby's garage. We can be off in minutes."

"You're driving me back to Kent?" But

what about Gray — the Connaught — all the unanswered questions . . .

Llewellyn turned at the edge of Jermyn Street. "I'd rather drive to Oxford, actually. The best Woolf expert in England is there. Will you come with me, Miss Bellamy?"

Another expert. Who might tell them, once and for all, that the notebook was nonsense. But she would have to risk it; she *had* to know.

"I think you'd better call me Jo," she told him.

Chapter Twelve

31 March 1941
Sissinghurst

"I must write *something* in reply," Vita protested this morning, when we had taken our tea and bread in the Priest's House, with its trestle table and painted cupboard, its heavy drapes of velvet. Watery sunshine through the leaded windows, the dourness of Sunday gone like a passing thought. Vita's Alsatian trotting across the barren steppe of the roses, narrow shoulders slumped in misery. There had been two of them once, hadn't there? The loneliness of the left-behind.

"To Vanessa, as well," she persisted. "Did I mention I've also had The News from your sister, in this morning's post? — You left a note for her, too, I presume?"

"I hoped she'd comfort Leonard. Tell him he did all he could, always."

"Then you lied, dearest. The failure of a marriage is never one person's fault."

"I ought not to have married him."

She laughed. "It's a practice I can't recommend to those who like having their own way!"

"Then why did you do it?"

She moved restlessly towards the window. "Good Lord — only think how Hadji and I live! In our separate spheres. I never go up to London if I can help it, unless it's to talk about marriage for the BBC. He comes down on the odd week-end and digs the garden; we each have our studies where neither may enter; and the boys take care of themselves. That's why I'm devoted to Hadji — he has never interfered in my splendid realm, but he adds to it immeasurably. Rather like a prime specimen tree set off to advantage by surrounding bed-fellows. What shall I tell them, your helpmeet and sister? That you're alive and well and breakfasting somewhere near Cranbrook?"

"You're lucky, Vita. You haven't the hatred that spoils relationships. Or the need either."

"I'm a cold fish, in other words?"

Vita, who will sit at my feet and allow me to brush her hair? Vita of the sensual eyes and drooping mouth? "Coldness . . . that's a word for me, not you. I'm girlish, Leonard says. Inviolate. *Impenetrable.* When what he means is cold. Vanessa says it, too."

"He tried, I suppose? Early on?"

I knew what she meant. The maidenhead. Impenetrable. My frantic anxiety those nights in France, the misery of his hands, our honeymoon, my every muscle flexed and fighting him.

"I was such a coward, a sexual coward. Don't you see," I went on, "— what we desire in others is what we lack in ourselves? And end up resenting. Hating. I have hated Vanessa for her children — even when poor Julian was killed, I envied her grief. Leonard —"

"Was *never* in love with his wife's sister."

"No. That was my crime. I fell in love with Clive."

"Oh, darling — call it *wanting,* surely? Not love. An hysterical impulse. *'I must have what Vanessa has. I must have it.'* Fairly typical of the age, I should think. And of sisters."

I worried a bread crumb with my fingernail. Vita was lavish with butter; we never saw it in Rodmell unless Vita sent it; she kept cows. They would be dead soon if the Germans landed, stomachs bloated and hooves sticking straight up into the air. "To cast out and incorporate in a person of the opposite sex all that we miss in ourselves and desire in the universe and detest in humanity is a deep and universal instinct on the part of both men and of women."

"You're quoting somebody."

"Myself. I wrote it ages ago." I unfolded from the table, drifted towards the garden door. "Send whatever you think proper to Vanessa and Leonard. Condolence. Sympathy. Guilt-ridden regret."

"You want me to pretend you're dead?"

"Maybe I am. Haunting Sissinghurst. A pale shade in a paler garden."

"You're very cruel, you know."

"I was taught to be."

She said nothing as I went out. Not yet noon, and already Vita reaches for the sherry decanter.

I stood at the gate to the north of the Priest's House; there is a statue worth looking at, half visible from here. My arms wrapped in my cardigan. Shivering. The Little Virgin, Vita calls her. Cold as lead. Draperies swirl about her knees, coy, suggestive. She is not for touching. I wish to be dead to Leonard and Vanessa.

The boy Jock was working in the garden — a barrow, hoe, tip basket, secateurs. Whistling. Free of war or marriage. Thinking only of green. Morning, he said. Was it still morning? He tipped his cap. Brought up to do so, I suppose, by his mother at Knole. *Tip yer 'at to the lady, now, Jock, there's a good boy.* And Vita hardly aware of them as she passed, trailing scarves and scent, her lambskin gloves clutched in one hand, bent on the car waiting in the drive —

"Fine morning," the boy said. Polite, but cautious.

I suppose the morning was fine. Sunlight and cold. I hugged my cardigan tighter. The crabbed claws of my hands searched for warmth. I ought to have put on my coat. I did not want to go back inside and learn what Vita was writing to them.

"You've a good deal to do here," I said neutrally.

"That I do, ma'am. But I was bred up to it," he replied, leaning on his hoe. "It's a garden worth the labour — not so grand as Knole, perhaps, but more human. Her ladyship understands the way things grow. I like to learn from her, when she can spare the time. It's a good place — provided Jerry leaves it be."

Jerry. Germans. The Home Guard at night.

"Do you stand watch in the Tower?" I asked.

He shook his head regretfully. "I've another year yet. Foolish, if you ask me. I'm old enough to do my bit."

"You're doing it here."

He grinned — and with a jolt I was reminded of Thoby, the years at Cambridge, his rooms with Leonard, Vanessa and I in our white dresses, the Apostles, the boats on the River, Rupert Brooke swimming, his body a god's but not for me; I swam like a swan with my head in the air, both of us writing poetry at that house on the riverbank. Thoby. Thoby. Who died too young and bequeathed his sisters to his friends . . .

"Ma'am," the boy was saying. "Are you all right? You'll catch your death of cold."

He had abandoned the hoe and was standing before me, slightly taller than I, sturdy, a line of worry between those clear brown eyes. He almost, but not quite, reached a hand to my elbow. As he might have to his grandmother. I wanted him to touch me. I wanted Thoby's hand on my arm.

"I shall go in."

"That's right," he said encouragingly. "You go in, now, ma'am. The dog will go with you; she needs the warm."

He was talking about the Alsatian, I realised, who had fallen in a heap at my feet.

"Not the same since that Martin went. It's early days yet."

"Martin?" I repeated.

"T'other dog. Her la'ship had to put him down, a week or so since; attacked the neighbour's prize hound."

I touched the dog's silky head; she thrust her nose into my palm.

141

"Shot Martin herself, la'ship did. It fair went to her heart. That's why I'm glad you've come, ma'am. She won't take so much of that sherry, now you're here."

Vita would be appalled if she knew how much this boy sees. The trailing scarves, the scent, the lambskin gloves — and yet he penetrates to the core of iron, Orlando on the battlements, shooting her dogs and keeping tight hold of her bare bodkin against the German advance. Alone and depressed in the blackout night, her decanter uncorked in South Cottage, silent except for the drone of planes.

The great ghostly barn owl flitting over the blackened garden.

"Come along, then," I said gently to the inconsolable dog, who gathered herself and followed me inside.

CHAPTER THIRTEEN

"Ever been to Oxford?" Peter Llewellyn asked as they forged west through London traffic toward the M40.

Jo was inclined to say: *I've never been anywhere,* but instead she settled for a shake of the head.

"It sometimes disappoints. People seem to expect an Austen film. Or *Brideshead.* When in fact Oxford is fairly urban. Americans like Cambridge better — it suits their idea of what an English university *should* look like."

He was just making conversation, she realized; talking about anything rather than the quest that had propelled them from Sotheby's front door. Already, Jo was regretting the impulse. She had completely abandoned Gray Westlake — who had flown six thousand miles solely to see her — and that complication, Gray in the solitary splendor of the Connaught, nagged at her. He was waiting. She should call. He was her client, for God's sake. He had said he was falling in love with her. *In love with her.* No. It made no sense. *Integrity,* Peter Llewellyn had said; a difficult word. How did you deal honestly with a client who wanted you, body and soul? Something had to be compromised. Your business, your heart, your whole life . . .

"— wonderful place not far from town," Peter was murmuring. "You've heard of it, no doubt. Le Manoir aux Quat' Saisons. Margaux and I took the cooking class with Raymond Blanc —"

Who was Margaux?

Who was Raymond Blanc?

She pulled her thoughts back to the car. Time enough in Oxford to let Gray know where she was. How long could this consultation take? She'd be back in London by dinnertime. At which point she'd simply tell him: *Gray, this will never work. I'm uncomfortable with the blend of business and pleasure. . . .* Her heart somersaulted with desire and regret. Was she insane, to be pushing a man like Gray Westlake away?

I'm not ready. She didn't think of herself as somebody who'd steal another woman's life. And she would never want Alicia's life, anyway. She wanted her own. But *Gray —*

144

". . . she ought to be able to spare us an hour. Given what it might mean. For *her* career. As well as ours," Llewellyn concluded.

He glanced at Jo expectantly, and his expression changed. "I say — are you all right?"

"I haven't heard a word," she told him truthfully. "You'd better start over."

Peter, it seemed, had studied English literature at a college with the odd name of Maudlin.

"It's spelled like the Fallen Woman in the Bible," he explained, "but pronounced like a lapse in good taste." From the offhand and apologetic way he described his years there, Jo concluded it was a great honor to have studied at Magdalen, and that he'd done uncommonly well. She detected, however, disappointment in Peter — that the best years of his life were behind him? That all his hard work and passion for words had ended in a desk at Sotheby's? Books, he explained, weren't what they used to be. Collections — the aristocratic hoard of rare first editions, lovingly bound in calf and tooled with gold, arranged on the polished shelves of spectacular libraries — were impossible for most individuals to maintain. They hadn't the interest, Peter said. Books went to universities, or national libraries with climate-controlled, hermetically sealed chambers designed for the preservation of paper. New money, when it logged onto the bidding website at Sotheby's, preferred to splurge on wine.

"Burgundies," he added gloomily. "And, of course, your subscription-only Cabernets. Can't say I blame them. There's nothing like a smashing glass of red."

The Book Expert, Jo gathered, was unhappy. And she suspected the woman named Margaux was partly to blame.

Not that Peter would admit it. He was too careful, still, for confidences. But Jo sensed an uneasiness whenever the English professor's name came up, as though Peter were two-stepping around a land mine. *Margaux Strand.* Literature don, Magdalen College. He'd known her for years, ever since they were at school together.

"First-rate in her field, Margaux is," he said with forced enthusiasm. "A Feminist interpreter, of course. Edits a journal on Women's Fiction. An acknowledged Woolf expert." They were cruising toward the Oxford skyline, Peter pointing out the dome of the Radcliffe Camera. "Margaux will tell us whether we've got something explosive

146

in your notebook — or just a bomb."

She'd prepared herself for grandeur — that was implicit in the idea of Oxford — but the quiet beauty of Magdalen took her completely by surprise. The college was at the end of the High Street, rising from a park that flanked the River Cherwell; a narrow bridge of Cotswold stone spanned the water, and punts lined the grassy bank. Somewhere, a bell tolled the half-hour; Jo's watch read three-thirty. She stood by the slow-moving brown water in the still October air, mentally improving the landscape with plant substitutions of her own design, while Peter Llewellyn stabbed at his cell phone; a pair of students in their twenties strolled across Magdalen Bridge, their flutey English voices drifting toward Jo. She almost pinched herself. What was she doing there?

"Margaux says we're to come up." Peter thrust his phone back in his coat pocket. His face was rather pale, Jo thought. "Her stair's just across the quad."

Chrysanthemums blazed in a central bed. A group of kids, undergraduates probably, strolled beneath the Gothic arches in black gowns. A bicycle whirred by. Gray's set face, that look of pain. He would order his jet back to New York tomorrow. It was probably better that way. But what about his garden? Would he fire her? Refuse to reimburse all her expenses? Why had she decided to stay at the George? Was there an equivalent of a Motel 6 in England?

"Through here," Peter said briskly, heaving open a massive oak door to reveal a set of stone steps. "Third entryway on the left."

Margaux Strand surprised her. Jo had formed an image of a tidy but plain woman, with brown hair rather like her own; a no-nonsense girl who dealt in ideas, not things. But Margaux was what Peter would have called *smashing.* She rose from her desk like Venus from the half-shell, sinuous and tall. Her hair was jet black and fell in waves; her lips were full and red; her eyes were liquid pools. When she smiled, it was as though a curtain had parted on a wondrous world. Jo stared at her, astounded; Peter reached for his necktie.

"Peter, *darling,*" Margaux breathed, and slid around her desk to greet them.

She wore a simple sheath that fell to her toned thighs, and black Chanel boots that rose above the knee. Involuntarily, Jo took a step back, wanting the support of the wall behind her. The woman was going to kiss

Peter. Not just on the cheek — but a full-body snog, fingers in his hair, curves leaning into his frame. "Gorgeous," Margaux murmured. "You always smell so delicious. Like saddle-soap and foxed pages. Isn't he *delicious?*"

She threw Jo a complicitous smile, as though they both understood Peter was catnip to women, and reached out one long-fingered hand. "Tell me all about yourself. I'm so *thrilled* to meet you."

"Margaux — Professor Strand, I should say —" Peter stuttered, his face flaming. "May I introduce Miss Jo Bellamy. From the United States. She's a client, as I mentioned on the phone."

"Where in the States?" Margaux enthused. "I just got back from New York last week! Still *dead tired,* of course — conferences are such a *body slam,* aren't they, and then we were clubbing until all hours, I'm afraid. I've been twined in the sheets ever since, can't *drag* myself out of bed —" A smoldering glance here for Peter.

Jo struggled to find something to say, but *I'm from Delaware* just didn't seem appropriate.

"Miss Bellamy's on rather a short lead today," Peter supplied. "Expected in Kent this evening. So perhaps we —"

"Sit down! Sit down! And let me see your treasure. You found it at Sissinghurst, Peter says? Among Vita's things? I've been tearing out my hair ever since I heard! I spent *months* going through the Sackville-West papers for my last book — *Sapphist Writers in Arcadia*. I can't imagine how I missed your notebook."

"It was among the gardener's things," Jo managed.

"Ah. That explains it." Margaux, from her tone, didn't do outbuildings.

Jo took a chair; Peter took the couch, and Margaux flung herself down beside him, legs drawn up helter-skelter beneath her. One arm rested lightly on Peter's shoulder; she was leaning over him like an eager child awaiting a bedtime story. Peter's frame stiffened and his breathing, Jo noticed, accelerated slightly. The expression she'd come to recognize — polite and apologetic — was replaced with one of almost wooden resolve. How much of Margaux's behavior was reflexive — the social habit of a mesmerizing woman — and how much was targeted deliberately at Peter? Was Margaux mad about him — or simply enjoying her obvious power over him?

Peter cleared his throat, then nodded at

Jo. "If we could see the notebook, Miss Bellamy?"

She took it from her purse and handed it to Margaux. "I may have noticed it when other people didn't, because it was labeled with my grandfather's first name. Jock. He worked at Sissinghurst in 1941."

Margaux turned the notebook over in her hands, studying the binding, and then her immense brown eyes came up to meet Jo's. "Where's the label now?"

"In my hotel in Cranbrook."

"The George?" She didn't bother to wait for Jo's answer but opened the notebook and took a sudden deep breath. "Good Lord. It certainly *looks* like Virginia's handwriting." Her gaze moved over the page. "But the dates! Peter — you *must know* the dates are all wrong."

"Of course." He said it calmly and without apology. "That's why we're here. The dates raise significant questions — if the writing is absolutely Woolf's."

Margaux went still for the space of three seconds. Jo saw the sex-kitten pose die out of her body as swiftly as the sun retreats behind cloud; then she uncurled herself from the sofa and crossed to her desk. She gathered a magnifying lens and a pair of gloves, shifted her laptop to the low table

151

near the sofa, and ignored them both for the next fifteen minutes.

Peter, during the course of Margaux's examination, visibly relaxed. His rigid limbs eased into the corner of the sofa; one loafered foot crossed over his knee; he even managed a smile and a raised brow for Jo. She was watching the don, however. Margaux was parsing the notebook's difficult handwriting effortlessly, employing her magnifying lens once in five pages. Every so often, she let out a chortle or gave a distracted nod.

"Where's the rest?" she demanded when she came to the end. She was studying the two-word phrase *Apostles Screed* with a faint line between her eyes. "Who's had a go with the knife?"

"We're not sure," Peter said. "There may not be any more."

Margaux rose restlessly and began to pace. "God, I wish I could smoke."

"Still off the weed, then?" Peter observed. "Good girl. Stuff was killing you. And it absolutely destroys the palate."

Jo glanced at her watch; nearly four-fifteen. If she was going to make it back to London by dinner, she'd have to push. "So what do you think? About the notebook? Could Woolf have written it?"

Margaux stood still for an instant, her back to both of them. She was staring out the leaded windows of her rooms, at the blazing autumn of Magdalen's quad. She looked, Jo thought, like some sort of diva; Brünnhilde in boots, from a modernist staging of Wagner. She was beautiful and terrible and potent and strange. She gathered her long hair into a swift knot. Her hands, Jo noticed, were shaking.

"I can't give you an opinion. Not absolutely. Not tonight. I'd need more time."

"But you're not totally ruling it out," Peter interjected. "That it could be Woolf, I mean."

Margaux sank back onto the sofa. This time, she kept her hands to herself and her eyes on the text. "All right. I'll run through my notes. As you've already observed, *whoever* wrote this knew enough about Virginia's life and history to be comfortable putting her at Sissinghurst. I presume the writer also knew something about your Jock." A swift obsidian glance at Jo. "But there are other things. Whole phrases lifted from certain works. The first few lines are almost a direct quote of an unpublished fragment — the bit about characters in books, haunting the minds of those who read them, like ghosts. She cribs 'Clarissa

Dalloway in Bond Street,' too, when she describes her walk through the London Blitz. And she mentions *Lapinova in the snare* —that's from a rather obscure short story about a couple who pretend they're rabbits, and are fond of each other as rabbits might be, until the husband declares that Lapinova — who stood for the wife — was strangled in a snare. It's generally interpreted as Woolf's veiled comment on her marriage. She and Leonard used to pretend they were monkeys, but it's assumed Leonard wearied of that bit of playacting. The snare can be read as his attempt to strangle her selfhood. Virginia was constantly fighting his control, you know — there's even a body of theory that regards her as entirely sane, and suggests her 'madness' was invented by those around her as a method of stifling her independent genius."

Peter rolled his eyes. "Is suicide the act of a sound mind?"

"Perhaps. If death represents the ultimate freedom."

"But she'd had bouts of madness before Woolf ever entered the picture! She'd tried suicide around World War One!"

"It is a woman's ultimate weapon to fight the social forces limiting her self-expression by withdrawing from that same society — by negating it through noninvolvement. Woolf established that idea as early as 1907 —"

It was an old argument between them, Jo could see, and it was growing more heated. "We don't know that she committed suicide," she interposed. "The notebook doesn't tell us."

They both turned to stare at her. Something in Margaux's face changed. She nodded once, swiftly, and leaned away from Peter. "Bang on. The notebook raises all kinds of questions. Did she leave Leonard, wanting desperately to live? And did he find her? Force her to go back? Driving her, in the end, into that swollen river?"

"Or was she pushed?" Peter said, with a sidelong glance at Jo.

Somewhere, a bell tolled twice, the half-hour.

"Bollocks," Margaux spat viciously. She rose and moved dismissively toward her desk. "Time for sherry with the department. There's a visiting French scholar I simply *must* greet — he may be hired — and then there's the Yearsley dinner — always such a bore, but an *absolute* command performance, Peter, you remember. I really must dash."

"But, Margaux —"

"I can't give you an opinion. I need more time. Look — what would be *really ideal* — what would help us all out — would be if you left this with me for a bit."

"A bit?" Jo repeated. It was a phrase the English seemed too fond of: elastic and conveniently vague. "I have to get back to London tonight. I have to leave right now. I appreciate your time —"

Margaux was ignoring her, her liquid gaze fixed imploringly on Peter's face. "If it's *honestly* a Woolf, the stuff in this notebook will set the entire field of Modern English on its ears, Peter, you know that —"

"Naturally! That's why I brought it to you!"

"And I'm *immensely* grateful." She wrapped herself around him again suddenly, her lips lingering on his. "*Delicious.* So you'll leave it with me? Just for tonight? I'll look it over once more in the wee hours and hand it *straight back* to you in the morning, with my best possible judgment?"

"Margaux —"

"Smashing," she breathed.

So that was where Peter'd picked up the habit.

Margaux stroked her long fingers through his hair, patted his head like a good puppy.

156

"Meet me at the Queen, eight o'clock tomorrow. Café au lait. We'll talk. It will be *just* like the old days. I'll bring the note-book."

Without pausing for a no, she slipped the small brown binding into a Hermès tote idling by her desk, waggled her fingers at Jo, and gave Peter one last caressing look. "Until tomorrow, then. You'll let yourselves out?"

"I can't believe you did that," Jo said bluntly as they crossed the Magdalen quad a few minutes later. "My plans didn't include Oxford tonight, Peter. I've got no time. There's a client of mine waiting in London —"

"Is that the bloke who tried to get you drunk in the middle of the morning?"

She stopped short and glared at him. "Is that any of your business?"

"Staying at the Connaught? Sending cars for his gardener? Buying a complete replica of the White Garden? I already loathe him."

"I don't see why! You've never met Gray."

"Oh, yes, I have. He's the sort who buys futures in Burgundy, my dear, merely so he can display the exorbitant labels in his climate-controlled *cave*."

"That's not the point," she retorted hotly.

"The point is that he sent me here — I'm traveling on his nickel. My time is Gray's own. And it doesn't include an overnight in Oxford. I'm supposed to have dinner with him."

"Perhaps you should have thought of that before you contacted me." Peter's tone was unexpectedly savage. He was walking fast, now, toward the car park, where he'd left his old Triumph, his eyes on the ground and his interest in Jo absolutely zero. "You don't open Pandora's box in order to slam shut the lid. It doesn't work that way."

"Are you talking about the notebook? Or that woman?"

His steps slowed. "What's that supposed to mean?"

"It's perfectly obvious you'd never pass up a chance to see Margaux Strand again. And my time and interests are being sacrificed to your . . . your . . ."

"Crotch?"

"I wasn't going to say that."

"You didn't have to." He gave Jo an unexpected, defeated smile. "I'm hopeless around her, I know it. She's had that effect on me for years. You're right, Jo — I owe you an apology."

His sudden capitulation was unsettling.

"You owe me the notebook and a ride

back to London."

He shook his head.

"Peter, I don't even have a toothbrush. And I have *no time.* I leave England in a few days —"

"But your notebook is temporarily un-available," he reminded her gently. "We'll never track Margaux tonight — I know her habits of old. We'll just have to hunt for a hotel instead."

CHAPTER FOURTEEN

They found rooms at The Old Parsonage, an inn on the Banbury Road better suited to Peter's tastes than either the Malmaison Oxford — a boutique hotel in a former prison, all neon and pulsing music — or the anonymity of a Best Western. Jo was beginning to realize that small details mattered intensely to Peter: the quality of what he ate, what he wore, where he slept. Authenticity was his touchstone. That explained a good deal about how he'd ended up at Sotheby's.

"They do a pub supper here that's simple but brilliant," he said as they parted on the stairs. "I'll be downstairs in a quarter-hour, if you're hungry."

She tried to evaluate the neutrality of this statement: Did he want her company? Or was he hoping she'd crash for the night, order room service (if the Parsonage even offered such a thing), and leave him free to prowl after Margaux? It was impossible to interpret the good manners of Englishmen. In a sudden fit of petulance, she slammed the bedroom door behind her and threw her purse on the bed.

Her first call was to the Head Gardener's office at Sissinghurst; she reached only an answering machine, and told Imogen she'd be back the following day, notebook in hand. Then she screwed up her courage and dialed Gray's cell.

"Where are you?" he said.

It was his usual question, and the note of hope in his voice almost undid her.

"Oxford."

There was silence.

"I had to consult this woman about the Woolf manuscript. Or the one I think might be Woolf's. And that meant a road trip."

"I see." His tone was careful, now.

"I should be back in London tomorrow," she said, "and I'm not expensing this sideline, Gray. I realize I'm not on your time clock right now. I hope you don't think I'm abusing the privilege of being sent to England —"

"Cut it out, Jo. What's going on?" There was a rustle as Gray sat down on what she presumed was his bed. "What is it, with this notebook?"

"I tried to tell you earlier."

"That you're a hopeless romantic?"

"Not just that. Gray — I've never mentioned my grandfather. He . . . died . . . a few months ago."

"I'm sorry." The automatic response.

"He worked at Sissinghurst as a kid. I didn't know that until I got here," she added in a rush. "And when I found the notebook — it had his name on it."

"— On this book you think was written by Virginia Woolf," he repeated, trying to understand.

"Exactly."

"So your grandfather owned it?"

"I don't know. He's actually *in* it. Like a character. Or . . . someone she met. Someone she knew."

"How is that possible?"

"That's what I'm trying to find out."

"Jo —" He sounded exasperated, now. "Isn't there a better way to go about this than chasing all over the English countryside? Couldn't you talk to a . . . book expert of some kind?"

"That's what I'm doing in Oxford, Gray."

He considered this. "Did I scare the hell out of you?"

"Yes." The word was out before she could stop it. "But I really meant to get back to

162

London tonight. I wanted to talk to you."

"That's all we do," he said. "Talk."

This time, it was she who fell silent.

"Look — I've got to go. Dinner. With a British fund manager. Can I call you tomorrow?"

"Of course." *From your plane,* she wanted to say, *or your hotel?*

After that, Jo had no interest whatsoever in food. She called down to the bar for a glass of wine, drank it in the bathtub, and curled up in front of the BBC.

The Queen, as Margaux Strand had called it, turned out to be a coffeehouse on the High Street, shoehorned between Queens' College and St. Giles.

"Claims to be the oldest coffeehouse in England," Peter confided, "but probably isn't. And now that they've tarted up the place, it's lost all character — might as well be a Starbucks. Used to be a claustrophobic hole. Did smashing fry-ups."

He glanced disapprovingly around the Queen's interior, which Jo gathered had suffered an expansion at some point in the past two decades, then sniffed at his coffee in its trendy glass mug. "Used to be filtered," he observed. "Now it's Americano. Can't think why Margaux bothers. Must be habit. Or convenience —"

Neither habit nor convenience seemed to drive Margaux this morning, however. She had ordered them to meet her at eight o'clock — Jo distinctly remembered her saying eight o'clock — but as the coffee drained from their mugs and the croissants were consumed, the doorway remained stubbornly Margaux free.

"Perhaps she meant nine," Peter attempted, as half-past eight came and went.

"I think she's blown us off."

"Sorry?" Peter's brow shot up, and his eyelids flickered; perhaps the phrase meant something nasty and sexual in England, Jo thought. But she was too furious to care at this point.

"Blown us off. Skipped her date. Gone elsewhere for breakfast," she emphasized.

"*Overslept,* perhaps —"

"Then it's time we woke her." Jo pushed back her chair from the table. "Know where she lives?"

"Of course. I'll just ring first."

He stabbed at his cell phone with nervous fingers. But Margaux, it appeared, wasn't answering this morning.

"Peter," Jo said with an effort at calm, "that woman has my notebook. *Where is she?*"

■ ■ ■ ■

Margaux lived in a Victorian "two up, two down" terraced flat in a part of Oxford Peter referred to as Jericho, just outside the old city walls. The neighborhood was bohemian and chic, sought-after and expensive; a canal, lined with houseboats, bordered one side.

"This is Hardy's bit of town," he explained, as though he'd known Thomas Hardy in his student days. "There's even a pub called Jude the Obscure. Sort of an homage."

Jo knew little about Thomas Hardy, and cared less. As Peter tapped on the oak door, then walked gingerly around to Margaux's front window, peering into the unlit room beyond, her anxiety mounted.

"She's gone, hasn't she?"

"I shouldn't think so," he replied with infuriating calm. "It's a Tuesday. She's got commitments. Obligations. *Students.*"

"She's got our book."

They stared at each other wordlessly. Then a window above their heads was thrust open.

"Looking for Margaux?"

The voice came from a curly black head now dangling over the sill. The face, Jo

165

noticed, was unshaven, gorgeous, and about ten years younger than Professor Strand's; what was visible of the body was unclothed.

"That would be the *commitment*," Jo murmured. "Or maybe just the *student*."

Something in Peter's face changed. He stabbed at his glasses and called up belligerently, "Of course we're bloody well looking for Margaux. She's late for breakfast."

"Must have slipped her mind," the youth said, grinning. "She was off early, this morning. Barely had time for tea."

"Do you know where she went?" Jo asked, fighting a desire to scream.

The Greek god shrugged. "Couldn't say. You can step inside. Leave a note if you like. — Half a tick."

He appeared at the door seconds later, his waist enshrined in a towel. "I'm Ian," he told them cheerfully, offering his hand. "Classics. University College."

Peter had apparently decided to ignore him; Jo introduced herself. A cursory glance around the sitting room and kitchen beyond did not reveal the notebook.

"I don't suppose you noticed a small brown book anywhere upstairs?" she asked Ian. "Lying on a table, for instance?"

"The Woolf manuscript, you mean?" He smiled. "She took it with her, of course."

166

"Where?" Peter's word had the force of a bullet.

"Didn't say." Ian tightened his towel. "Very cagey this morning, our Margaux. And now, if you don't mind — I've left the bathwater running. . . ."

CHAPTER FIFTEEN

"I'm sure she'll call," Peter said for the third time, "once she realizes she missed us."

"Missed us!" Jo stared at him incredulously. They were walking in the direction of Peter's old Triumph, which he'd left near the canal. "*Ditched* us, you mean. Lied to us, too. Margaux knew that notebook was written by Woolf — and she *stole* it, Peter. Put us off with all this garbage about *further analysis,* then lit out alone for God knows where."

"I'm sure you're mistaken." Peter stopped dead and whipped out his cell phone. "I'll just try her mobile, shall I?"

"Try away," Jo muttered. She was suddenly aflame with impatience and frustration. She'd abandoned Gray — wasted time better spent on the White Garden — and embarked on a wild-goose chase across the Thames Valley. She'd wanted to make sense of Jock's suicide. She'd been hopelessly stupid.

"No answer," Peter said miserably. "Quite unlike her. Usually picks up on the first ring."

"Right. But she can tell from her cell that *you're* the one calling, so she's letting you go straight into voice mail. And don't say *I'm sure you're mistaken.*" Jo strode on furiously toward the bottle-green Triumph. "I'm not mistaken. You're willfully blind."

"You're angry."

"Of course I'm angry!" She whirled and nearly stepped on his toes. "I've lost something priceless. Something important to me personally, as well as to the literary world. Never mind that it also belongs to Sissinghurst . . ."

"I understand. But you don't know Margaux. She wouldn't just . . ."

"— Run off with somebody else's property?"

"Not with a treasure of this magnitude. She has her scruples."

Jo rolled her eyes in disbelief. "You're telling me that woman's never left you standing on a curb before, Peter, while she pursued something more interesting? I don't believe you. I've met the Boy Toy."

"There's no call for personal attacks."

169

He drew his keys from his pocket and shoved them viciously into the Triumph's door.

Jo felt her face flush. "I'm sorry. It's none of my business how often your friend's betrayed you. But that notebook *is*, Peter. We've got to get it back."

He held open the left-hand passenger door silently.

"*You've* got to get it back," she persisted. "You know Margaux. I don't. Where do you think she's gone?"

"Any one of a number of places. To verify a hunch, perhaps. Cross-check her sources . . ."

"Sell to the highest bidder?"

Peter's eyes blazed. "Not that. Not yet. The fame of discovery is more Margaux's line. She'd want the coup, you see. The headlines. The thirty-second spot on Sky News."

"So is she talking to the London press right now?"

"I reckon that's premature. She's not hasty, Margaux. More of a *calculating* intelligence. She'd want to be *absolutely certain* before she went public with this. The cost to her career would be enormous if she got it wrong, do y'see? And if she talks to the press — she'll have to tell them how the notebook was found. There are complications attendant upon that."

Complications.

Sissinghurst. The Family. *Jo.*

"Is it possible," she began, feeling her way, "that Margaux's searching for . . . something to authenticate the notebook? Something that makes the authorship unequivocal?"

"— Like the other half, you mean?"

They stared at each other. *The missing pages,* Jo thought, her heart beginning to pound.

"Somebody cut those pages from the binding for a reason," Peter persisted. "Perhaps they bore a signature."

"— Or the facts of Woolf's death?"

Almost involuntarily, he reached for his cell phone.

Jo erupted in fury. "*She's not going to pick up,* Peter! She must be miles away by now. Are you planning to stand here in Jericho until she parades across your television screen? Or are you going to figure out where she's gone?"

"All *right,*" he retorted, his palm slamming the Triumph's window frame. "I understand the problem, thank you *very* much. Now would you get into the bloody car?"

Jo got in.

■ ■ ■ ■

Imogen Cantwell listened to Jo's message twice, stabbing hard at the answering machine's buttons to rewind and play, before heading out into the garden that Tuesday morning. *Sotheby's,* she'd said, and *Oxford.* Imogen felt a sharp thrust of anxiety that bordered on panic: This was all spiraling out of control. Jo's absence was beginning to look like theft — and she, Imogen, was responsible.

Terence was the first of her staff she encountered near the Powys Wall; he was clutching secateurs and hazel stakes, and was clearly bound for the Rose Garden. Sissinghurst closed for the season in five days, and Imogen felt a slight stab of nostalgia; Terence would not be returning when the garden reopened to the public in March. His internship was nearly done. Imogen had no great love for Terence, but she felt rather like a mother bird pushing her nestling into flight, all the same.

"Morning," he called cheerfully. "Just going to kick a few." Which meant he would be shoving his booted foot at the existing rose stakes, elaborate architectural affairs known as "benders" over which the long canes of Vita's old roses were trained in a circular fashion. If the benders snapped under the force of Terence's kick, they would be replaced with fresh; if they survived, they would endure the wet and sun of another season. Terence loved kicking benders; it was a bit of garden hooliganism, of a sort other men reserved for rival soccer fans.

Imogen doubted there were benders in Los Angeles. Poor Ter would be lost.

"Is the American coming today?" he called after her. He rather liked Jo Bellamy. They'd probably pulled a pint or two when Imogen wasn't looking.

"Gone up to London," she tossed back, and hurried on toward South Cottage before he could ask why.

When the garden closed, Imogen thought, The Family would be much more in evidence. Sissinghurst was completely theirs during Closed months. And it was possible, Imogen thought, that the loss of the anonymous notebook might be discovered. That questions would be asked. That *she* would be blamed.

The Cottage Garden's four stalwart yews rose up before her eyes, quartering the center of the space — which Vita had called her "sunset garden." It was the boldest of

Sissinghurst's rooms, all fiery orange and yellow and red, a vivid charge to the spirit. This late in the season the colors were dying out, of course — the deep rhomboid beds were the province of a few dahlias, Bishop of Llandaff and Yellow Hammer and the tangerine East Court. The tubers required overwintering in the nursery; in a few days she would dig them up, dust them with antifungal powder, and store them in dry containers labeled with their names. Just looking at the flagging plants, Imogen felt an unaccustomed weariness.

She pulled out her secateurs and began to deadhead the flowers. Tomorrow was Wednesday. A Closed Day. So she might treat herself to a bit of liberty this afternoon. She might, with complete justification, take her small Austin out of the garage and test the open carriageway. Her snipping blades hovered near the throat of a spent dahlia as she considered the prospect. Time was running out. She needed to find Jo Bellamy and the missing notebook — replace it in the miscellaneous box in the tool shed before The Family noticed it was gone. Or, better yet, present it casually as a discovery of her own. *I was shifting the garden books for better storage. I thought this might be of interest. It* couldn't *be a Woolf, could it? Do you think it's possible that Virginia inspired the White Garden? . . .*

Jo Bellamy be damned, Imogen thought, as her anvil hit her blade. What had *she* ever cared for Sissinghurst or its people, anyway? Imogen had been too trusting. She'd believed the woman was a gardener — that they understood each other. Valued the same things. She'd even told Jo about her funding worries and the woman ought to have understood what the discovery of an unknown Woolf might mean to Sissinghurst. Now Imogen felt betrayed. There was nothing for it, she decided as she lopped off an entire dahlia stem; she would have to drive up to London right now.

"Tell me how your grandfather died," Peter said, as the Triumph slid onto the M40.

And so Jo told him, as she had never been able to tell Gray, about the tractor chain and the garage beam. The look of gasping horror on Jock's face when she'd viewed his body in the morgue and the swollen blue mass of his beloved hands. The sixty-five-year-old letter positioned carefully in a wheelbarrow. The hedge she'd left half-destroyed and the front loader abandoned for weeks. She told Peter how much she'd loved Jock Bellamy, how much she'd learned

175

from him, how solitary she felt without her grandfather's guidance. She even told Peter her deepest, private fear: That her trip to Kent had precipitated Jock's death.

He did not say, as she expected, *That's ridiculous, Jo.* He did not try to comfort her with the idea that Jock must have been ill.

"Of course you feel responsible," he said. "That's the problem with suicide. Everyone who loved the man feels they caused his death — simply by not preventing it."

The Triumph chugged on toward London.

"He never told your gran he'd met Virginia Woolf? Never gave a hint of the notebook's existence?"

"Never," she replied.

"And he left nothing but that old letter from the war?"

"Not a thing. At least —"

"What?"

She hesitated. The phrase was meaningless. She'd almost forgotten it herself. "A line on a scrap of paper my grandmother found."

"A quotation? Bit of poetry? *Do not go gentle into that good night,* that sort of thing?"

"It was nonsense, really. Five words. It may have had nothing to do with his death, even. *Tell her pictures at Charleston,* it said.

176

When I doubt he'd ever been to South Carolina in his life —"

"Pictures at Charleston?" Peter had suddenly jammed on his brakes; the Triumph squealed, and behind them, an outraged driver tooted his horn.

"Yes. It makes no sense. What pictures? Why Charleston?"

Peter was rapidly downshifting the car and skittering across the M40's lanes. "Don't you see?"

"No," Jo retorted, bewildered. "Are you out of gas?"

"I'm headed in completely the wrong direction," he snapped, "because, God help us, you never thought to share *your only clue*. It's near Lewes, I think. Sussex, anyway. We can find the house when we get down there."

"What house?"

"*Charleston*. It was practically our Virginia's second home. Belonged to her sister, Vanessa Bell. Famous painter. The heart and soul of Bloomsbury. *Surely* you've heard of Vanessa Bell?"

Jo shook her head.

"But you're familiar with *Bloomsbury?* As an historical fact, I mean?"

"I've heard the term," she said cautiously.

"Christ," Peter muttered. "The colossal

ignorance of Americans. . . . All right. A brief summary of the principal achievements in British art and writing in the first three decades of the twentieth century: *That* would be Bloomsbury. Your Vita is regarded as a member. So was Virginia Woolf. And her sister, Vanessa. And most of the men they took up with — artists, writers, philosophers, the odd civil servant. The men were friends from their days in Cambridge, and they all lived and worked and shagged in the part of London called Bloomsbury. Near the British Museum — it's mostly the University of London now. Radicals, freethinkers, passionate homosexuals — the lot. The twentieth century wouldn't be the same without them."

"So by pictures," Jo broke in, "Jock meant *paintings?* But when would he have seen them?"

"That's what he wanted you to find out. *Tell her pictures at Charleston.* Your grandfather's Last Will and Testament."

"You think this is important?"

"Of course." Peter tossed her a map. "Charleston is never an *accident.* Find the Brighton–Eastbourne Road, would you? And pray that Margaux hasn't pillaged the place before us."

CHAPTER SIXTEEN

The Connaught's private butler served breakfast in Gray Westlake's solitary suite that Tuesday morning: coffee, Danish, fresh fruit, steel-cut rolled oats. Gray drank the coffee, which was poured out from a silver service by gloved hands, as he stood near the full-length windows studying the miserable London weather. It was dark at nine A.M. It would be dark again by four-thirty. He was familiar enough with the city to have expected this, and in the heat of Buenos Aires two days ago he had yearned for it. Autumn in England. Scotch by the fire. Tweeds and cashmere and the warmth of Jo Bellamy beside him. He had imagined buying her things. Giving her treats. Long dinners with wine and conversation. Touching her constantly, and feeling her hands on his skin.

He'd imagined breakfast differently, too; he hadn't expected to be alone.

179

A spitting rain turned the limestone of Mayfair a dingy yellow, and almost everyone hurrying along the sidewalks below was dressed in black or tan. Umbrellas bobbed and cars sent swooshes of dirty water over the pavement. It was unutterably dreary and his solitude was annoying. Gray ignored the discreet click of the butler's exit, and asked himself for the hundredth time why he had not checked out of the Connaught already.

Because you don't give up, said a voice in his mind. *You wait. For the refusal and the doubt to turn to acceptance.*

Acceptance? Is that all he wanted from Jo?

Restlessly, Gray set his cup in the middle of the snow-white tablecloth, frowning at the food he had no desire to eat. He was used to being thwarted. That was a fact of a financier's life. He was used to calculating odds, and manipulating perceptions, and forcing his desired conclusion through a mix of will and ruthlessness. But he did not know how to win Jo Bellamy. She was utterly unlike the women he knew best — women who might be clever or accomplished or ruthless on their own ground, but who masked that steel with deliberate polish. Women like Alicia, who had been his lawyer before she was his lover and eventually his wife. He understood women who could calculate his net worth, their degree of sexual leverage, and his possible generosity in prenuptial agreements — and make decisions based on self-interest.

Jo was nothing like that. Jo was simple. Frank. Open-hearted. True. She tortured Gray, kept him wakeful at night, as though she were a path into a hidden country of unimaginable happiness that he could choose to follow, or ignore at his cost. Now, standing by the rainy window, he understood that he'd miscalculated. Jo's path — Jo's invitation — was hers to extend, not his to take. And she had closed a gate carefully between them, and walked briskly off into the distant trees. . . .

He could give Jo nothing, Gray thought, that she would ever really need. *He could not buy her.* Not even with this gift of designing his garden . . .

He should fire her. She was afraid of that, Gray knew. He'd heard the desire to placate in her voice last night, when she'd called from Oxford.

Oxford. His pulse quickened suddenly, and he thrust his hands in the pockets of his wool pants, fiddling with loose change. Consulting a book expert, she'd said. But Jo would never have found such a person on her own. . . .

There'd been that call from Sotheby's yesterday. She'd raced off to meet someone in the Connaught's car. Who was this joker, Gray thought, that Jo preferred to *him?*

Half his furniture had been bought at Sotheby's. On impulse, Gray picked up the phone.

"I'd like to speak to somebody who knows books," he told the auction house's central receptionist. And waited for Marcus Symonds-Jones to come on the line.

CHAPTER SEVENTEEN

They reached the Place called Charleston a few minutes before noon.

"We'll hope someone's there," Peter told her as they slipped down the A27. "It's not a Trust property, and the hours are a bit odd. But if *we* can't get in, that means Margaux is equally stymied. We'll persuade her to give up the notebook, join forces, and treat us to lunch."

His irritation with Margaux had evaporated once they left Oxford, as though Jo's clue somehow absolved the woman of guilt. It was possible, however, that Peter was simply looking forward to a good meal. For a man who was fit and lean, Jo thought, he spent a significant part of his day considering where to dine.

"Food is important to you, isn't it?" she observed. "Do you cook much?"

"Every chance I get. Love nothing better," he confided. "I've actually *called in sick* just

183

so I could spend a few hours at a farmer's market, and the rest of the day in my hole of a kitchen. Margaux and I used to say —"

He stopped.

"Yes?" Jo prompted.

"Sorry. It's just that it still catches me unaware — how much I *assume* we're together. When clearly we're not. Force of habit, you see. It's a *sickness*. She left me seven months and fourteen days ago, Jo, although who's counting, really? — and still, I speak of her as though I'm sure of her. As though the future we mapped out together — the farmhouse somewhere in the country, the room-of-one's-own where she'd write — was still going to happen. When it's all effing *gone* and she's shagging idiots like Ian, you know? My whole life is *completely* gone."

"I'm sorry," Jo said inadequately. "You were hoping you'd . . . marry her?"

"I bloody well *did* marry her." His retort was outraged. "That's my ex-wife who's stolen your notebook, Jo Bellamy, and don't you forget it."

"Oh, God," she said, and stopped before she added the inevitable: *Why in the hell did I trust you, Peter? Your Woolf expert is just the woman you can't leave behind.* However justified, the words didn't come. Peter was trying. He was AWOL from work; he would probably be fired. They could both, Jo reflected, be arrested for stealing a treasure from Sissinghurst Castle. What was the equivalent of a federal offense in England, and did it apply to property taken from National Trust houses?

"The notebook mentions Vanessa, remember." Peter swung sharply off the A27; they were a mile from a village called Firle. "How the writer envied her. Wanted her life. Almost fell for her husband, and so on. It was that bit, really, that convinced me it must be Virginia — I mean, who *wouldn't* hate having Vanessa Bell for a sister?"

"Was she that awful?" Jo asked.

Peter sighed. He was suppressing the impulse, possibly, to decry the general ignorance of Americans. "Vanessa was a superstar. Simply gorgeous. The kind of woman that men write poetry about. Everybody was in love with her — except, possibly, the people who knew her best."

"Like Virginia?"

"Well — being a sister complicates adoration, don't you think?"

"I wouldn't know. I'm an only child."

"Ah." He glanced sideways at her. "Virginia had the opposite problem. Lost in a pack of brats, really. Vanessa was the elder;

Thoby, whom your notebook also mentions
—"

"He's the one who died?"

"A lot of them died. Thoby fell between the two girls in birth order; then there was Adrian, who was younger and never liked his sisters much; and four older half-siblings from each of the parents' first marriages. Virginia's mother died when she was thirteen, and then her elder half-sister went, and her father, and finally Thoby — of typhoid, after they'd all been to Turkey together. Enough to drive anybody to suicide, one would think."

"Ye-es," Jo said. She was sensitive on the subject. "But given that people were dying like flies all around her — I'm surprised she didn't cling to Vanessa."

"Oh, I daresay she did." Peter was peering anxiously through the Triumph's windscreen, searching for the Charleston sign. "They wrote and visited and generally lived in each other's pockets throughout their lives. But Virginia was always going mad, d'you see, and needing rest cures and attempting suicide —"

"So the River — what did you call it?"

"— Ouse. It's not far from here, by the way."

"— the plunge in the Ouse, *whenever* it

186

happened, wasn't a complete surprise?"

"Lord, no! There were bouts of overdosing, and so on, for years and years. Everybody who knew Woolf expected her to end it, one day. Although women, it seems, take several tries to kill themselves; it's men who bring vigor to the first attempt."

Jock, Jo thought. Had he given much thought to his last, terrible act? Agonized over it? Considered asking for help? Or simply walked out into the garage —

"But Vanessa" — Peter slowed the car and dived into a gravel opening in the surrounding brush — "was more of a brick. Fell in love with her painter friend Duncan Grant, and set up shop here at Charleston with utter disregard for the conventionalities. Her husband, Clive, visited the family between mistresses. Vanessa raised kids by both men in one rather unusual household and proceeded to paint every bare surface she could get her hands on."

"Sounds nuts in a different way."

"Maybe." His voice was wistful. "Devilish attractive, for all that. Everyone visited her — Maynard Keynes and E. M. Forster and Vita Sackville-West and Roger Fry and Lytton Strachey. Some of them even bought houses in the neighborhood; it was a sort of Bloomsbury-in-Exile. Virginia and Leonard

Woolf could walk over — Monk's House is only a matter of miles from here."

"That's Woolf's place?"

"Yes. In Rodmell. Perhaps we'll stop, if we've time."

"She *didn't* walk over, though, did she? At the end? She ran to Vita, not her sister."

"Perhaps Charleston was too close. To Leonard. Perhaps she thought Vanessa would send her back."

The Triumph jolted over the rutted road, demonstrating the limits of its suspension system.

"Did Virginia ruin her sister's marriage?" Jo could not help thinking of these tangled relationships in terms of herself. *Gray*. The shadow of adultery.

"Clive Bell didn't need a push to wander — he was a womanizer par excellence," Peter said disparagingly. "What Virginia craved was not her sister's husband, but her *sanity*. She wanted Vanessa's self-possession. Her earth-mother warmth. Christ, she wanted her *children*. Leonard decided early on that Virginia shouldn't have kids — he was convinced they'd drive her mad."

"So Vanessa had everything? And Virginia nothing?"

"It could look that way, yes. To Virginia, certainly. She was the sort to feel plaintive about her wants."

"I don't think any two people could have been happier than we were," Jo murmured. "She wrote that, to Leonard Woolf."

"But it reads as ironic in your notebook, doesn't it? That's the lie she left behind her, for kindness. Ah — here we are," he said, as Charleston came into view.

At first, the house didn't impress her as anything much. She had recently been walking the grounds of a fifteenth-century castle, after all.

Charleston was a solid, rectangular place of no particular age or style, with broadly sloping tile roofs, lapped all around by fields, the smoky suggestion of the Downs rising beyond. The buff-colored walls were built of a mixture of brick and flint, and the word *shabby* came to mind. The windows were massive eyes punched in the front façade, fringed with faded vines. There was a pond, edged with what Jo suspected were weeds, and a willow tree drooping over it. Hovering on the far bank she glimpsed something — a woman? Staring at them? — and clutched Peter's arm.

"She's going to throw herself in!"

"It's just a statue, Jo." He studied it with narrowed eyes. "Creepy, though, isn't it?

Like an unquiet ghost."

Only one other car sat in the gravel lot.

"Margaux?" Jo whispered — although the car was obviously empty.

Peter shook his head. "She's probably been and gone."

"But why would she even *come* here? She never knew Jock or what he wrote when he died. *Pictures at Charleston* is nowhere in the notebook —"

"The mention of Vanessa might have been enough. Something made her snatch the book and run."

Peter waited for her to precede him through the blue-painted gate that led from the car park to the front door. Standing before the entrance, they both hesitated. A bird called. Jo shivered. She couldn't shake the sense that someone was watching her — the ghost by the pond, perhaps.

"Do we look for pictures of Virginia?" she asked.

"I don't think there *are* many, really — she hated sitting for her portrait." Peter smoothed his blond hair away from his spectacles. "Shall we just start with the first room and go on to the second? Something is bound to strike you."

"Okay," she said uncertainly.

■ ■ ■ ■

But as she had expected, nothing really did. Except the obvious thing that struck everyone who walked through Charleston's front door — how extraordinary the house, in every detail, actually was.

The rooms were a jumble of the rare and the mundane, of walls stained with damp, of curtains and fabrics faded by the sun. There were fantastic objects — carnival masks, seashells, ceramic zebras — and ordinary ones, like fraying rugs. Some of the ceilings were low, and the light dim. Floorboards creaked underfoot. A faint tang of mold laced the air, and the scent of flowers, and possibly charcoal. It was a house that did not feel like a museum; but it felt, Jo thought, like the house of old people who were dying or dead. That saddened her. It must have been a vivid place when Vanessa lived there — because almost every wall was flamboyantly painted, with rounded nudes, or enormous flowers, or the figure of a dog. Tables and lamps and mantelpieces were painted, screens were positioned as trompe l'oeil doors.

She turned in place, her eyes sweeping the canvases that lined many of the walls, wondering how on earth they would find what Jock intended her to find — could they *lift* the paintings from their hooks, and feel with hopeless fingers for notebook pages stashed behind them? Or had Jock meant something was *hidden* in the vibrant images swirling all over the furniture? Peter was chatting in his correct English way to the guide who took their entrance fee and pressed a brochure upon them; he was asking whether she'd noticed his friend earlier that morning — a tallish woman, long dark hair? She had not. The guide was moon-faced; she wore a wool skirt and sweater against the chill of the house. She was obviously going to hover at their elbows as they walked through the rooms. Lifting a picture frame would be an impossible violation.

They drifted from Clive Bell's green and yellow study — books on teetering, makeshift shelves; an odd sort of stone hearth like piled slates, jutting from the fireplace — to the black and silver dining room, where the inky wallpaper was stenciled by Bloomsbury hands. More paintings here: still lifes, a man fingering a piano, a painted fire screen, but none of them could be Jock's hidden clue. They seemed a world apart from the White Garden, from the fevered words of the Lady's notebook so briefly in

Jo's hands; and doubt scrabbled at her mind. Vanessa Bell may have been the center of Bloomsbury, but what could she possibly have to do with the death of an elderly man in Delaware? Jo began to feel impatient. Peter had dragged them both on a wild-goose chase. It was something to see the tubes of paint and the stacked canvases in Duncan Grant's burlap-colored studio, to hear Peter discussing with the guide certain elements of Post-Impressionist paintings, the influence of Picasso, the legacy of Cézanne; but she longed suddenly to be outside in the open air, with dirt beneath her fingers, where things made sense.

They were mounting the stairs. A series of bedrooms. Clive's, with its painted bed and riotous textiles. The green bathroom, with a sprawling Duncan Grant nude on the tub enclosure. More paintings on the walls — none of Virginia. Duncan's room. Portraits of Vanessa: As a young woman. As a middle-aged woman, in a batlike gray cloak, hunched at her easel. Then regal as a queen on a throne, her hair gray and her eyes forbidding.

Abruptly, they came to the spare bedroom. Or what looked like a spare bedroom.

"This is Maynard Keynes's Room," the

193

guide announced, in what was obviously a memorized spiel. "John Maynard Keynes, the brilliant architect of the economic theory that bears his name, *Keynesian Economics,* was a great friend of Vanessa and Clive Bell. He was often at Charleston, and the family set aside this room for his use, although other family members certainly slept here. Baron Keynes later purchased Tilton House, not far from here."

It was a low-ceilinged room, with a single narrow bed covered in what looked like Indian cottons. There was a bookcase and several paintings, one of which Jo found vaguely troubling — two male nudes, sprawled on a brown bank, toweling their ribs after swimming. It might have been painted by Seurat; it reminded her somehow of crucifixion.

"The Bathers," Peter observed. "That's one of Grant's? He was quite close to Keynes, I believe?"

"Yes," the guide said primly, and closed her lips.

"Grant was gay," Peter explained for Jo's benefit, "regardless of his relationship with Vanessa. Most of male Bloomsbury slept with him. Including Keynes."

"I see," Jo managed. It was clear the guide had no intention of adding to Bloomsbury gossip, and would have liked them to move on; but still Jo lingered by the doorway. The room was somehow restful. It was so *white*. It murmured of sleep . . .

White. The walls were completely white.

"Peter," she said suddenly. "Don't you think it's weird? How *unpainted* this room is?"

He turned back and stood for an instant in the doorway, staring at the pristine walls. "Yes. *Very* weird. In a house where everything is daubed, a white wall screams for notice. I wonder . . ."

A cord across the doorway barred entrance. Birdlike, Peter peered over it, his gaze fixed on the whitewashed walls.

"It wasn't always plain," the guide said. These four words were the first unscripted ones she'd managed. She looked almost appalled.

Peter turned slightly, one shoulder propped against the doorframe. He did not quite look at her; but something about his silence must have been encouraging.

"There was a mural," the guide added. "Of a religious nature. Quite out of the common way, for Charleston. They weren't religious people."

"No," Peter agreed.

Jo felt her heartbeat quicken. She was

195

waiting, with a sense of suspense, for the important thing she knew was coming.

The guide folded her arms protectively beneath her breasts. "Mrs. Bell whitewashed the walls the year Maynard Keynes died."

"When was that?" Peter asked easily.

"Nineteen forty-six."

"Ah. So it was. Just after the war. Keynes saves the economies of the Western World with the notion of deficit spending, and goes home to Tilton to die." He nodded casually at the sterile walls. "Sad, that so much valuable art should be lost."

"She was always painting over things. We've found pictures inside of pictures. Canvases reused. Nobody knows how much there might have been."

Pictures inside of pictures. Jo almost said: *Were any of them of Virginia?* But something about Peter's face — a careful, listening quality — stopped her.

"There's a photograph on file," the guide offered. "Of the mural, I mean. If you'd like to see it."

"How enchanting," Peter enthused. "We'd *love* to."

Chapter Eighteen

Cities made Imogen Cantwell uncomfortable — the excessive traffic, the narrowness of certain streets, the confusing directional signs. A bare fifteen minutes into the heart of London she was cursing foully at the windscreen, which was spattered with the first drops of rain. The fact that she had forgotten to prepay the central London congestion charge, and would now owe a late fee in addition to the usual eight-pound toll, infuriated her further; she ought to have taken the train in from Kent. It was *idiotic* that she had chosen to drive. The miscalculation betrayed her country manners, her lack of sophistication, her general backwardness. It also further eroded her faltering self-confidence.

So that by Tuesday afternoon as she stood in front of Cissy, doorkeeper of Sotheby's Books and Manuscripts department, Imogen was flushed with self-loathing. Broad-hipped, in khaki trousers and a cotton jumper, her grizzled hair lank with rain, she seethed before the reception desk, while Cissy made a show of studying her computer screen.

"Have you an appointment?"

"No. I have *not.*"

"Then I'm afraid you must schedule, madam. The Experts are all booked —"

Cissy's languid drawl; her Sloane Ranger hair, carefully blonded every three weeks; her suggestion of being merely on loan to Sotheby's in the odd interval between modeling gigs — all infuriated Imogen. She leaned heavily over the reception desk, her breath coming in rapid snorts through her nose. "I'm here on a matter of some urgency, love. You people have nicked something that doesn't belong to you. And I want it back. You can turn me away now if you like — but it'll be a police matter before long."

A faint crease appeared between Cissy's perfect brows. She stared coldly at Imogen, then extended one polished talon to her phone. "If you'll sit down, madam, I'll inquire."

"Right," Imogen boomed. "Inquire away, love. And tell them it's about the Woolf notebook you're sitting on, the lot of you."

She cast a defiant look around the paneled waiting area, the row of comfortable seats dotted with well-heeled clients. None of them was sodden with rain. None looked ill at ease. One actually rose, as though to offer her a chair: a dark-haired man of middle height and wordless authority.

"Did you say *Woolf* notebook? As in, Virginia Woolf?" he asked.

"That's right." Imogen eyed him dubiously. "Could be priceless. And I've reason to believe it's here."

"Or perhaps in Oxford."

"*Ox*ford?"

The man smiled at her disarmingly; she realized, with sharp misgiving, that like Jo Bellamy he was American. He turned to the blonde at Reception. "It's all right, Cissy. I'll just bring Miss . . . ?"

"Cantwell."

". . . in with me."

"Very well." Cissy dimpled at him, and cradled her phone. "Marcus would be *delighted* to see you now, Mr. Westlake."

The photograph of the mural painted on the walls of Maynard Keynes's bedroom was obviously quite old.

The Charleston House guide — who informed them that her name was Glenna,

199

that she lived nearby in Firle and had taken the job half-time during the winter months, now that her youngest was at school — led them to a small office area crammed with heavy oak furniture that might once have belonged to the Bell family.

"We're a private trust," she explained, "sustained by publications, charity, and various Bell grandchildren. So we make do. Most of the funds go towards repairs, of course, and the maintenance of the garden, or recovery of paintings by artists associated with the house. So many canvases were sold — once English Post-Impressionism fell out of fashion, Vanessa and Duncan were rather hard up. They had to work to live."

"Don't we all," Peter muttered. And Jo realized, with a small jolt of awareness, that she was unlike the rest of the world in this — she lived to work. She loved nothing so much as planning, digging, and establishing a garden — even if, in the end, it was handed over to clients.

She stood next to Peter in the office doorway. There was only one available chair, and both of them were too conscious of the other to take it. Glenna pulled open file cabinet drawers and flipped through manila folders, edging photographs into the light just long enough to determine they were not the one she sought. Then she slammed the drawer with a decisive *click* and handed an eight-by-eleven print to Peter.

"Here it is. Not in the best condition, unfortunately, but it gives you an idea."

Together, they bent their heads over it.

A black-and-white image, slightly grainy as old photographs often are. The print was cracked and stained with age; one corner was dog-eared and another was missing entirely. A few words were scrawled in the white margin at the base; Jo could not make them out.

"What is the title?" Peter asked.

"Virgin and Apostle," Glenna replied. "As I say — a religious subject, really quite unusual for Mrs. Bell, but then again it's hardly an ordinary depiction, is it?"

Surreal would be a better word, Jo decided — complete with Magritte's bowler hat. One was lying in the foreground, as though it had just rolled off the head of the dark-haired man who was crouched at the base of a statue. He was seen in profile: brown-eyed, middle-aged, with a mustache and a pleading expression reminiscent of a bloodhound's. A rectangular briefcase stood at his left knee. Papers were scattered in the grass.

"Maynard Keynes?" Peter suggested.

"Possibly," said the guide. "Or possibly not. The quality of the photograph makes it difficult to say."

The man in the suit was venerating — or pleading with — a fluid feminine shape, all draperies and delicate ankles. Her arms were joined over the breast in what might have been prayer. Her head was unveiled, and suggested a Greek goddess; her hair was drawn back in a classical knot at the nape; her face was an ovoid blank.

"Virgin, Virginia." Jo said it for Peter, but it was Glenna who answered her.

"I doubt very much this is a portrait of Mrs. Woolf, if that's what you're suggesting. One of the grandchildren would surely have identified her."

"Although she *hated sitting for her portrait,*" Jo murmured. "When was this painted, I wonder?"

Peter turned the print over and glanced at the back side. "No date."

"We've talked of doing a bit of research," Glenna offered, "but with funds so short, and the mural *not* a priority —"

"What did Vanessa mean by calling Keynes the Apostle?" Jo asked. "Was he particularly devout?"

Peter frowned. "There's no mystery about *that,* surely. Keynes *was* an Apostle. A

Cambridge Apostle. He practically reformed the Society in his own image, I believe, during his days there."

"But we can't be sure this is a portrait of Keynes," Glenna interjected.

There were times, Jo thought, with a surge of irritation, when she understood too well the force of Winston Churchill's adage — that the English and Americans were one people divided by a common language. What in hell were the Cambridge Apostles? Peter referred to them as though they were as familiar as Christ's. Matthew, Mark, Luke, and Maynard . . . But the repetition of that single word — *Apostle* — had reminded her of the Lady's notebook, at least.

"Apostles Screed," Jo exclaimed. "It was written in the back of the notebook, right where the pages were torn out. Does that have to do with Cambridge, too?"

Peter's gaze was still fixed on the print of the mural, but he wasn't really looking at it anymore. He was chasing a rapid succession of thoughts Jo could track in the expressions that crossed his face.

"Screed. *Screed* — that could mean one of several things. Conversazione. The Ark, perhaps, or the Memoir Club," he muttered.

Jo snorted and rolled her eyes.

"No wonder Margaux's not here," he

persisted. "We've gone in *completely* the wrong direction, haven't we?"

"Are you saying we should be in Cambridge?"

But at that moment, Peter's cell phone rang.

CHAPTER NINETEEN

Marcus Symonds-Jones had spent the few hours between Gray Westlake's unexpected call and the man's appearance in Sotheby's book department conducting what he called due diligence. This meant an all-out assault on available information: online searches of biographic and financial data, reviews of past auction purchases, quick interrogations of Marcus's opposite numbers in Wine Sales and European Antiques. By the time Cissy tapped her fingernail against the paneled mahogany door and slid into the room, Marcus had a rough understanding of Gray Westlake's tastes. He knew that the man was worth somewhere in the neighborhood of half a billion dollars. He knew Gray was fifty-four years old. He knew that he bought rare cars and speculated in oil futures. He knew that Gray's first wife liked English antiques, his second American country, and his third, Mid-Century Modern. He knew that Gray drank Bordeaux and California Cabernets, that he was a member of golf clubs all over the world, and that his five homes were scattered, at the moment, on three continents.

About Imogen Cantwell, Marcus Symonds-Jones knew absolutely nothing.

At first, he thought the woman might be Westlake's bag carrier, but that notion was dismissed as soon as he caught a good look at her. He was surprised and slightly unnerved as he bared his teeth and extended his hand to grasp Gray's own; if the man had brought a manuscripts expert to his first meeting — and Imogen was just frumpy enough to pass for one — then the American was in deadly earnest.

"Do tell me how I can be of *help*," Marcus boomed, as Gray stood before his desk. He would have liked to have sat down himself, but the other man wasn't bending, and Marcus saw that he was waiting for Imogen Cantwell to take a seat first. She seemed oblivious of this, her gaze fixed malevolently on Marcus; he recoiled as she thrust out a work-hardened finger.

"Was it *you* that woman talked to? When she brought her stolen goods to market?"

"Sorry?"

"A book expert, she said. At Sotheby's.

Was it you?"

Marcus blinked, his eyes shifting to Gray Westlake's.

The American smiled. "Let's sit down, shall we? Miss Cantwell? Have a seat?"

Grudgingly, Imogen lowered her bulk into one of Marcus's beloved Bauhaus chairs — white leather and steel, he'd saved for months to buy them before they'd even gone on preview. Everything in his office was deliberately chosen to offset the fusty image of Rare Books and Manuscripts, to scream in the broadest visual accent: HEDGE FUND OPERATORS TAKE NOTE: WORDS ARE HIP, TOO!

He wanted to ask what the fuck these two were talking about, but as they obviously assumed he *knew,* he sank instead into his chair and made a pretense of stabbing his keyboard. "Right. It's a pleasure to have you at Sotheby's again, Mr. Westlake — and to welcome you to Rare Books! I understand you'd like Miss . . ."

"Cantwell," Imogen supplied.

". . . to sit in on our meeting?"

"I thought her information could be helpful." There was a hint of amusement in Gray's eyes that Marcus immediately resented.

"You said something about a Woolf manuscript, is that right? You think you've found one, or that perhaps we *have* one — am I correct? What sort of manuscript, exactly?"

"A bloody great find, which that woman snatched right out from under our noses, that's what you've got," Imogen Cantwell snarled. She was leaning toward Marcus now, her breasts swaying in her wool jumper. "She brought it here under false pretenses. I've come to get it back. It's as much as my job is worth if The Family finds out it's gone."

As Marcus stared at her, understanding broke like dawn over his reeling brain. The Family. A stolen book. A notion it was worth something. Imogen was a *servant,* obviously. But what in the bloody hell was Gray Westlake doing with her? And why had he forced her on Marcus?

"Mr. Jones," Gray said — and Marcus felt the familiar fury in his gut at the careless curtailing of his name, he was no mere *Jones,* no sodding shopkeeper from Wales with a single syllable indistinguishable from all the rest, he had worked hard to come up with Symonds, the perfect hyphenated expression of his aspiration — "it might be easier if I explained. My landscape architect, Jo Bellamy, was at Sissinghurst Castle in Kent this week, where Miss Cantwell is the

National Trust Head Gardener."

"Ah," Marcus said.

"Jo was observing operations in the garden, at Miss Cantwell's invitation, with a view to replicating certain aspects of Sissinghurst at my Long Island estate."

"Jesus," Imogen interjected. "You're the one who wants the White Garden? I'd have thought you'd more sense than to buy a *fake*."

Gray Westlake ignored her. "Jo tells me she found a notebook in some sort of shed —"

"And I led her right to it!" Imogen cried.

"She thinks it might have been written by Virginia Woolf. She brought it to London yesterday, to be assessed by your department."

"— Which she had no authority to do!" Imogen was working herself into a rage. "I never gave her permission! Wanted to read the book overnight, she said. Because of her precious grandfather. And now she's gone, and the notebook with her —"

Marcus stabbed at his speakerphone. "Cissy — did a Miss Jo . . . *Bellamy* . . . an American woman . . ." — he mouthed at Gray Westlake: *Young? Old?* — "in her mid-thirties, perhaps . . . approach the department yesterday?"

"He doesn't even know his job," Imogen muttered to Gray. "But you — if Jo's your architect, you *must* know where she is, surely?"

"Marcus?" Cissy purred through the speakerphone. "I sent her to Peter. The rest of the department were in conference."

"Peter," Marcus spat. "Of course. Still taking coffee in some bloody café, is he?"

"We've had a call this morning. Peter's on sick leave."

"Sick my arse!" Marcus shouted at the speakerphone. "Give me his mobile!"

"I think," Gray Westlake said as Cissy disconnected to search her database, "you'll find that Peter is in Oxford. . . ."

"Is it Margaux?" Jo asked.

"No." Peter thrust his cell phone in his coat pocket. "Work number. Marcus bloody Jones. I won't answer."

"Seen all you need to, then?" Glenna held out her hand for the mural photograph. "There's so much in these files. And so little order! The whole collection should be placed somewhere. University of Sussex, perhaps. With the Woolf papers."

"But how nice that it's here. In the house," Jo said politely. She turned to follow Peter through the doorway when a thought struck her. "Glenna — do you have any photographs of Vanessa Bell? Or anyone else who lived here?"

"Loads." The guide pulled open another file cabinet and spilled a sheaf of prints over the oak desk.

Her beauty, Jo saw, was bone-deep: as much to do with the deeply modeled sockets of the widespread eyes and the subtle squaring of the chin, that in her sister, Virginia, was elongated to the point of caricature. Vanessa had a luminous glory that must have haunted the men who loved her. In the aging photographs beneath Jo's hands, her liquid gaze held fated depths, her full lips invited touch. There was power, too, in her air of stillness: She might have been an Archangel, something winged and terrible come to rest. Yet her children huddled gladly within her arms.

"That's quite an early one of Vanessa with her boys — Julian by her shoulder and Quentin in her lap," Glenna said. "He passed on just a few years ago."

"And Julian?"

"Killed driving an ambulance in the Spanish Civil War."

There had been something, Jo remembered with a faint ribbon of unease in her stomach, about Julian in the notebook. The

211

envy the writer felt when she saw even Vanessa's grief. Vanessa had lost her son — and Virginia, if Virginia indeed was the writer, had envied her for it. As though anguish were as valuable as love.

Jo sifted through the photographs. Most had stickers on the reverse, with a date and subject noted. Duncan Grant was in many of them. A few showed Clive Bell, with his high forehead and balding pate, his expression of wounded dignity. Quentin grew older under Jo's fingers. *Pictures at Charleston,* Jock had said. *Tell her pictures at Charleston.* The final one was a group photograph: Virginia Woolf the most obvious face among them, a collection of men about her. She was sitting indolently, her long delicate feet extended, in a basket chair on the lawn. Her thin face with its hooked nose and pronounced underbite was suggestive of a horse, where her sister's had conjured an angel.

Jo glanced at the back of the picture. *Virginia and Apostles, 1933.* "Glenna — would it be possible to get a copy of this? And the one of the mural?"

"What — right off the machine?"

Jo shrugged. "I know it's asking a lot."

"It's criminal! One doesn't do that to old photographs. The light's bad for them."

"One doesn't store old photographs in file cabinets, either."

"Well —" Glenna looked at the scattered images on the surface of the desk. "I suppose it couldn't hurt. Just this once. Are you two scholars or something?"

"Yes," Jo said. *Something* just about covered the two of them. *Gardener and Expert, 2008.* Peter was moving restlessly near Charleston's front door, too polite to remind her he was waiting.

She took the photocopies Glenna gave her. "Here," she said, handing the woman a twenty-pound note in return. "A donation. For the Charleston Trust. I wish it were more."

The guide placed it carefully in a strong-box as Jo walked away.

CHAPTER TWENTY

"You'll need to find the M11." Peter tossed her the map as the Triumph hurtled up the road. "Although it might be wiser to just take the A1 north out of London. The traffic shouldn't be too bad at this hour — everyone's at luncheon."

"Except us," Jo observed. "Surely you've noticed the lack of food? Isn't there a Michelin three-star in your back pocket?"

"With time so short — oughtn't we to wait until Cambridge?"

"At which point, we're talking dinner."

"Tea," he corrected.

"Tea, then. Drop me in London as you fly by."

The Triumph swerved inadvertently as he turned to stare his outrage. "You're not serious!"

"I'm tired. I'm hungry. And I'm feeling *really* guilty. I ditched somebody yesterday who flew thousands of miles for the privilege. I promised I'd be back by tonight."

"This being the bloke who tried to get you drunk before lunchtime."

"Gray Westlake. Yes. My *client.*" Jo felt herself flush. "He gave me a glass of wine, okay? That hardly qualifies as —"

"Sorry. None of my business. I simply can't — I won't accept that you're pulling out of the chase."

"The chase? Is that what this is? — A hunt for the Missing Margaux?"

"Not Margaux," he retorted. "Never Margaux. I wouldn't risk the loss of lunch — much less my job — to hare after *her.* But this . . . Jo, *this thing* you've stumbled on is worth any amount of senseless driving and future unemployment. Don't tell me you don't agree. You want to know the truth more than I do. It's personal for you."

Jock, she thought. But she did not say anything. She was torn between halting the mad dash to Cambridge before it began, demanding that Peter find his ex-wife and restore her notebook, and the desire to plunge further into this inadvertent treasure hunt. There was a whisper of doubt, too, in her heart of hearts: Was she just avoiding London and Gray and the terror of choosing?

"I saw your face back there," Peter persisted. "What did you worm out of Glenna?"

"Photographs. Or copies of them." She tossed the pictures in Peter's lap and held the Triumph's wheel as he looked down. "I know I'm American and we never recognize anything more recent than our own birthdays, but could you *please* humor me and explain what an Apostle is?"

"Actually, you're not *supposed* to know," Peter said kindly. "Nobody is."

"Well, that's a relief."

He laughed. "The Cambridge Apostles are a Secret Society. Rather like your Skull and Bones in America — a group of hush-hush movers and shakers from a particular university, blood sworn to keep mum about what they do together. Or where. Or for how long."

"I've heard of Bonesmen," Jo said cautiously. She couldn't exactly quote the Skull & Bones rule book — if one existed — for Peter's benefit. But they surfaced occasionally in movies. She had a vague idea they were misogynistic and somehow tied to the CIA. Or was it the Mafia? There was something about a coffin. . . .

"The Apostles began way back in the Napoleonic period, I believe, as a kind of evangelical Christian movement. Hence the name. Although most people think it's because there's rarely more than twelve of them at any one time. Undergraduates, that is. The alumni group is much larger, of course — scattered through all walks of British life."

"What do they do?"

"I *think*," Peter answered carefully, "that they talk a lot. The other name for the group is the Cambridge Conversazione Society. The idea is that the Apostles gather in a room somewhere, every Saturday I believe, and somebody reads a paper he's written. Then the rest discuss it. And take a vote on something that came up in the conversation. They used to eat sardines on toast — one hopes the fare has improved now they've started admitting women — and then disband until the next week."

"Sounds incredibly dull."

"It does, doesn't it?" he agreed. "One sort of expects *sex* with a Secret Society, or at least one of the Seven Deadlies. But the unifying factor among Apostles has been *genius,* I think — some of the most extraordinary minds in Britain have been members."

"Keynes," Jo suggested.

"Keynes. Also Alfred, Lord Tennyson. Rupert Brooke, the godlike poet of World War One. Lytton Strachey — who was a

217

flaming queen and a damn good biographer
— E. M. Forster, who wrote *A Room with a View* and *Howards End*. And your Virginia's husband, of course — Leonard Woolf."

"So Virginia knew about them."

"Of course. She practically lived in their pockets. It's extraordinary, really — only a handful of people in the past two hundred years were chosen, and there they all are: the heart of Bloomsbury. One wonders whether the Bloomsbury Group would have existed, absent the Apostles."

"So you think the whitewashed mural is some kind of clue, pointing us toward Cambridge. What if Vanessa just decided she hated it? Once both Virginia and Keynes — if it *is* a portrait of Keynes — were dead?"

Thoughtfully, Peter shook his head. "It's too weird. I mean, why would Vanessa stick that picture in Keynes's old bedroom, long after he'd acquired a house of his own in the neighborhood? And think about the atmosphere of the piece. He's on his knees. It's like he's praying for forgiveness. There's guilt behind it. Don't you think?"

"So where in Cambridge do we look?"

Peter took his time answering this. They were coming into the southern suburbs of London now, skirting around the city on the ring road toward East Anglia. Jo glanced at the map, no longer interested in forcing Peter to drive to the Connaught and drop her there. She at least ought to call Gray. But she had turned off her cell phone to save the battery — her charger was back at the George Hotel in Kent, she hadn't expected to be gone this long — and a curious languor was sweeping over her. The first sign of starvation, probably.

What she wanted was to sit in a basket chair like Virginia, skirt pooling around her, dancer's feet extended. While the Apostles showed off their Genius . . .

"Apostles Screed," Peter muttered. "That phrase meant something to Margaux, obviously. She was studying the back cover of the notebook yesterday right before she kicked us out. And then she skipped her vital departmental dinner, rang somebody up — and set an appointment with the bloke for today. Who would it have been?"

"A present-day Apostle?"

"That's a start. Somebody with access at Cambridge. A professor, perhaps. Christ, it could be anyone! Pity they don't announce which of their dons is Apostolic, on the university website. We could just go down the list."

"Peter," Jo said, "we shouldn't bother

retracing Margaux's steps. She won't take your calls. She's not going to give up the notebook. And she's probably already left Cambridge."

"Are you declaring defeat, then?"

"No. I'm suggesting we beat her at her own game." Jo shifted in her seat so that she faced Peter's profile. "Margaux's set her course. We followed ours — to Charleston. We have to assume it's a race — and get to the finish before she does."

He shot her a glance, at once derisive and smug. "This, from the woman who was parting company at London."

"You said something back there, at Vanessa's house — when I referred to *Apostles Screed.* What were you thinking?"

"About the Ark," he said.

"The what?"

"It's supposed to be a sort of box. Actually, it must be countless numbers of boxes by now. Each week, after the chosen Apostle stands on the hearth rug and delivers his or her paper, a copy is stored in the Ark. The Apostolic Holy-of-Holies."

"Is that where Margaux will look first?"

"It's the obvious place. But the question is: Where exactly have the Apostles hidden it?"

Jo frowned. "You mean, you don't *know?*"

"Nobody does," he said calmly, "who isn't a member. Margaux *can't* know. And so she'll guess. She'll look at the fact that most Apostles hailed from certain colleges — King's and Trinity — and she'll nose around them."

"But, Peter — where do *you* think the Ark might be?"

"In the bowels of the Wren. That's the library at Trinity."

"Can we get access?"

"Possibly." He downshifted as a massive lorry thrust itself in front of the Triumph. "There's a fellow I know. Hamish Caruthers. Did him a favor, once. He's Head Librarian. I suppose he *might* just be an Apostle himself. I'd never ask, of course."

"But why would this guy violate his oath — and show us the Holy-of-Holies?"

Peter smiled cryptically. "Now that really *is* a secret. You'll have to pry it out of Hamish himself."

CHAPTER TWENTY-ONE

"It would seem," Marcus Symonds-Jones remarked, "that Mr. Llewellyn is out of mobile range at the moment."

"Why don't you tell us about the guy?" Gray Westlake was sitting at his ease in the Bauhaus chair, one tailored leg crossed over the other. Why, then, did Marcus sense the coil of a venomous snake?

"Oh, Peter's quite *sound,*" he murmured. "Or rather, he *has been.* Until lately. Excellent credentials. Knows his stuff. Magdalen man. Been working Rare Books for a decade at least. Twelve years, perhaps."

"Does he usually go AWOL with clients?"

"Sorry?" Marcus glanced at the Cantwell woman, but Imogen seemed as bewildered by the term as he was.

"Absent without leave."

"*Right.* Peter has never done a bunk like this in my knowledge of him. But to tell you the truth" — Marcus leaned over his desk with an air of confidentiality — "he hasn't been the same since the wife left him. Very hot property, that — legs right up to her neck —"

Imogen snorted.

"Trophy wife?" Gray suggested.

Marcus knew this phrase — trophy wives abounded in Sotheby's world, spending their husbands' wealth on furniture and jewelry and priceless works of art — but he shook his head emphatically. "Not at all. Margaux's something of a sensation on the literary scene. Completely out of Peter's class, of course. Highly regarded. She's a Fellow at Magdalen."

"Oxford or Cambridge?"

Point to you, Westlake, Marcus thought. Few Americans knew there were two colleges by the same name, one at each of the top universities. "Oxford. She and Llewellyn met there, as undergraduates."

"But Jo called from Oxford yesterday," Imogen objected. "She was there, with *my* notebook."

"Maybe Llewellyn took her," Gray added.

"You're suggesting he consulted his ex-wife about this pseudo Woolf property?" Marcus managed to sound incredulous.

"Is that so unlikely?" Gray smiled disarmingly at the frumpy woman beside him. "I talk to my former wives. Usually about money. Does this guy dislike his so much that he's cut her off?"

"Quite the reverse, I should have said," Marcus conceded. "Positively pining. He's done dick-all in the office, ever since the split —"

"Mr. Jones," Imogen broke in, "let us be clear with one another. I care *dick-all* for the details of Mr. Llewellyn's private affairs. I care *dick-all* for Mr. Llewellyn. I simply want my notebook back. It went missing on your watch. I expect you to find it. If you haven't located your bloody expert — and Jo Bellamy with him — by teatime today, I'm going to the police."

She thrust herself upward from Marcus's precious chair, as if determined to exit without another word, but Gray Westlake stopped her with a raised hand.

"Miss Cantwell. Going to the police will only get you fired from the National Trust."

"I doubt it'll come to that," she retorted. "Consider the scandal. *American Tourist Steals Priceless Manuscript from National Trust Property, Abetted by Auction House.* I reckon Mr. Git-Jones here will go his length to keep *that* pile of dung from hitting the fan."

"And who gave her the notebook in the

224

first instance?" Marcus sputtered.

"There's a simpler and better solution." Gray was studying Marcus now, with a look he recognized — the look of a Bidder about to raise his paddle. "We calm down, go after Jo, and let Sotheby's decide whether the notebook is genuine. If it's crap, we hand it back with pleasure to Miss Cantwell. If it's not, I pay market value for an undiscovered Woolf, donate the manuscript to Sissing-hurst, and Miss Cantwell's a hero. Nobody's accused of theft, nobody loses her job, and Sissinghurst snags a great display for its summer tours. Agreed?"

"What's in it for you?" Imogen demanded suspiciously.

Gray's eyelids flickered. "Jo Bellamy can't design my garden if you throw her into jail."

"Yeah, well — the White Garden's been designed for a good fifty years already," she snapped. "All this talk! Where does it leave us? The notebook's still bloody *AWOL*."

"It leaves us with the ex-wife." Gray looked expectantly at Marcus, who allowed himself an instant's thought. Then he stabbed Cissy's call button. Nobody in the office knew more about the private affairs of the Experts than Cissy; she would have Margaux Strand's mobile memorized.

Peter had a peculiar sense of humor, Jo mused as she surveyed Hamish Caruthers, the Head of Wren Library, a half-hour later.

Trinity's home for books was a massive block set over an open colonnade. To describe it thus was to demonstrate the failure of words: It was the most beautiful building Jo had ever seen.

Buff-colored stone, rectangular and classic; rank upon rank of soaring windows; and inside, a black-and-white checkerboard floor sweeping to vanishing point. At either side, sensibly perpendicular, were the stacks of books.

"Christopher Wren designed it," Peter told her as they sauntered across the marble. "You'll know him for —"

"St. Paul's."

"Grinling Gibbons carved the limewood figures at the end of the stacks. Four hundred–odd years old, I expect."

"And kids get to study here." Jo craned her neck to stare at the ceiling, awed.

"They get to take it for granted, which is more of a luxury. Look." He stopped by a glass case displaying rare books. "There's Milne's manuscript of *Winnie-the-Pooh*. And

Newton's first edition of *Principia*. And Byron, of course."

A looming statue of the Romantic poet, complete with windswept hair and elaborately tied cravat, held down one end of the main floor. "It was intended for Westminster Abbey," Peter said, "but was refused on account of Byron's wretched morals. Trinity jumped at it. And there's Hamish, God love him."

Hamish Caruthers was almost as large as the statue. A massive individual in a heathered wool Fair Isle sweater, white dress shirt, and Trinity bow tie, his brown hair was the color of mud and fell in loose strings to his collar; his cheeks were full and red; and his shoulders — rounded by years of bending over the Reading Room tables — were like the sloping sides of a railway embankment. He wore a pince-nez. Jo had never seen a pince-nez, but the phrase formed itself in her mind as she stared at the fussy wire frame balanced precariously on Hamish's fleshy nose. He glanced over the pince-nez with a forbidding expression as Peter murmured in her ear — presumably conversation was discouraged in the Wren — and Jo saw recognition dawn. Unbelievably, Hamish was staring at Peter Llewellyn with what could only be described as profound distaste.

"Hamish, mate," Peter said easily as he swung across the marble floor. "How're tricks? Moldering volumes moldering nicely? Trustees happy? Wife safely off wherever wives go, when they're not wanted?"

The Head Librarian of Trinity College reached for his pince-nez, folded it deliberately, and tucked it in his cardigan pocket. "Peter." His voice had the quality of unsulfured molasses. "What in bloody hell are you doing here?"

"I've brought a friend to see the college." Peter was smiling, Jo noticed, at a joke he refused to share with anyone. He'd lost his quiet air of desperation — the melancholy that had shaped him from the moment they'd met in Sotheby's café yesterday morning. She understood that his present glee was entirely at Hamish's expense. Hamish also knew this, and suspected Peter's companion was in on the joke.

She would never be able to pry a secret out of this man. What in God's name did he owe Peter?

"Right, then — I'll let you get on with the tour," the librarian grunted, and turned away. The movement was akin to the shifting of a cannon, and ought to have required

228

the effort of several sweating laborers, but Hamish managed it in a single heaving roll.

"Sorry, but you're Point of Interest Number One," Peter said. "In fact, Hamish, old bean, we've come direct from London on purpose to see you."

The librarian grunted again, and rather than heave himself back to face Peter, merely leaned against one of the oak tables. It creaked alarmingly.

"What's to do?" he asked.

His mouth, Jo noticed, was pursed as though he were sucking aspirin. Or something equally bitter.

"We require a few moments of your time. And your Keys to the Kingdom."

"My *keys?*"

"It's an Apostolic Matter."

For several seconds, there was silence among them. Jo resisted the impulse to glance over her shoulder. Peter continued to smile genially to himself. And then Hamish said, "Who's the lady, then?"

"I'm Jo Bellamy." She extended her hand.

"American."

"From Delaware, actually."

Hamish's eyes drifted from her face to Peter's. "Perhaps she can have a look at *Pooh.*"

"No." Peter shook his head decisively.

"That's not on, Hamish. Miss Bellamy is to be admitted to the Kingdom with full privileges."

"Bollocks!"

The oath came out as a snarl.

"It's okay, really," Jo said feebly as she retreated toward the display case. But Peter was ignoring her. His eyes remained fixed on the librarian's face with that same expression of unholy amusement.

"Oh, very *well*," Hamish muttered in exasperation. "If it must be. I'll sell my soul to the Devil on your *behalf,* Peter."

"Smashing." Peter reached for Jo's shoulder, his gaze still on the man he miraculously controlled. The touch of his fingertips, light but certain, sent a jolt of warmth through her body. Startled, she glanced at Peter's profile — but he appeared unconscious of his effect. He was falling into step behind Hamish. And then he dropped his hand.

Cheeks flushed, Jo quickened her pace to catch up with the librarian, Peter's lithe frame swinging protectively behind her.

They descended a back staircase, heels echoing on metal treads, to the depth of three floors. They must be beneath the colonnade by this time, Jo thought, and the weight of Wren's massive building pressed on her mind. The subterranean passages of the library were airless, windowless, a labyrinth of lost books. Hamish trudged toward an ancient elevator, the kind Jo had only seen in Hitchcock films: a wire cage framed in mahogany. She and Peter squeezed into it after the Head Librarian, who drew the accordion gate closed with his huge paw, and the whole delicate bauble swayed on its cable ominously.

Hamish had not spoken a word since his concession statement in the Reading Room above; he refused to make eye contact with either of them, his face stony, his lips pouting like a carp's. He threw a lever, and with a sharp lurch, the cage began to descend. Jo watched as layers of flooring — concrete, wood — slipped above her head inexorably. Three stories. Four. Darkness seeped like ink into the mesh cage and the air was filled with the sound of Hamish's wheezing. Peter began to whistle tunelessly; was he perhaps a martyr to claustrophobia? And then Jo's nostrils caught the wet-clay smell of damp earth, familiar from countless gardens but heavy now as the grave. The elevator shuddered to a halt.

Hamish peeled open the door.

Jo stepped out. Her shoes met hard earth.

Somewhere was a faint drip of water. And the temperature had fallen to shuddering point.

There was another scent now on the air — elusive, overlaid with gravedigger's clay, something vanilla and jasmine. She must be imagining it. She shook her head, deliberate as a dog, to clear her senses.

Peter touched her shoulder again. "Come on."

She walked between the two men, Hamish a moving mountain backlit by the small flashlight he'd drawn from his pocket. The passage was narrow and low, so that the librarian stooped, and even Jo — a good six inches shorter — felt tamped down and trapped. Peter's tuneless whistle drifted in the air. They turned a sharp corner, and then another, and came to an abrupt halt before a thick oak door bound with iron.

"Here." Hamish thrust the flashlight into Jo's palm and reached for a set of keys. "Train that thing on the lock, would you?"

Jo obeyed.

The librarian fitted an old-fashioned iron key into the door and turned it with both hands.

The heavy oak swung inward. Golden light spilled over the threshold. With it came the scent of midnight flowers, stronger and more cloying than a few moments before.

"Damn," Peter muttered. "I know that perfume. Margaux's been and gone, hasn't she?"

Hamish grunted. "She's friendly with a young Trinity man. An *Apostle.* He broke all his oaths for her, I'll be bound."

"He's not the first," Peter said brusquely, and stepped inside.

CHAPTER
TWENTY-TWO

Margaux Strand's heels clicked furiously across the paving stones of the King's College quadrangle. There was a don at King's she badly wanted to consult named Nadia Fenslow, who'd gone antifeminist and now made a career of celebrating the distinguished males who crowded the English canon in a slavish sort of neo-lit conservatism. Margaux had hoped she might be available, might remember the boozy lunch they had shared during last year's MLA conference. Nadia of all people would be up to her eyeballs in Apostles, swooning over E. M. Forster in a way that turned Margaux's stomach, or suggesting that Woolf was but a pale shadow to Lytton Strachey, who'd probably taught Virginia how to spell when she was just a little thing in white muslin. Nadia might have a notion what *Apostles Screed* meant. Only Nadia was in Reykjavik until the start of Hilary term, and the don who'd borrowed her office had smirked at Margaux as though she were Nadia's long-lost lesbian lover.

Margaux was seething.

Somewhere a bell tolled three o'clock. She was aware of an insistent curl of hunger in the pit of her stomach, ignored out of long dieting habit. What she wanted was a good glass of Bordeaux and a bit of cheese, possibly some biscuits, with a clever partner to gaze at her over candlelight. She needed somebody who understood her vocabulary and caught her references and knew where to look for the missing half of Woolf's notebook without demanding to share the limelight. That was the essential difficulty in Margaux's world at the moment: She had been sharing too much for too long. Other people's triumphs, for instance. Other people's credit. She'd contributed modestly to an article chiefly written by someone else, or shored up the course load of those too distinguished to be bothered with students anymore. She'd scrambled for a few crumbs of the Oxford pie to savor all by herself. At this point in her career, Margaux had reached the point she thought of as Lady Macbeth's Choice: Crush all obstacles in her path to power, or exit stage right, on maternity leave. Having jettisoned Peter, the latter choice was probably out for the nonce. Single motherhood was far too impoverishing.

Peter had looked quite forlorn, poor poppet, she decided fondly — trailing into her rooms with that regrettable American in her corduroy trousers, staring at Margaux with the eyes of a wounded hound, and handing her the means of being feared and envied for the rest of her literary days. Peter was too endearing; a failure in his own right, of course, but endlessly devoted. It was comforting to have a Peter in one's past. Just as it had been essential to leave him behind.

Margaux lurched suddenly as her stiletto caught between two paving stones. She cursed explosively. Across the quadrangle, a startled undergraduate turned his head. He couldn't have been more than thirteen. They were such *children* these days.

She balanced precariously on one foot, wrenched the other out of its granite vise, and swore again as she glimpsed the heel. The expensive leather was torn, the white plastic shoddiness exposed; and with her gift for the interpretation of metaphor she saw immediately that this might be construed as a statement about her life — possibly even about herself. She pushed the thought aside. Better to concentrate on finding that drink.

Limping slightly, she reached the quadrangle gate just as Sotheby's phoned her.

The Chamber of the Ark, as Jo would think of it ever afterward, was low-ceilinged and medieval, the sort of room that demanded an ecclesiastical sound track — monk's chanting or plainsong. The golden light came from an old oil lamp, set in the middle of a round oak table at the center of the room. Electric bulbs were easier on the eyes; but the Apostles, Jo was quickly discovering, were all about atmosphere.

Lining the walls were glass-fronted cabinets with Gothic arches; inside stood rank upon rank of rectangular cases, tooled in leather, and stamped with a date in gold. *1827. 1843. 1896. 1907 . . .*

"Did you talk to her?" Peter was saying.

"Margaux? Avoided her like the plague," Hamish growled. "She wasn't here long, mind you. Forty minutes, perhaps. Bit peevish as she left. Had words with our porter."

"Maybe he found something in her bag that didn't belong to her," Jo said.

Hamish gave her a wolfish smile. "I'm off. Back in an hour. Have to lock you in. Don't panic — nobody will hear you if you scream." A flicker of amusement crossed his blunt features — the shoe, Jo realized, was now decidedly on the other foot — and then with a salute, he pulled the heavy door closed.

Neither of them spoke as Hamish's footsteps shuffled down the dirt passageway. Peter drew his cell phone from his pocket, as if to call Margaux one more time — then thrust it away in disgust. There would be no signal so far underground.

"Where do we start?" Jo asked quietly.

"Nineteen forty-one, I should think." He crossed to the Gothic cabinets, scanning the volumes as he loosened the knot of his tie. He'd already undone the top buttons of his shirt, and the effect, Jo thought, was of the true Peter emerging from the shadows. All his attention was fixed on the task, but his elegant fingers were so blindly languorous that for an instant, Jo had to close her eyes. When she opened them, he had stuffed the tie in his coat pocket and dropped the coat itself over the back of a chair. He was briskly rolling up his sleeves, determined to get down to work. "Bring the oil lamp," he said, halting before one of the cabinets.

Jo snatched at it with trembling fingers; the knowledge that Margaux Strand had actually been in the chamber recently enough to leave her scent was infuriating. If they'd been quicker, Jo might have gotten Jock's notebook back.

"Better take 1940 as well," Peter said, and drew two leather-tooled cases from the shelves.

"What if Margaux took what we need?"

"She'd never recognize it," Peter replied. "She's good enough at literary analysis — *Woolf's obsession with drowning reflects the independent female's fear/fascination with orgasm, the unwillingness to submit to the annihilating vortex of the male psyche,* and so on — but terrifically dull when it comes to puzzles. I'll lay odds she completely missed whatever's here. Hence the row with the Wren porter. She'd need to rip up the closest available minion."

"Unless, of course," Jo murmured as she stared down at the empty interior of the case labeled 1940, "she just picked off everything available."

Peter stared at her wordlessly for a second, then lifted the lid of 1941.

"Fucking *Christ!*" he spluttered, and shoved the empty case away.

"So you see," Marcus Symonds-Jones was saying, "what we chiefly need is your help."

Margaux kept walking straight down

King's Parade, away from the college and its beastly gate, her mobile pressed to her ear. If Peter's boss wanted to find him, then Peter *hadn't* given up and taken his gardener back to London. He might be searching for her and the Woolf manuscript even now. Bloody *hell,* he might even be in Cambridge — Peter was no fool. Margaux's impulse was to tell Marcus Symonds-Jones to shag off, thank you *very* much, but before she stabbed the End Call button she hesitated. She *did* need help —

"What's it all about, Marcus? Has Peter been naughty again?"

"So naughty he's about to be arrested for theft," the department head retorted tartly, "and you with him. It *was* you that Peter and his client Jo Bellamy consulted in Oxford last night, wasn't it, Margaux?"

Shit. Shit shit shit —

"You *do realize,*" Marcus went on, "that the actual owner of that possible Woolf is either the National Trust or the Nicolson family, neither of which is going to take kindly to Peter's pilfering?"

"It's not Peter who's stealing, it's that American," Margaux sputtered indignantly. "She may look naïve, but I'll bet my knickers she's no innocent, Marcus. You know what Peter is. Always bending arse backwards to be of help —"

"So you *did* see him."

"What if I did? He's my ex-husband."

"Where he is now, Margaux?"

Her stiletto caught again in a paving crack, and Margaux lurched painfully. "I don't know. That's the truth."

"Look — Margaux . . ."

She remembered this wheedling tone; it was the one Marcus always used when he wanted sex. It meant that he *needed her*. Margaux was suddenly acutely alert. She came to a halt beneath a Tudor window, nursing her ankle, and listened.

"You wouldn't like Peter to lose his job. Or, heaven forbid, go to jail. Would you, Margaux?"

"I don't suppose so."

"What if I told you I had a deep-pockets buyer for the item who might be willing to put everything right? No loss to the Trust, no loss to The Family, no loss to you or us — Provided, of course, the Woolf is genuine?"

Margaux hesitated. "Money isn't the point, Marcus. *My work* is the point. My reputation —"

"—Will be rubbish, if the tale of this theft ever gets out."

The wheedling note had vanished. But

Margaux's mind was only half on Marcus's threats. She was thinking more clearly now. *No more sharing.*

"— As I'm afraid it will, if Peter isn't found. That's where you come in, Margaux. Find Peter, won't you, darling? Before we're obliged to call in the police?"

"Poor Marcus," she said, her heart suddenly lifting. "So thick, always. Peter is irrelevant. Why bother with *him* when I've got everything you could possibly need?"

CHAPTER
TWENTY-THREE

"So what do we do now?" Jo asked dispiritedly.

In a few minutes Hamish would reappear to release them from the Ark. She had spent most of their allotted hour listening to Peter rant about the maddening cheek of his ex-wife, elaborated in a series of piquant episodes that filled all possible gaps in Jo's knowledge of Margaux. She had said little during Peter's diatribe, too sick with worry to stem the flow. But their time was up.

"We'll have to find her," Peter said. "There's nothing else for it. Roust out the police, if we must."

"I should just go back to Kent. Tell Imogen everything. Make a clean breast of it, and get the Trust to help."

"But if we found Margaux —"

"We'd have to bind and gag her to get our stuff back! I've already lost twenty-four hours, Peter, on a wild-goose chase — and

I'm supposed to be *working* here!"

"Look — I know it's been a difficult day —"

"Make that two."

"But there *is* one more place in Cambridge we could look."

Jo stared at him with a mix of frustration and pity. "She's long gone, Peter. Give it up."

"Not look for *Margaux*," he persisted, "but for Keynes."

"What'll that do?" she asked, bewildered. "We've lost the manuscript *and* the contents of the Ark."

"But you said it yourself, remember? *We've got to beat Margaux at her own game.* She's amassing loads of stuff, all right, but I tell you — she hasn't a clue what it means. Forget the Ark. Let's outmaneuver her on her own ground."

He was standing now, and the oil lamp swept his shadow over the Gothic cabinets, wavering and wraithlike. Why did his intensity move her so much? Against her inner reason?

"What are you talking about?" she asked wearily.

"Economics," he replied. "Margaux could never stomach the subject. Too . . . *factual,* I think."

"And?"

"All Keynes's papers are held in an archive at King's College. She won't have thought to look."

Beyond the heavy oak door, Jo caught the sound of massive feet tramping. *Hamish.*

"All right," she said, feeling cornered. "But if there's nothing there, you'll take me straight to London?"

"Agreed," Peter answered without hesitation.

Ivy Gupta held out her hand for the folded piece of torn paper that bore Hamish Caruthers's scribbled introduction. It was usual for scholars to schedule access in advance; and as neither Jo nor Peter could present academic credentials, and the daylight was waning, Peter had imposed upon Hamish one last time. Ivy Gupta ran the King's College Library Archive, which was housed in an annex. She scanned Hamish's note of introduction, then said, "He urges me to lock and bar every door against you. Are you *really* an unscrupulous bugger who'll stop at nothing to gain your ends, Mr. Llewellyn?"

Peter smiled at her disarmingly. "Hamish and I have known each other for years. Familiarity gives him the right to sport with contempt."

"I see." She set the note to one side. "We close in two hours. I suppose it wouldn't hurt to let you use what time remains —"

"May we have the index to John Maynard Keynes's papers, please?"

It was obvious that Keynes had lived in a vanished era of paper and ink, when the smallest thought of every day was recorded and dispatched to somebody. Accessing the collection, Jo thought, was like wandering through Keynes's brain, a vast repository of individual moments cataloged under such headings as *Visits; Articles; Speeches and Broadcasts;* and her personal favorite — *Miscellaneous.* The word *Screed* was apt.

"I don't know the nature of your interest," Ivy Gupta said austerely as she handed Peter a printed copy of the Keynes online catalog, "but you'll see the total collection has been shifted about and reorganized over the years. You've only to note the files you wish to consult, submit the slips, and one of our people will fetch them. You've got an hour and forty-three minutes until closing. I'll stop in just prior to six o'clock."

"Right," Peter said briskly.

Jo leaned over the catalog he held. It was itemized by year, single-spaced, and ran to five pages.

Indian currency and finance, 1909–1913, 1 box.

Post-war reconstruction, 1916–1920, 1 box.
Economic consequences of the peace, 1919–1925, 4 boxes.

Committee on National Debt and Taxation (Colwyn Committee), 1924–1925, 1 envelope, paper . . .

"We're going to accomplish *squat*," she said. "We could sit here for a month and a half and never find anything."

"Don't be so defeatist." He reached for a pencil left helpfully in a bin on the table and began to check off items on the list. "We can ignore everything economic, I daresay, and concentrate on the personal. That rules out most of Keynes's life, frankly, as we're solely interested in the personal papers for the months surrounding Virginia's death — say, the autumn of 1940 through the spring of '41. Keynes died in '46. That should narrow the field considerably."

"You mean, like: *Letters, 1906–1946?*" she retorted, unhelpfully.

"There's a subcatalog for those." Peter seemed determined to forgive her acid tone. "Each letter is summarized, with the name of the correspondent and a few lines about

247

the subject. You might usefully skim the entries for our time span. I'll concentrate on the Tilton House papers — there's only one box of those, and they're bound to have references to the Charleston crowd, because they were neighbors. If we have any time after that, we can nose into the stuff found in the King's storeroom in 2006 — it's possible nobody's gone through that lot very thoroughly, as yet."

"Oh, goody. What's my subcatalog?"

"It's an index card file. Coded JMK/PP/ 45."

"You're kidding me. Index cards?"

Peter glared at her over the rim of his glasses. "Don't be so bloody *American*. Not everybody possesses digital scanners. The most they've achieved at this place is microfiche."

Jo sighed. The prospect of reaching London that night, much less her suitcase full of clothes and toiletries languishing in Kent, was growing more and more remote; and the stolen Woolf manuscript was just as gone. She was tired, she wanted a change of underwear by dawn, and the thought of Gray Westlake kept nipping at her mind like a small dog. She almost reached for her cell phone, but a large notice on the Annexe wall commanded that she KINDLY REFRAIN

FROM MOBILE USE in the Reading Room.

She turned instead to scan the heavy oaken bank of catalog drawers at one end of the reference area. Peter was already submitting his request for Keynes Collection item 58/TH: *Tilton House, 1 box* to the archive runners. And they had only an hour and thirty-four minutes, now, before closing.

Jo was handicapped, of course, by her inability to recognize almost all of the names of the people who'd animated Keynes's England — that place that was not *this* place, but another country, one on the edge of nightmare, an England where bombs rained nightly on London's streets and Cambridge itself was bathed in fire. So many of the letters written to Keynes in those months — personal letters from friends Jo had never heard of — were about the war. The summaries were clinical: *Brief description of ration programme in Sussex, June 1940; Death notice of childhood friend in bombing raid, August 1940; Decision of neighbour to slaughter milch cows in fear of German invasion. . . .* She could not afford to look at any of them, although they sang to her like a pack of Sirens. This was Jock's world, too — the world her grandfather had lost, and Jo found it tantalizing, a portal to a parallel universe. She shook herself slightly and tried to concentrate.

Peter was humming as he scanned the pages of the Tilton House papers — a box three feet long and one foot wide, propped on the table between them.

"I'm useless," Jo muttered. "None of these people means anything to me. I'm probably missing the whole point."

"Focus on content, then," Peter ordered. "I'll help with the names."

And so she read on.

It was twenty minutes before closing when at last she found what they were looking for.

CHAPTER
TWENTY-FOUR

"Margaux will meet us tomorrow at the Connaught," Marcus Symonds-Jones said as he cradled his phone. "Nine-ish, I should think. Coffee and croissants, no doubt. The cow quite liked the notion of holding court; a spot of breakfast should lull her into a false sense of complacency."

"Why false?" Gray Westlake demanded. "She has the manuscript. She has the upper hand."

"So she believes. But is the notebook a genuine Woolf?"

"Surely somebody here at Sotheby's can tell us that."

Marcus smiled. He thought, but did not say, *And set an excellent price for it, you poor bugger.*

"I'm coming to that meeting," Imogen Cantwell announced belligerently. "Someone must represent The Family's interest."

"Why not one of the Nicolsons themselves?" Gray suggested.

The change in Imogen's expression was comical to behold; she was at once appalled and flummoxed.

"Too soon," Marcus said smoothly. "And unnecessarily complicating. If we involve The Family, we involve the Trust, and our ability to contain the negative aspects of this unfortunate affair — for Imogen, and your friend Miss Bellamy — may be quite limited."

"Not to mention the nasty blowback for Sotheby's," Gray offered.

Marcus merely inclined his head.

"This woman — Margaux Strand — had no idea where her ex-husband might be?"

"None, I'm afraid."

Gray steepled his fingers thoughtfully, his gaze on a spot somewhere above Marcus's head.

"It's gone well beyond my ability to understand," Imogen said forcefully. "Jo scarpers with the notebook, brings your bloody man on, and then hands over the goods to his ex-wife without so much as a murmur. It doesn't seem likely to me. I smell something rotten. And it's coming from that Margaux woman's behind."

Gray Westlake rose abruptly, as though he could not endure another second in the department head's room; and Marcus thought, *He's wondering the same thing. Why has this bird of his run off with Llewellyn, if she's not authenticating the Woolf? And what, for that matter, is Peter up to? Margaux's nasty bit of news has thrown us all for a tumble, and no mistake. Steady, Marcus old sod; you'll have to manage things* quite cannily *at the Connaught tomorrow, or find yourself without a buyer. . . .*

He was grinning broadly as he ushered Gray and the Cantwell creature to the door. The American, he gathered, had handsomely offered to foot Imogen's hotel bill. Poor fool. He must really care about Jo Bellamy. But didn't Marcus recollect that there was a *Mrs.* Westlake somewhere?

That was a piece of information, he decided, as he closed his office door behind them, he really must research more thoroughly before morning.

In the end it was a name, after all, that got Jo's attention.

Letter from H. Nicolson to JMK, 4 April 1941.

"H. Nicolson," she murmured. "Harold? —Vita's Harold? Peter —"

He looked at her as though surfacing from deep water, blond hair scattered over his eyes.

"Harold Nicolson wrote to Keynes. A few days after Virginia may have shown up at Sissinghurst. Should I get the letter from the archive?"

"Might as well." He shrugged. "It's probably about the war. Everything was, then."

"Have you found anything?"

"Not much," he admitted grudgingly. "Mostly domestic accounts, notes about renovation projects at Tilton House, Keynes's plans for his garden — it looks like he borrowed Duncan Grant from Charleston to draft part of those, you'd find them interesting I daresay —"

"But we don't have time." She copied the letter notation from the index card carefully; it might have nothing to do with Virginia, after all, but she'd failed to discover anything else. And she was curious about Harold Nicolson. *Hadji.* He was a vague outline in the Woolf notebook, a Sissinghurst ghost, most present in Vita's loneliness.

The letter was on microfiche. It took seven precious minutes to retrieve it.

Sissinghurst
4 April 1941
    My dear Maynard —
    You will find it intolerable cheek, my writ-

ing to you like this, without warning or the delicate veils of diplomacy we two usually cast, over such trivialities as where to dine and with whom, the details as codified and mutually agreed as we once demanded of our treaties at Versailles — but I am uneasy in my mind, and as the uneasiness involves my wife, I will make no further apology for demanding what I may of your time.

Vita has had an unexpected visitor to stay at Sissinghurst. A visitor from the grave, one might almost say, and her appearance on the doorstep has tangled us in all the toils of broken marriage and fractured mind. Her history of nervous complaint and instability are strong marks against any tale she might tell — but I found myself compelled to listen when we spoke on Tuesday. I had gone down to Kent from London at my wife's request, and her friend's account of recent events in Sussex — as well as the part you and your Cambridge friends played there — can only be described as shocking. I do not pretend to know the workings of military intelligence; I am but a poor player on the Ministry of Information's stage; but it would seem to me that higher authority ought to have been consulted. You will argue that you, yourself, represent that authority; I decline to be persuaded.

Our friend has written an account of what she witnessed, and all she suspects. Some of it is quite fantastic — and I might regard it as another demonstration of her genius, a bit of dark fantasy brought on by this desperate war — had it not been for that unfortunate young Dutchman's death reported in *The Times* only yesterday morning. There will be an inquest, no doubt, and the matter will be properly hushed up — but it is all, as I say, quite shocking.

Our friend has placed the chief of her testimony in my hands for safekeeping. I might have dispatched it to her husband, along with the lady herself; but *The Times* has unsettled me, rather. I shall therefore place her pages where no one shall disturb them — set an angelic host about them, as it were — until such time as she may have need of them.

Should you wish to consult me on this matter, I am only too willing to make myself available.

Cordially,
Harold Nicolson

"It has to be Virginia," Jo said.

Peter was skimming the copy of the letter she'd printed from microfiche. "All very mysterious on Nicolson's part. And rather menacing, don't you think? *I know what you've done, Maynard, me lad, and so does Virginia.* Only, what'd he do? Who was the young Dutchman? And why should Harold or Keynes care that the fellow was dead?"

"Because Keynes was involved," Jo suggested. She was feeling her way through the density of Harold Nicolson's language. "Remember Vanessa Bell's mural — *Virgin and Apostle.* Keynes begging forgiveness, from a figure that could be Virginia. Keynes must have had a part in something that happened before she left her husband — something that haunted her, maybe even the thing that drove her away, in the end. A few days later, she confided in Harold Nicolson; and he sent off this letter."

"It's a threat, isn't it, from first to last? He might almost have said: *Harm her, and we publish.*"

"Except that he was too well-mannered. Invoking his wife. Apologizing for Virginia's nuttiness. And then throwing down his glove —"

"Only to fail." Peter's expression was uneasy. "Because if you're right — and she

257

didn't go into that river of her own accord
—"

Dread curled in the pit of Jo's stomach. "Why did she go to Harold Nicolson in the first place — Why couldn't her husband protect her?"

"Because Leonard Woolf was one of Keynes's 'Cambridge friends,' " Peter said patiently. "Leonard was an Apostle, remember?"

Ivy Gupta's slim brown form appeared in the doorway; she did not speak, but the very blandness of her expression was a summons. The Archive was closing.

Peter ignored the librarian. "Did you notice this faint handwriting at the foot of the letter?" He held the copy of the letter under the desk lamp that anchored one end of the research table. "It's not the same as Nicolson's. Much more crabbed. Can you make it out?"

Ms. Gupta cleared her throat warningly.

"I think that word is *burned,*" Jo suggested.

"Burned? Possibly . . . What about *buried?* Yes, I'm almost certain it's buried. *Buried Rodmell April.* Now what does that mean? If it's Keynes's hand —"

"Then he was closing the file, so to speak," Jo said thoughtfully. "Keynes buried some-

258

thing at Rodmell in April. Where's Rodmell? It sounds familiar."

"It should. Virginia lived there. I told you. A place called Monk's House. It's not far from Charleston."

Buried Rodmell April.

Jo's heart sank; of course there was a burial in April. At the close of that month in 1941, Virginia Woolf's body was fished from the River Ouse.

What if something *else* had been buried with her? Something that had worried Maynard Keynes far more than Virginia herself?

"Aren't you dying to know," Peter muttered as they returned the microfiche and the contents of the Tilton file, "who that Dutchman was — and why he died?"

Gray Westlake didn't even attempt to call Jo that evening. The knowledge that she'd lost the notebook she was supposed to be tracing — and was still running around England with this guy from Sotheby's, when she knew that he, Gray, had flown all the way to London simply to be with her — had changed his attitude in a matter of seconds. It was clear that Jo didn't give a shit about him. She'd turned her back when he'd opened his heart and mind in a way he'd no longer thought possible — when he'd shown her his trust, and vulnerability. Gray thought of some of the things he'd said before she ran out of his hotel suite, and felt searingly embarrassed. Jo hadn't even done him the courtesy of telling him the truth, to his face.

I can't buy her, goddamn it.

And with that thought, he missed her acutely. It was possible she was the only person who'd ever been out of his reach.

Gray had called the Connaught and reserved a room for Imogen Cantwell, packed her off in a taxi, and walked away down New Bond Street.

He'd toyed with the idea of heading for Gatwick, where his jet was idling. Maybe it was time to give up and go home. There would be a certain satisfaction in pulling out of this mess right now — Jo might even be arrested! — when he, Gray, could so easily save her. He had a sudden vision of the Woolf manuscript, retrieved from that Oxford professor tomorrow morning, and a tongue-tied Jo attempting to thank him for keeping her out of prison. He'd tell her then, with the ruthlessness he was known for, that she was no longer in charge of designing Westwind's gardens. That her expenses for this bizarre week in England were her own. But the impulse died a swift death. The notebook was no longer the point — she'd given it away. It didn't matter whether Gray bought it or not. There was no guarantee he'd ever see Jo again.

He walked on, heading south down the Strand toward the river. The absolute dark of a north European night was falling swiftly over the city; London was all black cabs, shining headlights, the sudden stab of neon. It was rare for Gray to be entirely alone — he hired people, he married them, in order to avoid solitude — but tonight the loneliness was welcome. It clarified his thoughts.

What was Peter Llewellyn like? What spell had he cast over Jo?

What does he have that I don't?

There was a restaurant just opposite — a simple sign, a sheltered doorway: RULES. Gray thought vaguely that he'd heard of it before. A steak, perhaps. A double scotch on the rocks. The table tucked into a fold of drapery, no one but the waiter coming near.

He would eat a good meal. Think things over. Then go back to the Connaught and ask them to hold all calls. He would fire up his laptop and compose an email — a private one, to the head of his investment firm's research department.

Find out all there is to know about Margaux Strand, Oxford professor, and Peter Llewel-

lyn, Sotheby's employee, before nine A.M.
Greenwich Mean Time.

CHAPTER
TWENTY-FIVE

"Here." Peter shifted his chair around so that Jo could view the computer screen. "That's our boy. Jan Willem Ter Braak. Found shot to death in an air raid shelter here in Cambridge, of all places, on the first of April, 1941."

Peter had accessed the online archives of *The Times* while they waited for Indian curry at an Internet café. He was drinking beer, while Jo opted for white Burgundy; the smell of roast chicken and yams was making her mouth water.

She focused on the death notice; it was extremely brief. *Dutchman Apparent Suicide,* ran the headline. The body had been discovered on the morning of April 1, 1941, with a gun beside it. Jan Willem Ter Braak was described as a Dutch refugee resident in England since the British evacuation of Dunkirk. No other details of the death were mentioned. Anyone with information regarding Ter Braak, the paper suggested, should inquire at the Cambridge police station.

"Not very useful, is it?" Peter observed.

"An air raid shelter! Weird place to commit suicide. How'd he know it'd be empty? — We have to assume it was empty, right? The article doesn't mention any witnesses."

"It doesn't mention much at all."

A waiter set down a plate of flatbreads, topped up Jo's water glass, and left a trail of wet spots over the plastic table. She tore into a pappadam; steam burst from the center.

Peter was at his keyboard again. "Here's a Wikipedia entry on the same fellow."

"He's that famous?"

"He wasn't Dutch at all. He was a German agent named Engelbertus Fukken."

"No wonder he preferred *Jan.* So you're saying he was a Nazi spy?"

"Rather. The article says Ter Braak parachuted into England six months or so before he killed himself. He took rooms in Cambridge, claiming to be a Dutch national evacuated with British forces from Dunkirk."

"But why kill himself if he was supposed to spy? That doesn't make sense."

"Apparently he ran out of money at the

end of March '41 and couldn't stick it."

"Because he was broke?" Jo frowned. "I'm sorry, but that doesn't seem very James Bondish to me. Couldn't he have robbed a bank?"

"Maybe he was afraid he'd be caught. And forced to betray the Reich. So he took the gentleman's way out."

"In an air raid shelter. That was unusually empty."

Peter seemed determined to ignore her contempt. "Here's something odd. Ter Braak went missing from his boardinghouse on the twenty-ninth of March."

"The same day our journal begins."

Peter looked at her. "But the body wasn't found for three days."

"It can't have been lying in the shelter all that time," Jo said decisively. "So Jan was somewhere else. And he definitely didn't shoot himself. He was kidnapped, killed, and finally dumped in that shelter April first."

Peter gazed at her pityingly. "Is it American, this need for drama? You never accept the obvious solution, do you? It's all conspiracy, in your mind. The national disease, where you come from."

"That's unfair." Jo took a bite of warm bread. There was a photograph in the Wiki-

265

pedia file, grainy and indistinct. Ter Braak was curled like a question mark on what looked like a tiled floor, clumps of dirt or perhaps concrete lying around him. His hair was dark. His face was visible in profile, left cheek uppermost; blood trailed over his mouth, to pool on the tile beneath him. He wore a trench coat and what Jo guessed might be a fedora hat, still perched near his head. Gloves. Black leather shoes. Pin-striped wool trousers. It seemed incongruous, all this bundled clothing, this need to protect against a cold that was now eternal. The gun lay on the tile almost too correctly, at a right angle to the limp hand.

Her mouthful of bread was suddenly difficult to swallow; she could not look at the body of this dead stranger without remembering Jock. She coughed, turned away, and felt Peter's hand rest lightly on her hair.

"Are you all right?"

"No," she managed. "But don't let that stop you. Why would the Nazis send this guy to Cambridge, anyway?"

"No idea." Peter was studying her frankly, a question in his eyes. "I suppose the university was of interest to the Reich — there's the Cavendish Laboratory, where some of the early atomic-bomb research went on."

"It all sounds fishy," Jo declared. She was determined to focus on Ter Braak, not the memory of Jock's dead face. "We're not getting the whole story."

"Agreed. This entry says that the details of the suicide, and the fact that Ter Braak was a German agent, were suppressed until after the war — the government didn't want to admit they'd let a spy run loose for so long. I imagine what few facts we're reading are the ones they chose to publish."

"Exactly. It's an official version. And I'm not saying that *just because* I'm American. We know from Harold Nicolson's letter that this . . . *suicide* was somehow linked to Virginia. And to J. M. Keynes. And to his *Cambridge friends.*"

"Has it occurred to you," Peter broke in, "that you have a major problem with suicide? You shove it straight out of your mind, like a child who can't bear to look under her bed."

She glared at him, open-mouthed. "Damn straight I do!"

"But that's just foolish. Look —" He leaned toward her, elbows draped anyhow on the restaurant table. "You seem to find your grandfather's death a personal challenge, a glove thrown smack in your face. When it's nothing like that. Sometimes ending one's life is just a *decision.* A final moment of chosen closure. It's about self-control, *autonomy.* I've always regarded Woolf's drowning in that vein — she was a middle-aged woman who fancied she could see the future, and it wasn't the one she wanted. Sure, the act leaves unspeakable pain in its wake. But that doesn't mean *you* caused it. Why are you clutching so tightly to this notion you failed Jock Bellamy?"

"Because . . ." She swallowed, shrugged hopelessly. "I should have stopped him. I should have seen how unhappy he was."

"Was he unhappy for a long time?"

"Not that I could tell. I was clueless enough to think he was fine. But then I told him —" She glanced away, her eyes filling with tears. "I told him, back in August, that I'd been hired to copy the White Garden. I was incredibly pumped about the job, you know? I mean, this was probably the biggest coup of my career. I've only been in business for myself for three years, and Gray's a *huge* client, huge. So I called up Jock and said I was flying to England to visit Sissinghurst in a couple months' time. He'd always been the guy who celebrated most for me, when things went well. He said all the right things. He was pleased and excited for me."

"And?" Peter prodded, when she didn't

continue.

"But I never saw him again. He hanged himself the next day."

There it was: The truth she'd never spoken aloud.

"I see." Peter's fingers stabbed at his hair. "So you feel responsible. I get it. But I'm telling you, Jo: Let this one go. Jock was, what, eighty?"

"Eighty-four."

"There you are, then. He'd had his innings. He knew what he was about, that day in the garage. He didn't ask your permission, yeah — but neither did he shower anyone with blame. He made his choice."

"And left me to deal with it."

"You're being incredibly egotistical, you know."

"What?"

"Thinking it all revolves around you. That you're the center of Jock's drama. I'd wager otherwise, my darling."

"I am *not* egotistical!" she cried, outraged.

"Disgustingly full of yourself. *He killed himself because of me.* I reckon you're wrong. Perhaps he couldn't face whatever he'd left behind at Sissinghurst — but that may have far more to do with Virginia Woolf than it will ever have to do with Jo Bellamy."

At his words, all the vehemence suddenly

died out of Jo's heart. She'd been about to argue passionately that Peter was wrong — that this guilt was completely hers to own, thank you very much, and no reasonable speech of *his* was going to change her mind. But he was right. Jock had made his choice. And she'd been operating for days, now, on the assumption that it had something to do with Sissinghurst's Lady.

"So how do we find what's missing from Ter Braak's story?" she asked wearily.

Plates of fragrant curry materialized under their noses. Peter took a deliberate draft of beer, set down his glass, and looked at Jo. Had he actually called her "my darling"?

"I say we go dig up whatever Keynes buried in Rodmell that April," he told her.

CHAPTER
TWENTY-SIX

She was a few minutes late for breakfast Wednesday, but Margaux felt that was only good business. Marcus *ought* to be kept salivating when the prize was a previously unknown Woolf manuscript.

Even if the manuscript was partial.

And unsigned.

Stop it, she scolded herself as she smiled at the Connaught doorman, aware of the dazzling effect of her high-heeled boots, slim black leather skirt, and cashmere shawl. *Stop sabotaging your own brilliance. You own Marcus Git-Jones.*

She strode up to Reception, heads turning in her wake, and purred Gray Westlake's name. A discreet phone call, while she tapped her lacquered nails on the polished counter. Then a smile and the firm suggestion of an escort to Westlake's room; the staff of the Connaught was not about to let her wander upstairs to the suite level alone,

one of the many perquisites afforded a guest of Westlake's wealth.

Floating beside the liveried butler, a man in his fifties who might have been mistaken for Mr. Bean, Margaux allowed her eyes to close briefly. She felt something akin to sexual arousal. She had no idea who Gray Westlake was, or how he made his money — only that Marcus had spoken coyly of him. Reverently. As though Westlake must be as fragile as china. And that meant gazillions.

All that cash. Waiting for her. She'd expected to meet Marcus at Sotheby's, or even at a coffee place on Oxford Street, not in the suite of a potential buyer. The Connaught had recently been renovated, hadn't it, the whole kit and caboodle tricked out with fresh paint, fresh fabrics, fresh art brought out of storage — the suites were said to be utterly top drawer, respectful of tradition without slavishly imitating it — they'd hired a female chef from Paris, a Michelin two-star, Peter would be envious that she'd even set *foot* in the place.

But she wouldn't, she thought hurriedly, be telling Peter about this adventure. Not right away.

"Here we are, madam," Mr. Bean said, and tapped at the door.

It opened immediately.

Gray Westlake had been waiting for her.

She felt a brief frisson of surprise: He was shorter than she. And far more informal. In his khakis and polo, he looked braced for nothing more challenging than a round of golf.

"Miss Strand, sir," the butler said.

"Thank you. Dr. Strand — I'm Gray Westlake. Please come in."

He stepped backward into the room. Gave her a cool look of appraisal, a slight smile, and bloody *hell* — she was actually tongue-tied! Edging past him as though she didn't know where to put her feet, or whether she had the courage to meet those calculating eyes. *Ridiculous.* She was the one with the power. It was sitting safely in a pocket of her black leather briefcase, a bomb roughly the size and weight of an Inland Revenue return.

"Margaux!"

Marcus was grinning with all his white teeth, arms extended like a major domo's as he walked toward her. He wore a suit that suggested his antecedents lay somewhere in Sicily, and a pumpkin-colored dress shirt. *Unbelievable.* She gave him her cheek, murmured a few syllables to convey he was irresistible, and looked past him to the frumpy, middle-aged woman who'd risen from the plush beige sofa in the suite's massive living room.

Blimey, was this Westlake's wife?

"Allow me to introduce Imogen Cantwell. She's . . . an interested party," Marcus gushed through his teeth. "In the Woolf, that is."

"You might as well say I'm the owner, and have done," Imogen snapped irritably.

"But you're *not,* sweet," Marcus crooned. "We're all avoiding the actual ownership issue, at the moment, and I'd advise you to keep quiet on that score. Margaux, do sit down. May I fetch you tea?"

"Coffee, actually."

There was a silver service on a Regency sideboard; a platter of mouthwatering pastries; succulent fruit, well out of season. No one was eating. It was sad, really, Margaux thought — how it would all go to waste, Mr. Bean or somebody else tipping the whole lot into the rubbish bins. Was that what money *really* bought? Waste and empty gestures?

Defiantly, she strode over to the sideboard and filled a bone china plate with raspberries and almond croissants. Marcus was hovering with a coffee cup.

"I take it fairly white," she said. "A bad

habit acquired during a term in Paris."

He grinned again — what a dreadful habit; he ought to marry or acquire a competent gay partner, the right person would stop him making an absolute *ass* of himself. She let him carry the cup over to her chair. A plush club chair, drawn up to the fire. And good God in heaven, it was *working.* A real coal fire in the heart of a hotel. She closed her eyes for a second time, almost swooning.

"Dr. Strand —"

"Call me Margaux, please." She smiled at Gray Westlake, who'd seated himself next to the Cantwell creature. He was such a relief for the eyes after Git-Jones; self-possessed. The sort of person who'd seen most things in the world, and remained unimpressed. She flushed slightly, suspecting from his indifferent gaze that she might be one of those unimpressive things — it was not a sensation to which she was accustomed.

"Margaux," Gray said. "You have something to show us, I think?"

So much for food and pleasantries.

She reached into her briefcase and drew forth the notebook. Then hesitated, the worn little clutch of paper in her hands. "To think," she half-whispered, "that *Virginia* once touched this . . ."

Imogen Cantwell rose from her seat, leaning ponderously over the elaborate flowers that dominated the sofa table.

"That's it!" she crowed. "Minus the ribbon, and the tag with her grandpa's name on it. I should never have let her take it —"

"May I?" Marcus interrupted. He was gazing at Margaux, but she was looking at Westlake.

The American's mouth quirked slightly. "By all means."

Marcus sighed as she handed him the notebook. He slipped a pair of reading glasses on his nose and a pair of cotton gloves on his fingers. His brow furrowed. He was swiftly transformed from an impossible salesman to a connoisseur of formidable standing; and despite herself, Margaux was impressed as he fluttered the leaves of the notebook with supreme delicacy, lost to the huddled group and their cooling coffee, intent, an original reader. For the space of several heartbeats the room was completely silent.

"No signature," he noted.

"None," she agreed. "But I've compared the handwriting to several examples in my possession . . ."

"Photocopies, however?"

"Of course. My budget doesn't run to

original Woolfs."

Marcus's nostrils contracted; he looked as though he were reserving judgment. He almost, but not quite, shrugged. "Yes — well, we'll have the whole subject of handwriting thoroughly sussed before declaring our position. One that can *only* be heavily caveated, of course. The thing's not even in good condition."

He held up the notebook for Gray's inspection, albeit with an antiquarian's care. For an instant, all four of them studied the ravaged spine. A good half of the pages were missing.

"I'd be prepared to offer my professional opinion," Margaux said, with faint irritation.

"Naturally." The teeth bared again. "And we can verify such data as the composition of the notebook paper and probable binding origins — factories, year of issue, and so on — but you will admit it's impossible to label such a thing *an absolute Woolf.* Fragmentary and without the slightest foothold in the established historical record as it is. And, of course, there's the problem of the dates."

Margaux stiffened.

"Dates?" Gray queried.

"The notebook begins the day *after*

Woolf's suicide," Marcus said brightly. "Rather precludes her having written it, one would think — and a host of critics will certainly argue. I assume you noted that anomaly, Margaux?"

"Naturally." Her irritation was undisguised now. "But when one takes the time to read the text, it becomes obvious that Woolf *didn't* drown herself in the Ouse on the twenty-eighth of March. Rather, she ran away. From her miserable husband. Which any conscious scholar of Woolf and her oeuvre would be only too willing to applaud, Marcus. I assume you noted that *extraordinary reversal* of an entire school of literary analysis?"

"Hey," Gray said. He was holding up his hands as though about to receive a basketball, a supplication for peace. "Let's not squabble about this. The book is what it is. We need a team of impartial people to study it, and determine what they can. How long would Sotheby's want to look at the manuscript, Marcus?"

"It's already Wednesday."

"But you could pay people overtime. Bring them in all weekend."

"That *might* be possible," Marcus agreed, glancing at Gray sidelong.

"Say until Monday, then."

Margaux straightened. "Marcus, I can't agree —"

"I'm taking the thing home!" Imogen Cantwell cried at exactly the same moment.

"By what right?" Margaux sneered.

"Oh, shut up, you great cow," Imogen retorted. "You're no better than the rest of them — thinking your authority, that handful of letters pegged after your name, gives you a dog in this fight. You'd none of you be in this room if I hadn't been such a fool as to give the notebook to Jo Bellamy. That Woolf belongs to The Family, and I want it back. If one of you tries to make off with it, I'll go to the police and make a clean breast of the whole affair. I'll have the Law on you."

The simplicity of this statement brought everyone to a full stop. Margaux stared at Imogen, and Imogen stared at Marcus, while Gray still smiled faintly at something only he could see. They had all been tacitly playing a game for high stakes, and Imogen had just overturned the table.

"Miss Cantwell," Gray said gently — he did not do her the injustice of assuming he should call her Imogen — "if you are determined to bring in the police, I suggest you call them now." He held out a wireless phone receiver. "That way, they can take possession of the notebook while you make your statement."

"Take *possession?* I've just said . . ."

"Because you *do realize* that none of us will let you leave this room with a potentially priceless manuscript. One that belongs to the National Trust . . . or perhaps to the Nicolson family . . . but that absolutely does *not* belong to you. That would be the height of irresponsibility on all our parts, don't you agree?"

Imogen looked slightly sick. She opened her mouth to protest, then shut it again. Margaux imagined the scenes suddenly flooding the older woman's mind: herself, explaining to the police why she was reporting the theft of a notebook clearly sitting on the cocktail table. Herself, explaining the whole debacle to various members of the National Trust, while they considered the best way to fire her.

Margaux's heart rate accelerated. A bubble of mirth rose inconveniently in her throat. She could not take her eyes off Gray Westlake — his carefully bland expression, his slightly quirked eyebrow. The man was brilliant. No wonder he'd made millions.

"You bastard." Imogen thrust herself to her feet, her face blooming red. "Taking my part in that auction house, so you could nose into my business. Putting me up in your fancy hotel, then showing me the door. Life's too easy for the likes of you. I hope that Jo Bellamy makes a complete fool of you."

She was searching hopelessly for her handbag, which Margaux knew was resting on a shield-back chair in the front entry; rage or perhaps tears were blinding Imogen to the obvious. Marcus rose solicitously from his seat but it was Gray Westlake who placed a hand on the woman's shoulder and said, "Please don't go."

She shrugged him off. "I'm not likely to stay where I'm threatened with the police."

This was so patently hilarious that Margaux snorted.

"Miss Cantwell," Gray persisted, "we're trying to save you from yourself."

Something in his tone stopped her at last. She went still, studying him, and then with a sudden expulsion of breath, like a child done sobbing, she sank back down on the sofa. "What is it you want?"

"A few days. Three, maybe four."

"That's what *she* said. And it turned into a whole bloody week!"

"But the manuscript is back in safe hands. To convince you it's safe, and to limit your liability, I propose —" Gray glanced for confirmation at Marcus — "we write up a series of brief statements everyone can sign. Mr. Symonds-Jones will acknowledge receipt of the notebook itself, over his signature; Dr. Strand will state her professional opinion as to its authenticity —"

"— and receive in return an assurance of exclusive access to the material for a period of five years," Margaux bargained smoothly, "and an exclusive appointment as Manuscript Consultant during any publicity campaign that might follow the notebook's authentication."

"Hasty, hasty," Marcus murmured.

"But small pence, when without my aid and concern you'd never have set eyes on the thing," Margaux retorted.

"And I get sod-all," Imogen muttered, "just a nod and pat on the bottom as you shove me back to Kent. What I'd like to know is what *you* get out of this, Westlake?"

"The satisfaction of preserving your job." He smiled at her almost sadly. "If the notebook is determined to be as rare as some of you think it is, I would suggest we then approach the National Trust and The Family. Explain that Miss Cantwell has made a Find, and consulted Dr. Strand, and that a generous donor would be prepared to buy the item, support its preservation, and donate it back to Sissinghurst. That should untangle any looming legal snarls and make Miss Cantwell look like a saint."

Imogen's sour expression softened. If she still had doubts, she kept them firmly between her teeth.

"Who will type up the statements?" Margaux asked, as she bit into her almond croissant. *Delicious.*

"Already done." Marcus pulled a sheaf of papers from his black leather Filofax and handed them around, beaming.

It was only then that Margaux saw how completely they had been managed, from first to last. Gray Westlake had anticipated whatever she or Imogen could muster. Oddly enough — she didn't really mind.

It was only after the women had left, clutching their signed copies according them rights without any particular responsibilities, that Gray Westlake used the intelligence he'd received from his research department that morning.

Marcus Symonds-Jones was chattering in his usual fashion, a mixture of flattery and false intimacy, sprinkled with thanks for the seamless way Gray had handled the business, and offers of assistance in any way possible, present or future. Gray let him run on as he gathered up his documents and secured the Woolf notebook in a plastic bag. Then, as Marcus drew off his plastic gloves and threw one last smile Gray's way, preparatory to making his exit, Gray said mildly, "You slept with her, didn't you? Margaux Strand. That's what destroyed her marriage."

The man's mouth fell open, then after a stunned second, snapped closed. "I'm hardly the first."

"Obviously. Her husband, at least, was before you."

As Marcus started to protest, Gray raised his hand. "I'm not interested in discussing the woman's morals, okay? It's Llewellyn's reaction I find fascinating. He kicked her out, but he kept working for you. Doesn't that strike you as odd?"

Marcus shrugged. "She was the one who betrayed him."

"Not you? Not his boss? No hard feelings between friends?"

"As I've said," Marcus mouthed deliberately, "I wasn't the first to tickle her knickers."

"So you're not concerned — that he lit out with a client and a valuable auction prospect, and is still wandering the country unaccounted for? It'd make me sweat a little, Marcus. If I were you, I'd be waiting for the other shoe to drop."

"What are you saying, Westlake?" The expert frowned, trying to work it out.

Gray shrugged, already bored. "A guy who works for you, and has every reason to hate your guts, gave that notebook to his ex-wife . . . who brought it straight back to you. Don't you feel, Marcus, like you're being set up?"

CHAPTER TWENTY-SEVEN

Peter slept late Wednesday, and sat alone over tea and toast in the cavernous dining room of the University Arms hotel, a decidedly gloomy Victorian pile that overlooked a sward of green just off Regent Street in Cambridge. The place was half empty, the hallways echoing, but they had settled on it without debate the previous night as the most obvious place to fall into their separate beds.

Jo'd been rather quiet after the Indian curry, and Peter suspected she was worrying about her client again. Reviewing his own high-handed behavior during the past few days, he was awash in guilt; there was no other way to describe his miserable feeling. Guilt was the British national disease, after all, the baseline emotion beaten into every public schoolboy, and he'd carried it abjectly from childhood straight into his relationship with Margaux at Oxford —

something she'd taken for granted and knew how to use. Whenever he was uncomplicatedly happy — as now — a shadow of doubt would loom, a gnawing conviction that the bubble must burst as a result of his stupidity and self-indulgence. He'd selfishly seized on this lark as an escape from boredom. Jo, however, had come to England with a job to do — and he'd prevented her from doing it. He might even get her fired.

It was absurd, in the clear light of day, to consider chasing south to Rodmell, much less his harebrained plan of invading the Monk's House garden under cover of darkness. They would both be arrested. And Jo wasn't even a British subject! The consequences might be dreadful.

No, Peter thought — compelling as the adventure was, it could not go on. When she came down to breakfast, he'd offer to drive Jo straight back to London. He poured a third cup of tea, found it was lukewarm and bitter when he tasted it, and set it aside. Life was so damnably depressing.

And then his head came around as unconsciously he recognized her step on the marble flooring. She was wide awake, showered, her hair falling loose about her shoulders for the first time since he'd met her; and she'd changed her clothes.

She'd changed her clothes.

"Morning," he said, rising from his chair. "You look fresh."

"I've been out shopping." She was smiling ecstatically. "New underwear, Peter. New jeans. A silk sweater. I paid a fortune for this stuff, given the exchange rate — but I don't even care. It's like . . . rain after a day of heat. Pure bliss."

Pure bliss. New underthings. He found he was blushing, imagining Jo with her long hair down, in the bath, of all places.

"You look smashing," he managed. "Tea?"

She shook her head. "I found a Starbucks in town. Let's check out of this place and *go* already!"

And at the sight of her happiness, he hadn't the heart to tell her it was over. He merely paid his bill, stowed her shopping in the Triumph's boot, and pointed its nose toward Rodmell.

It was three hours before they dropped off the A27 near Kingston and slowed to a creeping pace as they entered the village of Rodmell. Rape fields lapped the handful of cottages, a few of them old enough to be half-timbered and thatched. Beech trees lined the fields; a gray, square-sided church tower pierced the distance. The soft,

288

huddled shape of the South Downs rose behind. Children were at play in the school-yard as the clock slid past noon, their high, piping voices calling as unintelligibly as cranes through the village stillness.

"There's the pub," Peter told Jo. "The Abergavenny Arms. Quite old, actually, and known for really smashing house ales. We turn left into The Street — that's what they call this main road through Rodmell — and Monk's House is perhaps half a mile on."

It was a clear autumn day, crisp, with no hint of rain, not even a mass of clouds over the Downs. Stiff from the drive, Jo said, "Let's walk."

They left the car near the pub and set out together up The Street. Nothing seemed more natural than Peter taking Jo's hand as they paced down the verge. "I love this sort of place," he said. "I don't know Sussex well, but one finds these smallish villages all over England, despite the ugliness of Town Councils and public works; and they call to me. Rather as I imagine gardens call to you."

"Then why don't you get out of London?"

He smiled faintly. "How would I live?"

"Cook. You know you want to. Just make a plan," Jo answered sensibly. "Figure out how much money you need to set up a restaurant in a destination spot — one like this, only maybe *not* this exactly, but a village with some kind of draw. Tourists or weekenders. Antiques hunters. University people. That sort of thing. And just . . . go for it. Peter's Place."

"You make it sound so simple."

"I started my own business." She shrugged. "I *know* that it's not simple. But I also know the more effort it takes, the more you love the result. You've got to follow your bliss, Peter. Not just do what you're told."

"I don't know. . . ." He let go of her hand. "I was never good at . . . risk-taking. It's not my strength. Margaux was always the one who walked out on a limb; my job was to make sure the tree never fell."

"And so you're still standing here, solid as a rock, while she's skipped off into thin air?" Jo asked quietly.

He turned and, without warning, kissed her. It was unexpectedly fierce, that kiss: filled with a lifetime of Peter's dreams and guilt and longing. Jo's knees gave way and her breath suddenly stopped in her throat. Her hands came up to his shoulders.

"Jesus," she breathed. "Where did that come from?"

"Sorry."

He would have walked on, drooping with embarrassment, but she grasped his wrist.

"Don't. That was wonderful. I'd hate it if you never did it again."

Wordlessly, he reached for her.

A passing car honked irritably as it swerved to avoid them.

Monk's House, to their disappointment, was closed.

"Damn," Peter said. "At least we know Margaux hasn't been here."

"Can we get into the garden?"

He glanced over his shoulder. "Not without an audience."

It was true that the place was completely exposed to the wondering eyes of Rodmell folk. The house sat right up next to The Street, separated only by a narrow flint wall backed with shrubs. The wall was topped with rounded bricks, and reached only to hip height; Jo could easily imagine swinging over it in the darkness. There was a plain wooden gate with a sign that proclaimed the house's name; the building itself was faced in white clapboard, with double-hung windows, shutterless, and a right-angled front entry jutting out like a carbuncle. It reminded her of the Federal farmhouses of the Delaware Valley; a place of simple elegance and sufficiency. It was decidedly unlike the flamboyance of Charleston. And that told her something about the sisters, Vanessa and Virginia.

"It's really all about the garden, which you can't see from here," Peter murmured in her ear. "Leonard Woolf was an avid horticulturalist. Started the local society, and so on. Greenhouses, beehives, vegetable plots, an orchard. To say nothing of the flowers. There's even a bowls lawn."

"A what?"

He grinned at her. "Like boccie or pétanque, only with a straightforward British name. Perhaps we should walk round to the back, by the church and school — they run alongside Monk's House. We might find a better view."

Trying not to appear conspicuous, they walked. The way led them by the old Norman church and its wide-open, sunlit plot of ground, dotted with graves. The sound of children's voices from the school next door had faded. Presumably the lads and lasses of Rodmell had gone back to their books.

"See the hedge?" Peter pointed. "It borders the bowls lawn. There used to be two elm trees growing in the middle of it — one called Virginia, and the other, Leonard. They leaned toward each other, as though seeking comfort."

"What happened to them?" Jo asked, her

voice hushed.

"Virginia's blew down in a gale sometime after her death. Leonard's died, I think, of Dutch elm disease."

Jo looked at Peter. "And?"

"Leonard buried his wife's ashes under the tree called Virginia."

"April 1941. Rodmell."

"Yes."

She drew a deep breath. "How will we find the spot, now the tree's gone?"

"The memorial plaque is still there. With a quotation from her novel *The Waves*."

Jo sighed. "It all looks so beautiful — as though someone still lives here."

"Somebody does," said a voice behind them.

They turned.

A young girl with ill-cut, sandy-colored hair was easing herself out of a red Austin. She was holding a grocery bag and had a purse slung over her shoulder; keys dangled from one hand. "There are caretakers. Full-time. Only they're not home at present. I'm house-sitting for the house-sitters. They're friends of my parents."

"Ah," Peter said. "That's helpful, thank you. It looks . . . very well tended."

"Better than when the Wolves were here. That's what I call them. Leonard and

293

Virginia. They were perpetually short on funds. Used an earth closet, if you can believe it — no running water. All the effort went into the garden." She set the grocery bag on the bonnet of the car and went round to the boot. Peter and Jo exchanged glances. Time to scarper.

The girl was engaged in lifting a suitcase to the ground. Another was firmly wedged near the spare tire.

"Can we be of help?"

"That'd be brilliant — thanks."

Peter hefted the second case from the boot, took the other in his free hand, and said smoothly, "Lead on."

She led.

There was a back gate to the property, and a path to a second gate in the walled garden; she opened this with some difficulty, the iron hasp being long since rusted into obduracy. "It's just through here," she said. "You can drop the cases at the back door — I'll fetch them in."

Peter set down the luggage carefully on the brick path and dusted his hands. Jo was trailing along behind, her eyes on the autumnal remains of the mixed borders. Leonard's tastes had run to the exotic, it seemed — if indeed the plantings were representative of those that had grown in his day.

"Unfortunate that the house is closed," Peter remarked. "We drove down from Cambridge on purpose to see it."

"Cambridge? Which college?"

"King's," Jo said automatically.

"I've a mate at Magdalene," the girl offered. "I'm Lucy, by the way."

"Peter. And that's Jo." He held out his hand. "Well, we won't keep you. Enjoy your time here."

"Thanks. I'll probably be stark, staring mad in another week — they'll have to scrape me off the floor of the Arms."

"Not keen on solitude?"

She stared at him, her lips slightly parted. "In *this* place? It's the end of the earth. I only agreed to house-sit *again* because I had the loan of the car. As soon as I start talking to myself, I'm off to Lewes for the evening."

"Smashing," Peter murmured. "Well, Jo, it's a pity we came on the wrong day — but we'll just have to see the place on your *next* trip to England."

"Whenever *that* is," Jo mourned. She gave Lucy a brave smile.

"Are you American?" the girl asked.

"Yes. I'm from L.A.," Jo invented, remembering Ter. "California. *Hollywood.* You've heard of it?"

"I should say so!" Lucy said scornfully. "Not that I think much of the place, mind. The way those people treat poor Posh and Becks. It's inhuman."

"He should never have left West Ham," Peter observed.

"You mean Manchester United."

"Yes, well, I'm heading back tomorrow," Jo persisted. "And the whole point of my trip, really, was to see Virginia's house."

"You're having me on," Lucy said.

As they were undoubtedly lying through their teeth, Jo was momentarily flummoxed by this comment, but Peter said hastily, "It's true. Jo's life dream has been to stand in this very spot. She's a writer, you know."

"Oh. *Books,*" said Lucy dispiritedly.

"Movies, actually. That's why I live in L.A. We're thinking of doing something on Virginia. Sort of like *The Hours,* only less . . ."

"Dreary." The girl eyed Jo suspiciously, as if uncertain whether to believe her, and said: "Ever met Brangelina, then?"

Jo shook her head regretfully. "But my friend's niece was one of their nannies. They have several, you know."

"Well, they *would,* wouldn't they?"

"Jo, we *really* should be going." Peter's voice was that of the long-suffering Englishman forced to endure more Hollywood gossip than anyone should, over the past few days.

Lucy licked her lips and glanced hurriedly over one shoulder, as though the ghost of the Woolfs might be watching. "Look, if you'd like to come in for a few minutes — it seems a shame, you've come all this way . . ."

"*Really?*" Jo cried. Without waiting for an answer, she bounded forward and hugged the girl impulsively. "You're just too sweet. I'll never forget this. It'll make my whole trip worthwhile!"

"I've always wanted to see California, myself," Lucy said. Her cheeks were flushed and hectic, like a nineteenth-century consumptive's.

It was a small, low-ceilinged place lit by only a few windows; and the pervading sense was of green: green shadows, green walls, faded wood the color of slate, chairs sagging from use. It was a restful house; but inescapably of a period — impossible to imagine Lucy's friends truly *living* here. It was probable, Jo thought, that the caretakers had a modern apartment somewhere on the premises. It would not do to betray nosiness, and ask.

Lucy was chattering on about a Jennifer — there were so many possibilities with that name, it might be Lopez or Aniston; Jo murmured something about Madonna, and diverted her immediately.

A succession of tables filled the sitting room; Jo could imagine books stacked and spread out to be read, or manuscript pages fluttering. A pot of tea and a plate of something simple — Virginia was a notoriously spare eater, an anorexic, probably. There was a poky old kitchen and two bedrooms. Virginia's sitting room was closed to the public.

"In good weather, she liked to write in what she called the Lodge — the old gardener's hut at the bottom of the garden," Peter murmured.

Jo followed his gaze through the back window and saw it: a perfect little room of one's own, with a porch.

"One of the suicide notes was found there. On her desk."

"Why kill yourself," Jo asked wistfully, "when you've got all this?"

Lucy was hovering, probably regretting her impulse to let them in; Jo smiled at her encouragingly. "Who's your favorite British actor?"

And received a disquisition on several raffish young men of dubious sexual orientation.

Peter was bent over a glass case, studying some pictures. There were albums, too, all of them very old. "Jo," he said. "Still have that photocopy from Charleston?"

"The mural?"

"The group snap."

She fished in her purse and drew it out.

"I thought so. There's another version of the same people displayed here — only they're named, this time."

She looked from her photograph to Peter's. It was dated 1936. *Quentin Bell, Maynard Keynes,* she read; *Roger Fry, Clive Bell, Julian Bell, Anthony Blunt.* The final figure was Leonard Woolf; thin and spare even in his middle period, his nose strong as a ship's prow, his hair swept back from a broad forehead. The most interesting face in the bunch — besides Virginia's suffering one.

"Lucy," Peter said firmly, "you've been too lovely — but we mustn't trespass any longer. Enjoy your evening in Lewes. Try not to go mad amongst all these ghosts."

"I won't charge you entry fees," the girl said tentatively. "It being a Closed Day. I wouldn't like to have to explain to the Trust."

"Very right," Peter agreed. He slipped her a ten-pound note. "Have a pint or two at the Arms, won't you? With our thanks?"

CHAPTER
TWENTY-EIGHT

Gray expected Margaux to keep him waiting that Wednesday evening. Still, he arrived
at Bar 190 a few minutes early; ordered a
very dry gin martini; and sank back against
the dark oak paneling. He was adept at stillness, and in his charcoal-colored jacket and
simple white shirt he might have disappeared into the crowd. It was his compo-
sure, however, that drew attention. Most
men, left alone with a drink, would have
immediately accessed their BlackBerries
and trolled through email, or dialed someone on a cell phone. Gray simply sat, one
hand lying casually on the table before him,
the other thoughtfully stroking the stem of
his martini glass. His self-containment suggested he was somebody; and it is possible
that more than one person drinking at the
Gore Hotel that evening wondered *who*.

Margaux had left her contact number on
the document she'd signed that morning. It

was a simple matter to persuade her to meet for drinks; and Gray let her choose the bar. He knew that posed a difficulty: How to guess what Gray liked? Or what would impress him? What could appear too tawdry, too hip, too cheap? He expected Margaux to settle for the obvious and safe choice of the Connaught itself — and was pleased when she didn't.

And there she was: Dramatic in black and red, a variation on the theme of the morning. Black matte jersey wrap dress, the hemline well above her knees; black leather boots almost reaching them. A red swing coat. Her black hair falling nearly to her waist in a mass of waves. She was a gorgeous woman, without question — but Gray was unmoved. He had seen so many gorgeous women before. They always knew their worth — and expected it to buy them more than it did. His lips quirked slightly as he thought of a woman who remained unforgettable, despite being long gone: His mother, Barbara. *Lightning doesn't strike twice,* she used to say. Meaning: If she's gorgeous, she's probably lacking a soul. Or a heart. Or a mind. It was rare to find all three, and beauty, too, in the same person. Although Barbara Westlake had certainly managed it.

Gray raised his glass to her memory as Margaux swept toward him, turning heads all through Bar 190. She ignored them. She turned heads every day.

"Gray." She extended a hand but didn't lean in, as he expected, to brush his cheek with hers. "Sorry I'm late — my last meeting ran hideously long, but then they always do."

He suspected she'd spent the hours since he'd last seen her shopping. How many changes of clothing could she have brought, realistically, for a single morning appointment? But perhaps he wronged her. Perhaps, as she clearly intended him to think, her life was one long series of important commitments. Or maybe she kept a flat in London filled with black and red clothes.

"Please. Sit down." A waiter had already materialized. "What would you like?"

"Pellegrino and a lime," she said briskly. "I can't afford to be muddle-headed when talking to the smartest man in the room."

And now she certainly had surprised him.

Gray slid his glass to one side of the table and studied her.

She studied him frankly in return. "Although I should like to take the compliment, I don't reckon you met me here tonight on the strength of my good looks.

Am I right?"

"Not *solely* on the strength of your good looks. No."

That won a smile. "Excellent. It gets so old, that sort of thing."

"Male admiration?"

"Male underestimation." She turned her head slightly as the Pellegrino appeared, and reached for it with one long-fingered hand. "I've spent years persuading a world populated by males that I've a brain inside this head of mine."

"You could always cut your hair," he suggested.

"That's just another way of losing the battle, isn't it? Why scarify myself to be taken seriously?"

The bar was beginning to fill; a steady buzz of voices made it necessary to shout. Gray had no desire to broadcast his message to the better part of London; he spoke at a normal level. As he'd hoped, Margaux leaned toward him.

"You're correct in thinking I wanted to talk to you. Without the rest of those folks from this morning pitching in."

She nodded, waiting.

"I want to know why Jo Bellamy gave you that notebook."

Margaux frowned. "Surely I told you? My

304

ex-husband is a Book Expert. He brought it to me to be verified."

"Understood. But that doesn't explain why you still had it this morning. I'm surprised Jo parted with the thing. It's very important to her."

Margaux's eyes slid away; she shrugged slightly, a beautiful movement, her breasts rising slightly with her sculpted shoulders in a fluid shift of jersey. "Peter — my ex — can be fairly vague. I think we agreed to talk over the next several days. I merely kept the notebook with me for safety's sake."

"And handed it off without a second thought to Marcus Symonds-Jones."

"Well, he *is* Peter's bloody employer!"

"Have you talked to your ex? Since Monday?"

She took a sip of Pellegrino, buying time. "Actually, no, I haven't. May I ask what this tends towards, Gray? An examination of my mobile-use habits, or of the status of my divorce?"

She was attempting umbrage, a mood that suited her; it went well with the flowing hair and chocolate eyes.

"Why were you in Cambridge last night?"

"I'm often in Cambridge. I'm a *don.*"

Gray held her gaze. "Somehow I don't think you were showing the notebook to a colleague. This is too important to share."

Her lip curled. "Too bloody well right."

"— Even with the people who gave it to you: Jo, and your ex-husband."

For once, she had no answer.

"What do you think they're doing, right now? Why haven't they come back to London?"

"Why do you care so much?"

Gray eased back in his seat, his fingers still caressing the stem of his martini glass. "I understand your hesitation to be frank with *me* — after all, we only met ten hours ago — but I confess I'm surprised that you're lying to Marcus. He could cut off your access to the material completely. Should he learn of it."

"I'm not lying!" Her voice had risen; she was leaning so far over the table toward him, she was nearly prone. In other circumstances, he would have enjoyed this view of her cleavage. In this case, he kept his eyes steadily on her face and held a finger to his lips. A warning. *Steady.*

She glanced sidelong, then raised herself upright. "I took the effing notebook Monday night and told Peter I'd give it back in the morning. Only I decided to go to Cambridge instead."

"Why?"

"You saw that there are pages missing from the back?"

"Maybe Woolf didn't like what she wrote."

"I doubt it. I think someone else edited that manuscript for her. There's a tantalizing phrase scribbled on the inside of the back cover. Peter saw it, too, I'm sure he did — a sort of envoi. A *clue*. In any case, I thought it possible the rest of the manuscript was hidden for a reason. And that it might be found."

"At Cambridge?"

"Cambridge was supposed to tell me where to look. But I'm not as good at solving puzzles as Peter is — making abstruse connections. I'm better at emotional analysis."

Abstruse connections. Gray's pulse had suddenly accelerated. *Peter Llewellyn was hunting for the rest of the notebook. And Jo with him.*

"It's frustrating to see the possibilities and lack the technique," Margaux was saying. "Honestly, I was ready to chuck the whole thing in the River Cam when Marcus called."

"But you decided instead to make the best of a . . . partial . . . situation."

"Exactly." She placed her hands on the table, fingers linked. "I don't want cash,

Gray. I'm not in it for a payoff. This isn't about greed."

"Of a *financial* kind."

"It's about access," she pushed on, ignoring his gibe. "I want exclusive rights to this new material — no sharing, for the first time in my entire career. Marcus has the power to stipulate my terms — *you* have the power to grant them."

Gray frowned. "Limit access to information? That's profoundly un-American. I'm not sure I can agree."

"You already signed a paper to that effect this morning."

"Paper, as we've seen, can be torn in half."

Margaux's teeth worried at her lower lip. "Tell me you've never closed communications about a deal you've decided to make. A fund you intend to set up. A client whose millions you've decided to squander. I won't believe you."

"But in those cases I control the deal. It's a closed system, like playing tug-of-war with both ends of the rope. You, unfortunately, have got only one."

She stared at him. "Now we come to it. *Your terms.* What is it you want, Mr. Graydon Westlake? How much body and soul do I have to sell?"

"I want you to drink this martini," he

replied, sliding it across the table toward her. "And then I want you to call your ex-husband."

CHAPTER
TWENTY-NINE

Peter and Jo walked back to the Abergavenny Arms feeling as though every eye
in the small village of Rodmell was upon
them. Jo succeeded in looking over her
shoulder only once; Lucy was not, as she'd
feared, posted in Monk's House's front
door staring balefully after them.

"I'd make a lousy criminal."

"It's all in the practice," Peter said impatiently. "I'm sure you'd take to it, with time.
Look at Anthony Blunt, for God's sake.
Right there in the Monk's House display
case, innocent as a lamb. Nobody suspected
him."

"Who's Anthony Blunt?" Jo demanded,
bewildered.

"An Apostle to end all Apostles. And one
of the Cambridge Five."

"I thought there were twelve."

"No, no — the Cambridge *Five,*" Peter
insisted, as though repeating the phrase

might make it comprehensible. "Surely you've heard of them?"

"I know the Jackson Five, but . . ."

"Oh, *Christ.* Burgess and Maclean? Ring a bell?"

"I'm sorry. Were they theater people?"

"They were *spies*," he said with immense patience. "Double agents. In the pay of the Soviets. For most of the Cold War. Kim Philby? Heard of him? I won't even ask about John Cairncross."

"Philby sounds familiar," Jo offered tentatively. "But isn't he American?"

Peter sighed. "Look — Guy Burgess and Donald Maclean defected to the Soviet Union in the early fifties. They'd been up at Cambridge together, and Burgess was an Apostle. He was also one of the more flamboyant sons of King's. Part of a group of Golden Youth that cut their political teeth in the age of Fascism, and the Spanish Civil War —"

"Like Vanessa's son. Julian Bell."

"Exactly." Peter stopped short in the middle of The Street. "Guy Burgess was elected to the Apostles the same year as Julian, in fact. Anthony Blunt probably nominated him — Blunt was a few years older and fairly influential in the Apostles at the time. He took up with Julian Bell through the Society,

311

which accounts for Blunt's appearance in that photograph we just saw."

"A bunch of Apostles."

"In the heart of Bloomsbury. What the Bells and the Woolfs appear to have missed, however, is that Blunt and Guy Burgess were systematically selling out Establishment Britain from about 1936 onwards. Along with Kim Philby, another prominent Cambridge man, and Maclean and Cairncross. The five, taken together, were the crown jewels of Soviet foreign intelligence."

"Julian Bell was a *spy?*" Jo was feeling rather deflated, as though the peaceful world she'd glimpsed at Charleston had been lifted, turned upside down, and shaken vigorously — causing several dead spiders to drop out.

"He didn't live long enough. But if the Spanish war had spared him — ? Who's to say? They were a group of young men who valued friendship *almost* more than politics. E. M. Forster — who you'll remember was an Apostle — is famous for saying: *If I were forced to choose between betraying my friends and betraying my country, I hope I should have the guts to betray my country.*"

Jo reached inside her purse and drew out the photocopy of the group snap, as Peter called it. She was familiar enough with the faces by this time. Leonard Woolf's narrow, ascetic profile; Keynes's balding pate and dark mustache; Julian's jovial, bearlike figure; his father's urbane expanse of forehead. And there was Blunt: composed, grave, almost insolent as he stared at the camera. The most inscrutable of the bunch. "Was he an economist, like Keynes?"

"Not at all. Art historian. Aesthete. Director of the Courtauld and surveyor of the Queen's Pictures. The old guard at Sotheby's used to consult him frequently when authenticating paintings — until Margaret Thatcher exposed him as a Soviet spy. There was a fearful row when that happened. A lot of long knives came out and all Blunt's old friends disavowed him. He was stripped of his knighthood, and died not long after."

"But he wasn't shot, or anything."

"No," Peter agreed, smiling faintly. "He lost his good name — and in Blunt's world, that was worse than a firing squad. Look, it's going on half-four and you probably want your tea, but we ought to run down to Lewes before the shops close. It's only a few miles back up the road, but you never know — they might lock up early. Can you manage without food for a bit?"

"What are we buying?"

"A shovel, two pairs of gloves, a stout bag,

313

and a smallish torch," he said, guiding her to his car. "Oh, and possibly a room for the night. It won't do to linger in Rodmell once we're done digging."

Digging.

Jo halted by the Triumph's passenger door. "Are we really going to exhume Virginia Woolf's ashes?"

"I shouldn't think there's many to be found, after sixty-eight years," Peter said dispassionately. "But I know what you mean. Disturbing sacred ground, and so on. That's why Leonard buried whatever spooked Maynard Keynes at the same time he buried Virginia. He expected the place never to be disturbed."

In Lewes, they found everything they needed at a store called Bunce's.

"Doing the autumn tidy this weekend, are we?" the clerk asked as Peter offered his credit card.

"We're putting in bulbs," Jo supplied.

"You're late. Mine were in a good three weeks ago."

"Ah," Peter said. "We'll just have to hope for the best, then, shan't we?"

Feeling chastened, they stowed their gear awkwardly in the Triumph — Jo would be cradling the iron head of the shovel in her

lap during the brief return to Rodmell —
and walked back up the High Street in
search of a pub.

"I'm getting bloody well tired of these
soulless meals," Peter muttered.

"I'm not even hungry," Jo said.

"Rubbish!"

"I'm a little nervous. And it's turned cold."

He steered her immediately into a small
café — perhaps ten tables, only three of
them occupied — that glowed warmly with
candlelight; logs burned in an open hearth.

"What you need," he declared firmly, "is a
restorative soup. Something creamy, like
crab bisque. We're quite close to the sea
here, you know. And then a good steak and
a green salad. Warm bread. All strictly
comfort food, washed down with red wine.
Cheese to follow."

It was a simple meal, but a thoroughly
delicious one; and Peter was right: She *did*
feel her borderline panic recede as the
comfort rolled in. She pushed all thought of
their midnight errand from her mind and
listened to Peter talk, which was something
he had begun to do, she noticed — he was
easy enough in her company now that he
didn't edit what he said.

"I've been thinking about your idea —
Peter's Place. It'd have to be named some-

thing else entirely, of course, and God knows where we'd put it — but there would be a few fundamentals. Locally sustainable produce, for one. Organic if possible. Local beef and poultry, naturally raised. And a limited menu — say, six entrées on any given night, but all of them *exquisite.* Inspired food that takes the best of several culinary traditions and fuses them well."

"I'd eat there," Jo said. "What would it look like?"

He stared off into space for a moment. "I love the texture of old buildings. By that I mean all that's authentic about them."

There it was again — the connoisseur in Peter, his instinct for what was true. It was the quality Jo trusted most.

"Serviceable buildings that had a utility once," he continued. "A group of oast houses, for instance, or an ancient barn. I'd like bare timbers and stone floors and a *really massive* hearth people could sit in with their wineglasses. Rustic, relaxed, but absolutely top drawer. Know what I mean?"

"Yes. I do."

"Ideally, there'd be a working potager in the back."

"Peter." Jo set down her wineglass. "I just designed the most *fabulous* potager for Gray. An entire walled acre, divided into

316

quadrants — espaliered fruit trees, season-ally rotated heirloom and organic veg-etables, everything from five types of beet to eleven types of lettuce. It's going to be the most magnificent symphony of color and texture and flavor imaginable —"

"Gray being your abandoned client?"

Jo screwed up her face. "Yes."

"And what's the bugger going to do with so much veg, then? Feed an orphanage?"

Despite herself, she burst out laughing. "I don't think he has any concept of how much food he's going to produce. And knowing Gray, he'll only live in the Hamptons about eight weeks a year. He owns five houses."

"So he's bought the *look* of a potager," Peter said thoughtfully, "and will probably toss most of the stuff back on the compost pile to rot. I should set up Peter's Place directly on the far side of his garden wall. And hire you to garden for me."

He looked at her then, and Jo flushed. But she only raised her glass and said, "To Peter's Place. Wherever it may be."

It was eleven before they noticed that the fire had fallen to embers, and they were the only ones left in the café.

Monk's House was completely dark when they rolled slowly past its flint wall and turned toward the churchyard beyond. Lucy might be at the pub, or she might be asleep. *Which?* Jo thought, her panic returning.

"The principal thing," Peter said, as he pulled the Triumph into the deserted school car park and killed the engine, "is to use the torch as little as possible. Can you see in the dark?"

"Usually. But this is pitch black."

True country night was wrapped around Rodmell. If there were stars somewhere above, their light was masked by a bank of cloud and the heavy weight of the Downs looming on the horizon.

"The easiest possible course is also the most exposed," Peter said. "That's to walk back round to the front and nip over the flint wall. Then we can simply amble along the side of the house to the back garden."

"Somebody'll see us," Jo argued. "Can't we just cross the field and cut through the hedge? You said the two elm trees once stood there."

"I did," Peter agreed, "but have you ever tried to cut through a hedge?"

"I do it all the time."

He frowned at her. "What *are* you talking about?"

Jo reached for her purse and scrabbled in its depths. "While you were inspecting shovels, I bought a pair of secateurs. Autumn's the time to prune, you know. I'll do a passable job. It won't hurt the hedge."

"Smashing," Peter said. "I'll get the shovel."

It took Jo twelve minutes to carve a break in the soaring wall that divided field from garden. She chose a spot roughly around where Peter thought he remembered having once seen the marker to Virginia's memory. So late in October, the yew was brittle: she was glad of the gloves, for the sharp evergreen would undoubtedly have drawn blood. She held back the tough stems and motioned silently to Peter. He swam through and she followed.

He had dropped to his knees on the far side of the hedge, and was probing the ground blindly with his fingers. She crouched down and followed him. They were like two rats, she thought, scuttling along in the dark, the shovel trailing between them. But they had not yet used the flashlight.

Suddenly, Peter stiffened, then to her astonishment rolled like a log against the base of the hedge, his gloved hands covering his blond hair. The unmistakable sound of swearing came to Jo's ears; she flattened herself against the yew, heart pounding so loudly it had to be audible to the girl who was now standing outside the rear gate where they'd first encountered her that morning, trying to shove her unwilling key into the old lock.

Lucy. She'd probably walked to the Abergavenny Arms; it couldn't be more than half a mile away. But had she drunk enough to be blind to two bodies lying half-exposed in the darkness of the hedge?

The lock turned and the gate swung open, creaking on its hinges. Lucy staggered up the walk, and Jo — who was so far under the yew it was sticking painfully into her neck — watched her make her determined way toward the rear gate into the walled garden that surrounded Monk's House. Then she stopped short and turned. For an instant, she seemed to stare right at Jo, breathless and paralyzed on the ground.

A tiny orange light flared; Lucy, lighting a cigarette. She took a greedy draft of smoke and lingered by the garden wall, staring up at the chilly sky.

Go through the gate, Jo urged. *Go inside. For Chrissake, you must be freezing.* But maybe smoking wasn't allowed in National Trust properties. Another burden Lucy had to bear, when staying at Monk's House.

There was no sign of life from Peter; had he seen the girl, motionless but for the pendulum of her right arm, lifting predictably to her lips?

Suddenly, Lucy dropped the butt and ground it beneath her heel. She lifted the iron hasp on the gate and swung through it, securing it behind her. Perhaps a minute later the house door slammed and a light bloomed in the window.

Jo exhaled.

"You all right?" Peter whispered from somewhere ahead of her.

"I'm scared to death," she hissed. "Do we leave?"

His answer was drowned by a sudden swell of sound coming from Monk's House — a cacophonic blare of music played at deafening volume. Jo could just make out a sporadic clapping as Lucy kept poor time to the music; and then a snatch of the girl's voice, lifted in off-key song.

"Blimey," Peter whispered. He had crawled up next to Jo. "She's having her own little rave, right there in the caretaker's apartment. Look at her!"

And, in fact, craning to spy over the wall, Jo could just see the twirling form passing before one window, then the next; lost to everything but the metal frenzy.

"Right." Peter reached forward with his fingers again, searching the ground. "Let's find this bloody marker, shall we?"

Against you I will fling myself, unvanquished and unyielding, O Death!

Brave words, Jo thought, as she read the few lines illuminated by Peter's penlight. But what had the woman who'd written them, so long ago, felt as the water closed over her head, filled her mouth and lungs, cut her off from the sunlight and the bird singing triumphantly, *Life, life, life?*

How had Virginia come to the river, in the end?

Peter switched off the light and reached for the shovel. "Let's hope it's not too far down," he said.

It was a slow and careful business. Peter's plan, formulated on the fly, was to dig first at one side of the marker to avoid disturbing it too much; he would then angle under it and probe for several feet beneath. Jo kept watch alternately on the growing mound of dirt and the solitary party going on inside Monk's House, which after seventeen minutes had begun to turn maudlin. Lucy had substituted torch songs for head-bangers, most of them by female artists, and was singing emotionally and wretchedly at the top of her lungs. How much *had* the girl drunk?

"Jo," Peter said.

He lifted the shovel slantwise from the earth and then thrust it back in again. She heard a faint metallic clang.

"Shit," she said. "Do you think it's a . . . cremation urn or something?"

"Dunno." He dragged a cautious bit of soil from the hole. "I'll just . . . feel for it, shall I?"

Peter's arm disappeared up to his shoulder.

"Doesn't feel like an urn. Feels like a . . . a sort of box. Flattish and long." He grunted slightly with exertion, then pulled the object out of the ground.

For an instant, Jo thought he was holding a book.

"What is it?"

Peter rubbed at the clods of earth with his garden glove. "A Peek Freans biscuit tin. Probably prewar. They stopped making them in 1939 — couldn't spare the metal." He sat down beside her, removed his gloves, and reached for the penlight. A narrow beam played over the tin's surface.

"Peter — it's shaped like a book!"

"Yes — they were rather elaborate in those days, a marketing ploy on the part of the biscuit makers. Quite collectible now. Sold at auction, in fact. This one's gone a bit wonky, however — probably all the damp in the ground." He attempted to pry off the lid and failed. "Corrosion."

"Let me." Jo tore off her gloves. Her fingernails were never long — that was impractical for a gardener — but her fingertips were more delicate than Peter's. She found an edge and applied pressure. The lid moved.

Peter played the beam along the edge. "Here. Use the edge of the shovel. Like a lever —"

Together, they pried off the tin's cover.

Inside was what looked like a rubber bag.

"Oilskin, I think," Peter said, and lifted it out. "Jo — you ought to open this."

"What if it's ashes?" she whispered.

He shook his head. "It's not. I can *feel* it."

Whatever it was, however, would have to wait. Lucy had suddenly stopped singing.

CHAPTER
THIRTY

The lights were still on, but Monk's House was utterly silent. It was as though, Jo thought, Lucy and her tunes had been taken out by a neutron bomb.

"She's coming into the garden," Peter breathed, as the back door creaked open. "As long as she stays in the walled bit, we're fine; but let's hope she hasn't forgot something in the car."

"Do we run?"

"I hate leaving that mound of dirt."

This was so unexpected — and so entirely like Peter's sense of responsibility — that Jo nearly snorted with laughter. She caught herself, however, and tried to avoid breathing.

What could Lucy be doing? Impossible to see from their position. Gazing at the starless sky? Talking on her cell phone? But no, there was still no sound, and Jo imagined the girl was an emphatic talker. Then the scent of burning tobacco drifted across the garden wall, and Jo sighed inwardly. A bedtime smoke. Lucy definitely had a habit.

They waited wordlessly while the cigarette burned down. Then they heard the house door open and groan closed, and watched as one by one, the lights were extinguished.

Peter made fast work of filling the hole he'd dug. Then they went through the hedge a final time, and positively ran to the Triumph parked in the schoolyard, Jo clutching the Peek Freans tin to her chest. She was laughing with hysterical relief and Peter had just turned the ignition, when his cell phone rang.

"Bloody *hell*," he said as he stared at the number glowing green in the darkness. "Margaux."

"Pick up!" Jo hissed. "No, better yet — let me." She wrenched the phone from his hand, stabbed a button, and shouted, "Where's my notebook, bitch?"

"You might ask yourself instead," said a cool voice in her ear, "how many different ways Peter is using you. Could I speak to him, please?"

Scowling, Jo handed off the phone.

"Right, hello, sorry about that," Peter said.

Sorry? When Margaux had deliberately

screwed them and left without a word? Jo glared at him sidelong. And what did Margaux mean about Peter *using* her? That he wasn't really interested in the Woolf manuscript? Or . . . that he didn't believe it was *real?*

". . . not asleep, actually, I'm behind the wheel. Yes. *Driving.* Where are you?"

There was a pause. Peter shifted into reverse and the Triumph wheeled backward, turning toward the Abergavenny Arms. "You *what?*" he spluttered. The car swerved and Jo clutched at the swing strap. The ancient biscuit tin slipped off her lap and burst open.

"Well, that's bloody well put the cat among the pigeons, hasn't it? And you actually thought it was a *good idea?* I'll be fired, darling, if I'm not arrested —"

Darling.

Jo tried to remember that she had no claim on Peter. Of a romantic kind. He was just a nice guy who was helping her out. By handing her precious manuscript to his ex-wife, who promptly stole it . . . He'd landed Jo in a very difficult position with Sissinghurst. . . . Why had he decided it was okay to drop everything and leave London? Had he been *forced* to get out of town quick, and she'd provided an excuse?

The tin bounced at Jo's feet as the car negotiated a curve. She lifted the oilskin package and held it up in her hands. It was dark umber in color, tied like a parcel with blackened twine. She began to work at the old knots with her fingers. What she needed was a pair of scissors — or her secateurs. But no, she'd left them behind at the hedge. *Damn.*

"I don't know. I'll have to talk to Jo," Peter was saying. "I'm not entirely sure where we'll be. I owe it to her to discuss —" Another pause, and this time she distinctly heard Margaux's voice through the receiver, both strident and pleading. "I think you tossed that claim in the rubbish a year ago, along with half the contents of the Islington flat. Now look — I'll call in the morning. Get some sleep. *Night.*"

His voice, Jo thought, was a shade gentler on that final word, a caress half remembered. It made her stomach clench.

He snapped the phone shut and exhaled gustily. "*Lord.* She was put on earth to drive men mad."

"What did she say?"

I love you, Peter, I miss you, it was all a stupid mistake. . . .

"She said she was unavoidably delayed in Oxford yesterday morning —"

Boy toy, Jo thought.

"— couldn't reach us because her mobile was dead, so she just took the notebook into my office. And found that nobody knew where I was."

"She took the Woolf manuscript to Sotheby's?" Jo cried, outraged.

"My own particular boss put her through the Inquisition, rather." Frustration and amusement in Peter's voice, now. "She thought she'd help by saying I'd been at Oxford. The long and short of it is that Marcus has the notebook, it's being analyzed by our in-house experts over the weekend, and they're pursuing the issue of legal ownership as best they can. So you've no need to worry any longer. The notebook is safe."

"Are you out of your mind? I've just lost complete control! Your nightmare of a wife handed off my grandfather's book."

"... which you *filched* from a tool shed at Sissinghurst, Jo! It never *belonged* to you."

"That's not the point!"

"Then what *is?*"

She was so furious with him — his sudden defection into the reasonable world — that for a moment she was speechless. "The point," she snapped, "is finding out what happened. To Virginia. And Jock."

"Which we've tried to do. Who *owns* the

bloody thing in the end is irrelevant. Sotheby's might as well establish that as anyone."

"Given that you work there," she said with deadly calm.

"Now, what is *that* supposed to mean?"

"Peter, are you getting some sort of *commission* for all this?"

"I'm probably losing my job," he retorted acidly.

"What did that woman want? At two o'clock in the morning?"

"To hear my voice," he said distinctly. "She was . . . lonely."

There was a tense silence. The Triumph left Rodmell behind and picked up Swanborough Hollow — the road north, toward Lewes.

"You never asked about the Ark," Jo said. "What she found yesterday, or what she did with it —"

Peter cleared his throat uncomfortably. "To be honest, I completely forgot about the thing. It was a shock, actually — her calling like that. In the middle of the bloody night."

"So much of a shock, in fact, that you wasted the sole opportunity you had to grill the woman! Jesus, Peter — she's ripped us off twice, and all you do is scold her like a wayward child!"

"Haven't I just *explained* that she never meant to steal the damn notebook?"

"If that were true," Jo retorted, "she wouldn't have run off to Cambridge. I'm not that stupid, even if you *want* to be."

"All right — all *right.*" Peter lifted his hands from the wheel in exasperation. "Maybe she lied. It's a habit of Margaux's. But she's not all bad, you know. She tried to deal with the notebook honorably by turning it over to my boss. And she'd like to make amends. She's tumbled to the fact that we're searching for the rest of the manuscript — and she offered to help."

Jo grasped the twine securing the oilskin package and pulled.

"We're not searching anymore, Peter," she said.

CHAPTER
THIRTY-ONE

Peter pulled the Triumph onto the left-hand verge of the road and killed the engine. He snapped on his penlight.

"What have we got?" he asked quietly.

The book — for it was a slim bound volume, not a letter or notebook or even torn pages, as they'd expected — had no title stamped on its pale blue cloth cover. But there was a yellowed envelope resting on top of it, with an inky smear of handwritten words.

To the Grave Robbers, it read.

"Do we open it?"

Peter glanced at her. "Well — it *is* addressed to us. I suspect that's Leonard's writing."

Feeling decidedly guilty, Jo tried to pry up the flap. It parted damply in her hands, not so much torn as disintegrating.

There was a single piece of folded paper inside.

If offered the choice of betraying my friends or betraying my wife, I hope I should have the courage to do neither.

Or perhaps both.

How does one keep faith with anyone in such wretched times? Much less keep faith with all?

I have tried. I have done what Maynard asked, and destroyed the pages of Virginia's book that caused him such anxiety.

But to honour her whom this writing almost certainly killed, I typeset those pages before I burned them.

And so I have kept both my promises: to bury the truth, and to publish it to the world.

Do with this book what seems best to you.

But know that the unquiet mind of the author lives in it still, and will haunt you.

As she has always haunted me.
                    Leonard Woolf,
                    Monk's House,
                    30 April 1941

Peter reached for the book — he was, Jo remembered suddenly, an expert in exactly this object, in the typeface and the cloth bindings and the nature of paper.

"Leonard must have hand-set this on a small press they kept at Rodmell," he said. "The actual Hogarth Press — the company the Woolfs founded in 1917 — was moved out of London in 1940 to protect it from being bombed. No jacket — they often got Vanessa to design those, but apparently she wasn't in on the secret of this. Here's the colophon, however — the symbol of the Hogarth Press. Vanessa designed that, too."

He showed Jo the book's spine; stamped on it in gold was the head of a wolf, in profile. "The text is printed in a serif font, probably some form of Baskerville. Quite common. Leonard loved composing forms —— beds of type — but they were only practical for short print runs. Too labor-intensive otherwise. The first thing Hogarth ever hand-published was a pamphlet of two short stories — the Woolfs each wrote one. Virginia's became quite famous — it's called 'A Mark on the Wall.' They put together the covers themselves, gluing cloth on boards and assembling the books on the dining room table. He must have done this one alone."

Jo had a sudden vision of a silver head, a narrow profile, an oil lamp behind a black-out shade. The middle of the night. The silence of an abandoned house. The smell of lead on his fingers . . .

"We've got to read this."

Peter looked at her searchingly. "Aren't you exhausted?"

"What does that have to do with anything?"

"It's a polite way of asking whether you trust me enough — despite Margaux."

"Ah." She looked down at her hands. "I guess I trust you . . . *enough.* Let's stop driving for what's left of the night. Read Leonard's book. And I'll turn it over to Sotheby's as quietly as a lamb in the morning."

Peter smiled at her faintly. "A lamb. *Bollocks.* Jo, you don't know the meaning of the word."

"I've ordered it for dinner numerous times," she said with dignity.

"All right. But no cheating." He flicked off the penlight. "No reading until I've found us a room."

It was nearly two-thirty by the time they roused a night clerk at the White Hart in Lewes, an old coaching inn transformed into a modern hotel, with potted palms near its indoor swimming pool. Jo was tired enough to accept this as merely one part of a hallucinatory night. She was, after all, holding a Peek Freans tin dug up from Virginia Woolf's grave and yet again she was out of clean underwear; all of this was of a piece, part of the surreal world she'd inhabited since leaving Sissinghurst three days ago.

She decided not to correct the clerk when he referred to them as "Mr. and Mrs. Llewellyn," although it took her an instant to digest that he had only one room to offer them. She didn't care. She'd be reading for what remained of the night.

"I'll sleep on the floor," Peter suggested when they'd closed the door behind them. For all the hotel's half-timbered charm the room was rather claustrophobic, with a sloping roof and a worn bedspread.

"Whatever," she said. "I'll make coffee."

She found a pouch of Breakfast Brew near the minibar and filled the carafe. Peter tossed his jacket on a chair and began to roll up his sleeves. *Why* did the sight of him in a loosened dress shirt, even a wrinkled one he'd been wearing for days, affect her so powerfully? The word for Peter, she decided, was *debonair.* He looked as though he'd been born to hold a glass of gin on the sidelines of a cricket pitch.

He propped the bed pillows against the headboard and stretched out on the mattress. "It's considered bad form on the Continent to use a bed for anything other than sleeping, did you know? Only Americans sit on them to read. Or hold an intimate conversation. Mention this to a confirmed European and they'll explain that's why we invented *chairs.* But I've always thought a bed was the best place to get to know another person. The English have so many defenses, Jo — all we can't or won't say. But not when we're lying down."

He looked at her then, and she realized he'd taken off his glasses — so she'd be safely out of focus? His eyes were pale green, not gray as she'd thought.

"What can't you say standing up, Peter?"

"That I'm falling in love with you."

She stood rooted to the carpet, unable to speak. Nor could she look away from him, from the dreamy green eyes and the faint smile on his lips. She could feel herself go

337

hot, then cold.

*Ask yourself how many different ways Peter
is using you.*

"Make the coffee, Jo."

She turned blindly and poured the water
into the machine, her hands working of
themselves.

"Now where's that book?"

He spoke calmly, as though he hadn't just
dropped a massive stone in the quiet pool
of the room, as though the ripples weren't
spreading out to engulf her. But she could
see, even from the distance of the minibar,
the pulse at the base of his throat throb-
bing.

"Peter —"

"Ah. Here it is."

He pulled the cookie tin toward him.

The coffee began to drain into the carafe.
Jo waited. "How do you take it?" she asked.

"Would it kill you if I said I'd much rather
have good, strong English tea?"

At that, she began to laugh and the knot
of tension inside her slipped loose and
rolled away. They were friends again instead
of possible lovers or enemies and she was
able to bring two mugs to the bedside table
and stretch out beside him.

"It tastes like liquid cardboard and you're
going to drink it and like it," she said, tak-

ing a scalding sip of the truly lamentable brew. "Open the tin. I can't wait any longer."

He lifted the lid. The oilskin packet and Leonard's letter sat in the bottom.

Peter balanced the book between them, his head close to hers. The room was very quiet, and the clock, Jo noticed, read 2:41 A.M.

"Ready?" he asked.

"Ready," she said.

CHAPTER
THIRTY-TWO

Tuesday, 1 April 1941
Sissinghurst
NOTES ON THE MAKING OF A WHITE GARDEN:
PART II

Harold came down from London this afternoon on purpose to see me.

It was the sort of day that makes one believe it possible some fragile beauty will survive the war, some species of hope. I know in my heart that is a fallacy and a stupid comfort. My mind persists in wishing that the bird spoke truth when it sang of life. But the bird, too, was hoping, hoping — it is the bitterest joke of all, that as the world opens its heart, green shoots leafing, persistent stems rising, the golden beads of pollen streaming in the air — the lid of the box closes, the roof caves in. Earth will stop my mouth.

Vita was up early, at work in her garden

with the boy Jock. What is to be done in time of war, in such a place? Weeding. The cutting of hazel from the coppice below the meadow, and the setting of stakes in the herbaceous border. A cool breeze buffets her hair and cheek, which are no longer opulent, no longer the trappings of the harem. The bones of her fingers are knobbed and the skin tough and spotted. She has left off wearing gloves but still sports her jodhpurs, a cigarette dangling from the corner of her mouth as she digs. It is healing for her, this plunging of hands into the soil, and perhaps even the boy is healing — his uncomplicated strength, his willingness to lift and carry without comment, his deftness with the spade and pruning knife. Jock whistles as he trundles barrows in the garden. He does not dream of horror at night. In this he reminds me of Julian, who was like a bear in his strength, who went laughing to his death in Spain.

But for myself I think that to make things bloom while the bombs are falling is so much whistling in the dark. I could almost despise Vita for it.

I told her last night about November. The boy falling from the sky. The sprained ankle and the smell of fear and white patches around his mouth where the gag was bound.

The men coming in the night in black cars and the boy whimpering as they bundled him into the back. You wouldn't like it, I said. If it were Ben or Nigel or even Jock. A few days after I'd finished *Between the Acts,* I said, and the typesetting already begun. The smell of lead on his fingers when he put his hands over my mouth, to stop me screaming.

"Oh, my dear," she said absently, her eyes on the burgeoning yew, "I should stay out of it all, if I were you. Surely they know best, these people from MI5?"

But she must have telegraphed to Harold. There he was this afternoon, fresh from the 3:35 train, wandering up to take tea with us in the Priest's House, the boy Jock having fetched him from the station.

The spring day had quite faded by that time, and it was chill, with a mist off the moat; I wrapped a sweater of Vita's about me and hugged myself, the tea incapable of warming.

How to describe Harold Nicolson?

There is the obvious: black bowler hat, excellently tailored suit appropriate to Westminster, but rather worn, now, given the shortages of wartime and funds at home; the soft tissues of the face and the wide, mild eyes; the correct moustache —

Harold's attempt at manliness, I always think, a gesture he shares with Maynard Keynes. There is the weakness about the mouth and the softness of the fingers and the sense of warmth whenever he greets one — Harold cannot hide his easy affection, his interest in everything, though he attempts to do so with his studied wit.

He adores Vita and could not live, I think, without her, and yet she is the most supremely selfish being one could possibly meet; even when he ran for Parliament she politely declined to mount the hustings at his side, she magnificently ignored the gossip regarding their unusual marriage and would not play at the dutiful wife. She has discarded his name and resumed her own. She is steadfastly unfaithful with a variety of lovers, as he generally is with men and boys; and yet not a day passes without their exchange of letters. In their deep loyalty and constant choice of one another's friendship, Harold and Vita are unassailable. He accepts her narcissism and worries about her drinking; she ignores his perpetual unhappiness at the failure of his career.

And it is a measure of how much he cares for her that he dropped everything at the Ministry of Information this morning, and came down to Kent the moment she summoned.

"Hallo, darling," he said as he bent to kiss her cheek. "Hallo, Virginia. You're looking fit. So happy you could keep Mar company in her castle. She grows quite fidgety with all the regulations. Men posted in the tower. *Rations.* Been working the garden, Mar?"

Mar is his particular name for Vita; Hadji is hers for Harold.

"Virginia thinks we should plant white flowers," Vita said, gesturing out the cottage window, "so that the glow might light our way to bed."

"Then by all means, set Jock to uprooting the roses," Harold suggested. "Care to take a turn in the garden, Virginia? You might show me what you intend."

As I guessed poor Harold had come expressly from London to give me a scolding, I felt obliged to rise from my chair and saunter with him into the chill of the falling dusk, the bare rose canes enmeshing us with all the splendour of the trenches. Vita stayed behind. I had an idea of her reaching for her hip flask, and spiking her tea with brandy.

"And so you've run off, have you?" Harold took my cold fingers between his own and chafed them gently. "Poor Virginia. Has

Leonard been beastly to you?"

I said nothing. I would consent to listen, but not to speak. Not yet. There was too much I feared. The complicity of the men of Westminster.

"You've upset everyone terribly, you know. Leonard's dragging the river. There are parties of men and dogs along the banks."

This last brought me up short, my hand at my throat. *Dogs.* Torches. The flickering silhouettes of the search party and the sound of baying on the air. Slavering jaws mouthing the cold flesh —

I retched.

Harold's arm came briefly to my back; a faint pressure of comfort. "You must write to them. You must *explain.* It would relieve their minds —"

He strolled onwards, serene and infallible, while I stood like a plinth in the midst of Vita's garden. He did not look back as he walked, a darker shadow in the deepening dusk, past the Chinese jar and through the gap in the hedge that led to the statue of the Little Virgin.

I knew that spot well. Beyond the garden gate and several feet below its level; beyond the sight of the Priest's House windows. We could be private, there. I could tell him what he asked to know.

I took my courage in my hands and followed him.

CHAPTER
THIRTY-THREE

1 April 1941
Sissinghurst

"I love this old lady," Harold said, stroking the statue. "Vita would say I prefer Dionysius, but she's wrong. The Little Virgin's my pet."

"How did she come here?"

"A fellow named Tomas Rosandic carved her for us out of wood. But I had the original cast in lead, some years ago — wood never lasts." He glanced around. "I'm not happy with her here. The drop in grade means her legs are all but invisible from the gate — and that seems a shame, doesn't it? A statue should serve to focus the eye, draw the viewer along an axis. This is all wrong."

"She belongs in the White Garden — when you make it."

"Have you seen Delos? Vita's Attic Wilderness?" He took my hand, and tucked it under his arm. "It's even more hopeless now there's nobody to cultivate chaos. Let's stroll, shall we?"

The footing was very bad, and I clung to him. The night, and this familiar stranger; my heart beat quicker. Harold was silent.

"How are things at the Ministry?" I asked.

"Funny you should ask," he murmured. "Only a writer of novels could understand — I've become a vehicle for falsities and lies and hopeful declarations. I am never so full of bile as when forced to censor an upright journalist, before his truth terrifies half the kingdom."

"Hypocrisy," I said.

"Oh, yes — much more than I found in all my years with the Foreign Office. But perhaps I was simply callow, then, and unaware."

"No." I uttered the word as though I spat bullets. "People want lies, now. Like children before bed. Do even *you* grow to love lying, Harold?"

He stopped by a great chunk of rock — one of the ruins of Sissinghurst scattered about the ground Vita calls Delos — and stared at me soberly. "I hate it. But I've found lies are indispensable in wartime. What about you?"

"I left Leonard because of a lie. Or several. They beget each other, you know."

He sat down on a flat plane of the rock and patted it gently. "Tell me all about it, old thing."

"Last November," I began, "a young man fell out of the sky."

Harold's eyelids flickered. "One of ours, or one of theirs?"

I hardly knew how to answer the question. It suggested a world of absolutes, where I'd never lived.

"He was certainly German, if that's what you mean. But he claimed to be Dutch. He fell into one of the meadows near the river at half-past three in the morning, on a night of no moon. He told us his name was Jan. Jan Willem Ter Braak. I had just finished my book the day before. I couldn't sleep and I heard the dog barking."

How to explain to Harold that whenever the words left me, I was empty as a husk lying on the threshing-room floor? Empty as a woman whose birth has aborted? Impossible to sleep in such a state. Impossible not to hate oneself, knowing the words had spilled irretrievably, that there was no taking them back, that Leonard would *force me to print* when the thing was dreadful — paltry words, lifeless, without art, *shaming?* I wanted to burn my book, I wanted to drown it.

"*Between the Acts?*" Harold said easily. "Leonard says it's as good as *The Waves.*"

"Leonard lies."

I could not look at him, beside me on the rock. *Come under the shadow of this red rock.*

Harold fumbled for something in his pocket; a pipe. Then the match flaring, the comfort of tobacco smoke. "So a German parachuted into your back garden. What then?"

"The dog found him. Baying and whining in the middle of the night. He'd sprained his ankle, you see, and was stumbling. Leonard went out after the dog."

Harold puffed on his pipe. "What did Leonard do?"

"Jan tried to run and the pain made him faint. Leonard tied his hands and feet and left the dog to guard him. Then Leonard locked me inside the house and got on his bicycle and rode into Lewes, where there's a telephone."

"And a constable?"

"He didn't wake the constable."

"No?"

"He rang up his friends." I looked at Harold now. "You know some of them. In government. *Cambridge* people."

He smiled. "My poor darling, you make

them sound like Nazis."

I refused to notice this. "One of them is Guy Burgess."

"Delightful fellow. Works at the BBC. Radio interviews."

"You've slept with him, haven't you," I said, "so of course you think he's grand."

Harold drew his pipe deliberately from his mouth. "Did Vita tell you that?"

"No. Guy did."

"I see." He was still serene, without affront; there is no one more truly the gentleman than Harold Nicolson. "I shall have to beg the little sod to be more discreet. Was he the person Leonard rang?"

"Leonard put through a call to Maynard, who lives in Tilton — not far from Rodmell, as the crow flies. Maynard rang the other two in London. They share a flat. I couldn't think why they'd be wanted — Tony's an art critic and Guy a drunk — but eventually I understood. Tony Blunt's with military intelligence. He does something with German agents. And Leonard knew Jan was no Dutchman."

Think what the local bobby would do if he got his hands on the poor bugger, Leonard had said. *They all remember Dunkirk. Probably kill him by morning. Better to ring someone sensible and make sure the fool survives.*

"They came direct from London, in two black cars, and bundled Jan in the back. He was conscious by that time, and he tried to fight them, but it was no good."

Harold rapped his pipe against the rock, scattering the tobacco. "Disturbing, admittedly — but I have yet to detect Leonard in a lie."

"That came later." I hugged my sweater close. "There were bombers, you see, in waves overhead during the autumn, and talk of Germans coming. *Invasion.* My brother gave us morphia so we might kill ourselves, and Leonard hid it in a drawer. And then the planes stopped, Harold. *They stopped.* At first I felt relief, but then I began to listen to things the others said when they came. Your Burgess. And Tony."

"Leonard's Apostles. I'm only a poor Oxford man, but what is it they say — 'If forced to choose between betraying my friends, and betraying my country . . .' "

"Yes!" Perhaps Harold would understand, after all. "They came at night, after the curfew. They had special police passes, extra petrol. They talked to Leonard about Jan."

"The fellow was still alive?"

"He was being . . . controlled." I looked at him desperately. "They set him free, on a very long leash. He was sent to Cambridge, where Maynard might watch him, with money and his radio set, and ordered what to tell the Germans."

"—Which were lies."

"Yes."

"Sounds bloody brilliant to me."

"It was." My fingers twisted together, as though the bones were twigs I could break. "It was *inspired,* Harold. And Jan isn't the only one. There's a whole group involved — the Twenty Committee. Tony says every German agent dropped into England has been turned. The alternative to cooperation is death, of course."

"Virginia," Harold said gently. "We're at war with Hitler. Death is *always* the alternative. Tony and the others are simply doing their jobs. Why has this upset you so?"

I rose from my red rock and began to pace the wilderness of Delos. Weeds snatching at my ankles. While Vita drank her sherry in the Priest's House, a bramble grew steadily to surround Sleeping Beauty's castle. She would be walled up alive, soon.

"Because of the proofs. Leonard set the type for my book, Harold. All through the winter he was composing formes on the hand press. He hadn't really used it in years — but he said it was a distraction for him. From the war."

"Probably was."

"He gave me one set of proofs to correct. He kept another. But I mislaid mine, once, when Leonard was out — I found his set and started to read. He had changed the text in places, Harold. *He had put in other words.* Do you understand what I mean?"

"I'm afraid —"

The book is excellent. The finest you've written. Of course we're going to publish. But you must devote yourself to your proofs, Virginia. You must read and read them. . . . While he hid his poisonous screed in the forest of words.

"A sentence here, a sentence there," I persisted. "Tony Blunt told him what to say, and Guy would deliver it. My book was to be the handmaiden, Harold. *My proofs.* Passed to someone else. Who'd know exactly how to read them."

Harold stared at me. No longer the aesthete in the garden, but a man of Westminster. "Are you trying to tell me Leonard is a spy?"

"He lies." I whispered it.

"What did he print?"

I closed my eyes and repeated from memory.

"Special for Stalin: Hitler to invade Russia."

CHAPTER THIRTY-FOUR

"Why is that so terrible?" Jo asked. "I thought Churchill and Stalin were buddies."

"*After* Hitler broke the Non-Aggression Pact, they were," Peter conceded, "but that came in June, when the Nazis attacked Russia. In April, when Virginia's writing, Stalin was the enemy."

"And Leonard Woolf was passing information to him?"

"Or trying to. He could have been shot as a traitor. And Virginia with him. The message was in her book."

"Why would Leonard do such a thing?"

Peter shrugged. "The Woolfs were always to the Left. And a lot of people believed that if you were against Fascism — like the Russians — you were worth helping. That included Stalin."

"And then there were Leonard's Apostle friends. Tony and Burgess, the Soviet spies."

Peter rubbed his eyes wearily. "Virginia

mentions the Twenty Committee — there was another name for it. The Double-Cross System. It came from the Roman numeral for twenty —"

"Double Xs?"

"Yes. It was one of the most successful deceptions of the entire war, and the intelligence service were at pains to keep it secret. Leonard could have done immense damage with those few words in a book — letting Stalin know the Germans were coming might have blown the whole Double-Cross operation."

"Do you think Blunt got Hitler's plans out of Jan Ter Braak?"

"He must have. And Blunt — or Burgess — was desperate to get the message to Stalin. There was no Russian embassy in London at the time. France was occupied by the Germans. So they thought of Leonard and the press. They could *send* the message in a proof somewhere — say, Switzerland? But something went wrong — because Stalin was shocked when Germany invaded. He never saw Operation Barbarossa coming."

"Virginia," Jo surmised.

"Or Harold Nicolson."

"But Blunt and Burgess weren't exposed as Soviet spies," Jo pointed out. "At least, not then."

"Well, they *were* Apostles, after all. Keynes probably protected them."

"He persuaded Harold to send him Virginia's account," Jo suggested, "and then convinced Leonard to burn it. Only Leonard printed it, first."

They were silent a moment, considering it all.

"So why did poor Jan Ter Braak shoot himself?" Jo asked.

"Or *was shot?*" Peter countered meaningfully.

"Keep reading," she said.

It is to Harold Nicolson's credit that very little astounds him. That comes, I suppose, of having been born in Teheran — of being born to a diplomatic family, I mean, in a place that was never England. Harold is quite free of certain hypocrisies regarding our national character — that gentlemen are honourable, that allegiances are always clear. That there is a right way of living, and a wrong.

Harold understands that people lie; that self-deception is the most powerful technique for survival; that we are all riddled with competing loyalties that confuse and divide us. He is, after all, a father — who loves to sleep with young men exactly his sons' ages. He is a husband — whose wife has never been faithful. He has lived behind the protective screen of prevarication all his days; our world does not tolerate Harold's complexities.

"Hitler is going to stab Stalin in the back?" he said.

"That's what Jan claims."

"And this means, I take it, that Hitler is *not* going to invade us? Jolly good. Do we know when this delightful event will occur?"

I shook my head. "They've been trying to get the date out of Jan. But he doesn't seem to know. Tony is convinced he's just pretending to be stupid. *They're going to have to get tougher.* That's what Burgess said."

Harold glanced at me from under his brows. "You didn't learn all that from a proof, my dear."

"No. I've been listening to them. The men of Westminster. When they call on Leonard, late at night. Everything those two learn from Jan, they mean to pass on to the Russians."

"Dear me," Harold murmured, reaching once more for his pipe. "Did you tell Leonard how you felt, before you ran away?"

"No."

"Simply wrote your farewell, and bolted?"

"He thinks I killed myself. He told Vita so, in a letter. He thinks it was all to do with me — my madness, not his."

"Men are often obtuse in that way," he said neutrally. There was an interval with the pipe, the tobacco pouch, the tamping down of fires. "I wonder if you haven't blundered into something more significant than you know, Vee. And I'm beginning to regret my susceptibility to the charming Mr. Burgess, more than I can say. . . ."

The darkness had utterly fallen by this time, and the night was chill. Harold helped me back to the Priest's House, where Vita was preparing to set out for her sitting room in the South Cottage. The sentinel was posted in Orlando's tower. There was no drone of engines in the air. The Germans would not, after all, be coming.

Harold said nothing of all we'd discussed before his wife. When she had gone upstairs, however, he gathered his newspaper and a book and his spectacles and turned to me with his endearing — his perpetually gentle — smile.

"Vee, you must write to Leonard. You owe it to him. He can't have realised how he hurt you. And it's unfair to let him believe you've drowned. You're all of life to him, you know —"

Not quite *all* of life. There will always be a part of Leonard's mind I cannot enter — the part created and sustained so early in youth by the Apostles.

I did not promise Harold anything. But I slept, for the first time in weeks, without dreaming.

And woke to the news of my death in *The Times.*

CHAPTER THIRTY-FIVE

Wednesday, 2 April 1941
Sissinghurst

It was Vita who saw the paper first.

She purchased the afternoon edition when she dropped Harold for his London train. I am sure that she is heartily wishing I were on it, too — Vita loathes the invasion of friends, however much she feels her isolation when they are gone. And she is worried about my future — I see it in her looks — although I am sure Harold told her little of our conversation. Vita assumes I have left Leonard because I could no longer bear to live with him. She asks nothing further; and for once, I am grateful for her easy assumptions.

I met Harold this morning as I walked amongst the limes; he was dressed in his Saturday clothes, as he calls them, being most often at Sissinghurst at the week-end. He could not resist the call of the damp spring earth, although fully intending to return to the Ministry in a matter of hours; he knelt on the concrete pavers in tweeds quite bagged at the knees, turning the earth around the thin shoots of spring bulbs.

"My life's work," he said, when he saw me. "The Lime Walk. Vita never comes here, with her spade and her notions; this is *my* bit of earth. I carved it out of nothing, you know. A necessary axis to connect the Nuttery with the Kitchen Garden. I'm forever attempting to bring Platonic order to Vita's wilderness; and I'm forever frustrated. Sissinghurst is magnificent, but obtuse. It resists all attempts to contain it."

I studied him narrowly: loam on his fingers, light in his eye. This is what he's fighting to save — a bed of earth on an April morning. "Vita's endless columns about the making of gardens," I observed, "are so much bosh, aren't they? You're the real genius of Sissinghurst. You've plotted every line."

"I did a few sketches when we bought the place," he conceded unwillingly, "but Mar is better at colour and flourish — the place would be a sad bore if left in my hands. Well — one has only to look at this!" He gestured dismissively towards the marching limes. "No labour, no time, no funds because of this bloody war . . . but if the fighting ends one day, I'll turn it into a demi-Eden. Anemones in profusion. Tulips. Primroses. Have you thought what is to be done?"

"To your Lime Walk?"

"No. With Leonard and the others."

I shifted from foot to foot.

"Here is what I propose," he said briskly. "I shall write to Maynard — he'll nip the foolishness in the bud. Whatever his friends have got up to, Maynard is a sensible man."

My heart froze. He could have no idea of the midnight talks, the single bulb behind the blackout shade. The thread of spittle on Blunt's lips. The German boy bundled into the black car.

"Sense," I choked.

"You've known Maynard all your life!"

"He is Westminster. *Baron* Tilton."

"Vee —"

The hysteria closing my throat. I shook my head, emphatic, mute. The smell of lead on Leonard's fingers. The taste of it when I screamed.

"This is war we're talking of," Harold urged. "*Treason.* Violence."

There was sun on the heavy pavers, and the good green smell of earth rising in the air. The draught of a tomb. Harold's fingers on my arm.

"Have you breakfasted, Vee?"

I shook my head again. *Food.* Revolting.

The boy Jock's face, hovering like a ghost's beyond the bacchante statue.

Harold left for London a few hours later.

While the house was empty, I sat down in the cheerless library and compiled my notes. *On the Making of a White Garden.* A pure space, serene. *Life, life, life!*

"How incongruous," Vita murmured over tea in the Priest's Cottage as the dusk fell, "to be having buttered toast with Virginia, whilst reading Virginia's obituary. . . ."

She passed me the section of paper.

There were two notices, one a simple statement of death so abrupt and painful that I could almost hear Leonard's pen scratch as he wrote to George Dawson, the editor; and the other a more fulsome celebration of my literary genius, drawn up by a member of *The Times* staff.

I put my hand to my throat.

"Poor Leonard," Vita said. "Only think what this will bring down on his head! Letters of condolence from every person who ever met or loved you, and more from those who never did."

I was strangely calm now, the flood of

words having left me, the notebook tied with its neat label. "He might have had the decency to find a body."

"P'raps he has. There are always a few lying about, in wartime." Vita leaned over my shoulder to read the obituary. "They think rather a lot of *Mrs. Dalloway,* don't they? And dear Lord, they've thrown in *Orlando,* with a gibe at me. But I would imagine Leonard's still dragging the river. It's tidal, isn't it?"

"Yes. The current is cruelly strong." Water, tugging like a toddler at my clinging skirts. The insistent bird.

"In her letter to me, Vanessa wrote that she hoped the Ouse would carry you out to sea — because you loved it so."

"*The Waves* meeting the waves. How like her. It's the picture of death she contemplates; not the stench."

"What shall you do?"

I might have said: *I have done it.* Instead I told her: "Compose a letter to *The Times* disputing their judgement of my work — and suggesting they verify their facts before publication."

"I meant about Leonard. And your sister."

I folded the paper and rose from the table. "Please thank Mrs. Staples for the butter. The apotheosis of ordinary bread, don't you think? Especially in these oleo times."

"I do," Vita said. "But you cannot hide in my tower forever, dearest. I won't let you."

And now it is finished. Dinner eaten, the fire burned low, the last measure of the world taken before the blackout goes down. I have seen what I should not in a small column of *The Times*. Another suicide, meaningless in Cambridge. He disappeared the day after I ran.

I was right to fear them, the men of Westminster, in their Apostolic hats.

I wait for the light to vanish behind Vita's door. Then go in search of Jock, who sleeps above the stables.

(Concluding note by Leonard Woolf:)
I know that V. will not come across the garden from the Lodge, and yet I look in that direction for her.

I know that she is drowned and yet I listen for her to come in at the door.

I know that this is her final page, and yet I turn it over.

There is no limit to one's stupidity and selfishness.

CHAPTER THIRTY-SIX

"So what happened to her, Peter?"

They had come to the end of the slim bound volume. It was one hour before dawn, and the coffee was tepid and bitter.

"God knows." He closed the book gently, his fingers lingering on the cloth cover. "Poor Leonard. Whatever he did — or whatever she *thought* he did — he felt her death acutely."

"Egotistical of him," Jo said. "Disgustingly full of himself."

Peter looked at her keenly. "I didn't mean . . . I wasn't referring to . . ."

"To me or my guilt? Of course you weren't. I'll stop trying to be the center of Leonard's drama as well as my own." It was a bitter little speech, and Peter really didn't deserve it. "Ignore me, Peter — this is just my nasty way of telling you you're right. Leonard was no more responsible for Virginia's choices than I am for Jock's death, but each of us chose to wallow in guilt. There's a certain amount of victimhood in that. I can see it more clearly in someone other than myself."

"It's the normal response," Peter attempted. "You'd be less than human if you didn't feel regret about Jock's suicide."

"Regret!" She closed her eyes briefly; the lids were grainy as sandpaper. "This whole tortured trail's awash in it! Vanessa, painting her mural of Virgin and Apostle. Vita and her White Garden. Leonard and his bound volume. They were all struggling with guilt. Begging for forgiveness. So which of them killed her?"

"To answer that, we need to know what she did after she wrote her last word."

"Went looking for my grandfather," Jo said.

"And gave him *Notes on the Making of a White Garden?*"

"Maybe." She slid off the bed, her body stiff from lying too long in the same position. "That would explain the label on the notebook. And Jock, being a kid with nobody to turn to, passed it on to Harold Nicolson — who tore out half the pages."

"That works," Peter said. "We know Harold got the manuscript somehow, because he told Keynes as much. By the time he wrote that letter, he'd probably seen the Cambridge death notice in the paper, and didn't like the implications."

"Jan Ter Braak."

"Yes. It's the turncoat spy's suicide — or murder — that seems to have put the wind up everybody, wouldn't you say?"

"Dead because he didn't know the date of Hitler's Russian invasion." Jo scrabbled her hair into a pathetic ponytail, her fingers working as she spoke. "Virginia gives the book to Jock — who gives it to Harold —"

"— but somehow the dangerous bits end up in Leonard Woolf's hands. Because we know he printed and then burned them."

"Why in heaven's name would Harold Nicolson betray Virginia?"

"Because she was dead," Peter answered flatly.

He didn't have to add: *How or why, we'll never know.*

"I can't accept it, Peter. We've come too far. If only we had more information — a sense of where all these people were, in the days after the notebook ends. If there was *someone* who knew more about Virginia and her friends — where they might have converged —"

His expression stopped her.

"What?" she demanded.

"Bloody hell," he muttered. "You're conjuring Margaux. And whatever she pinched from the Ark. Aren't you?"

She asked them to meet her in Oxford's Bodleian Library by nine A.M. Thursday morning.

"I don't trust her," Jo insisted. "She doesn't help for free. There's an agenda behind all this, Peter."

"You don't know her. She's anxious to make amends."

"She's anxious to make a buck!"

"Give her a chance. *Please.*"

"If she doesn't show," Jo muttered as the Triumph chugged out of Lewes, "we'll head for London. We'll confront this boss of yours."

"She'll show."

Last night's ease had deserted Peter; he was tense and brusque. But then, Jo reasoned, he was no longer lying on a bed. He'd warned her about the limits of English openness. And how easily Margaux could manipulate him.

What, Jo thought again, *do* you *want out of all this, Peter Llewellyn?*

"Whatever Margaux's faults," he attempted, "she's a sound scholar. And that's what we chiefly need at the moment."

370

He was too far away from her by that time to be told she couldn't believe him, either.

The Bodley, as Peter casually called it, was actually several libraries housed in magnificent buildings in the heart of Oxford, all joined by footpaths and even underground tunnels; most of the vast book collections, he explained to Jo, were stored beneath the city streets and ancient squares. These were also mostly barred to cars — and so Peter had abandoned the Triumph at a park-and-ride lot on the edge of town, and hopped a shuttle with Jo. As a result, they walked the last few hundred yards, and she was treated to the breathtaking sight of the morning sun gilding the spires of Oxford above her.

There was the New Bodleian, the Clarendon Building, the Old Bodleian — which included something called Duke Humfrey's that Jo thought sounded like it should offer ales on tap — and the Radcliffe Camera. This last turned out to have nothing to do with photography, *camera* being the ancient Greek word for vaulted chamber. It was a roundish building of golden stone topped with a dome that Jo realized was vaguely familiar; she'd probably seen it in movies.

"Margaux will be in the New Bodleian," Peter said. "Which is actually pretty old —

1940, I think. She likes the ethernet in the Reading Room there."

And it goes so well with her outfit, Jo thought waspishly.

They were trudging up Catte Street, just past Radcliffe Square, and he pointed to the most distant of the library buildings, done in what he called "ziggurat style." It sat on the corner of Broad Street and Parks Road; Jo noted, with a degree of relief that suggested she'd already been in England too long, that the King's Arms pub was directly across the way.

Peter led her up the main staircase toward the back of the building, where a wall of windows flooded the quiet carrels with gray Oxford light. So early in the day, the Reading Room was nearly empty — except for the black-haired woman seated before her laptop in the far corner of the room.

"Peter darling!" She gathered him up like a lost schoolboy and kissed him lingeringly on the lips. "Don't *you* look like you just rolled off somebody's sofa! I've never seen you so rumpled! Did you sleep in a dustbin?"

Jo stiffened as Margaux brushed back Peter's hair. He was far too passive, she thought, in the face of this onslaught; he should be backing away, including her, making at least an *attempt* at resisting his ex-wife's charm — but no. He was gazing at Margaux as though Jo had faded into the mist, as though even the library itself had dissolved. And then the don's gaze slid over to meet Jo's. In quite a different tone she said, "You brought the rest of the note-book?"

"We did," Jo replied brusquely. "Although I have no desire to let you see it. Given what happened last time."

"Sorry." Margaux released Peter and sank down once more in her chair. "I can't *possibly* help, you know, if I'm not in posses-sion of all the material."

"Funny," Jo said. "That's just what we were thinking in the bowels of the Wren two days ago. Before I so much as offer a peek at the rest of the notebook, Margaux, how about telling us what you stole from the Ark?"

For the first time in their brief acquain-tance, Margaux Strand was thrown off bal-ance. She had no idea, Jo guessed, that they'd penetrated Hamish's defenses and followed her into the Apostles' lair.

"I don't know what you mean."

"The boxes for 1940 and '41," Peter said patiently. "Empty, Margaux. A bare half-hour, perhaps, after you'd been and gone.

Hamish tells us there was a row with the Wren porter."

She shrugged, unable to meet Peter's eyes. "He confiscated the papers, actually. I don't know *how* he came to realize I had anything but lipstick in my purse. Demanded to search my bag after I'd gone through the metal detector — though no bells went off. Outrageous, really."

"Maybe your name pops up on the porter's file whenever you enter a Cambridge library," Jo suggested. "Margaux Strand, Sneak Thief."

"Peter," the don said icily, "I don't have to take this shit, you know."

"Of course you don't." He leaned toward her fondly. "But you will. Because you want to be involved, don't you? You want the access?"

She stared at him, frowning.

"What did the porter take?" he persisted.

"Oh, very well. It's nothing of any importance, really." Margaux shrugged. "After I'd nearly sold my soul to an imbecilic junior Fellow at King's, too. He got me down into that sewer line they call an Ark, and shut the two of us into the room — and all that was left in those boxes was a typewritten note from Maynard Keynes."

Jo glanced at Peter, her excitement rising.

"What did it say?"

"*It is hereby noted that the Cambridge Conversazione Society, otherwise known as the Apostles, suspended all meetings for the academic year 1940, the membership being engaged in activities better suited to the defence of the realm,*" Margaux recited. "A bloody great dead end. The same thing was in the box for '41 as well. I *knew* there was something important about the Apostles — that phrase in the back of Woolf's manuscript could only mean Cambridge — but I hadn't the first idea how to sort it out. So I pocketed the papers and hoped I'd find someone who'd be willing to look at them."

"And only succeeded in having yourself blacklisted from the Wren," Peter mused. "Poor Margaux."

"Poor Margaux!" Jo cried. "You actually *believe* her?"

He nodded distractedly. "It's entirely typical. I told you she was no good at puzzles."

But supremely adept, Jo raged without saying it, *at managing you. Are you right about all this? Or has she got some missing piece of Ark information tucked tidily in her brassiere?*

"Fair's fair," Margaux told them. "I told you what I found. Now it's time to show me your treasure."

She was holding out her hand. It was a beautiful hand, utterly unlike Jo's earth-roughened one, with long, slender fingers and French-manicured nails.

There was a pause. Peter stared at Jo quizzically, offering no quarter, no refuge. Slowly, she reached into her shoulder bag and withdrew the oilskin package.

Margaux's nose wrinkled. "Christ, you really *did* rob a grave, didn't you?"

"I prefer to think of it as digging a hole in the garden," Jo said; and was rewarded with one of Peter's rare smiles.

"Draw up some chairs," Margaux ordered. "I want to read this before we talk."

"You sit, Jo," Peter said. "I'll get us some coffee."

And as he swung out of the Reading Room, with precision timing, Gray Westlake walked in.

CHAPTER
THIRTY-SEVEN

"Got a minute?" he asked.

"Gray . . ." Jo rose. "What are you doing here?"

"Let's take a walk."

Her eyes strayed to Margaux. The don was smiling to herself, fiercely intent upon Leonard Woolf's letter, which she'd found tucked into the book and had removed from its envelope. Jo wasn't fooled by appearances; the letter didn't take that long to read. She found it interesting that Margaux was utterly indifferent to Gray. Almost as though she knew who he was — and had expected him to be there.

"I'm not comfortable leaving my stuff," she told him.

"Then bring it with you." He turned on his heel and made for the Reading Room door.

It was impossible for Jo to wrench the bound volume out of Margaux's hands, now that she had it before her on the desk. And Peter was coming back . . .

Peter. Had he deliberately exited as Gray walked in? Was everybody in on this little meeting?

"How do you know Gray Westlake?" she demanded suddenly.

Margaux looked at her with cat's eyes that revealed nothing. "I would call it more of an acquaintance, actually. Of *very* recent formation."

Jo felt a spurt of anger; who the hell did Gray think he was, using Peter's ex-wife to spy on her? Never mind how they'd met — what did Gray think he was doing, walking into the New Bodleian as though he owned the place, and demanding she follow him?

He had paused in the doorway and was staring at her grimly.

"You leave this room," she snarled at Margaux, "and so help me God I'll track you down and rip your head off, got it? Tell Peter I'll be back in five."

"Cheers," Margaux replied, already engrossed in the bound volume.

Gray took her by the arm and led her briskly down the stairs she'd just ascended.

"I'm not leaving," she said through her

teeth. "What the fuck do you think you're doing?"

He did not reply, did not even look at her, but hustled her out of the New Bodleian door. It was there she succeeded in shaking him off, and stood rooted on the steps, glaring at him.

"This is ridiculous. You came all the way from London to drag me back against my will?"

"I came to talk to you. Since you're incapable of picking up your phone."

"I ran out of battery. I haven't got my charger."

"You've run out of a lot more than that, Jo. My patience, for instance. And time. You're completely out of time."

"Gray —"

"I sent you here to work on plans for my garden."

"Which I've done. And I told you the past few days were my own. A personal matter, having to do with my grandfather's death. But you seem to have difficulty separating *my* life from *yours.*"

"The two have been pretty tangled lately," he retorted with a harsh laugh.

"Did you pay that woman to track us down?"

His expression changed — from aggressive to careful.

"I have no idea what you mean."

"Oh, *right.* You just *guessed* I'd be in Oxford, at the Bodleian, this morning."

"Actually," he said evenly, "it was your friend Peter who called in to Sotheby's and told them where you were. I gather he's getting pretty tired of this jaunt all over England. Have you completely lost your *mind,* Jo, asking a complete stranger to run your errands for you?"

The words fell on her ears like shards of ice. Stinging. Unexpected. Unstoppable.

Peter. She'd had no idea what a pain in the ass she'd been. What a burden. When he'd probably been trying to get back to Margaux for days —

"Do you realize that but for me," Gray continued tensely, "you'd have every cop in Great Britain trailing you right now?"

"What are you talking about?"

"That little prank you pulled, Jo. At Sissinghurst. When you were in *my employ.* Stealing from a National Trust house! *Jesus* — Imogen Cantwell is ready to start World War Three! If I hadn't bought her off during a delicate round of negotiation, she'd have gone to the police."

"I see." Jo swallowed. *Peter.* "I should have

communicated better. I left her a message —"

"— Before your battery ran out. Right." Gray grinned at her humorlessly. "Between Imogen crying for blood and the head of Sotheby's book department furious at your unfortunate friend, I've had my hands full. And you don't even have the damn decency to get in touch."

"I'm sorry," she said. *Peter.* She needed to get far, far away from all of them and figure out how to crawl home. "It never occurred to me that you'd be involved in this. Why *are* you involved, Gray?"

"Because I care about you." He took a step toward her. "I just want you to forget this whole mess and come home."

"That's not what I mean." She shook her head, puzzling it out. "How did you meet Imogen? Why pose as a buyer? And you obviously know Margaux. This is all too weird."

"Yes," he agreed, "it's weird, and it's time it ended. Leave the notebook with your friend from Sotheby's, Jo, and come back to London. It's time to let this adventure go."

Let it go.

Why? a voice inside her asked. *Why should I let Jock's book go?*

Gray's arms had come around her and her

head was against his shoulder. His hands smoothing her mangled ponytail. She was supposed to feel grateful, feel comforted, like a little girl rescued from a train wreck.

"Unh-unh," she said stubbornly, and stepped away from him.

He stared at her, eyes narrowed. "You know, Jo, I can always tell Sotheby's I'm not interested in the sale. And let you negotiate terms from a jail cell."

"Now you're threatening me." She took another step backward. "Which do you need more in your women, Gray — fear, or gratitude?"

"I'm the reason you came to England in the first place!"

"And for that I've been grateful. But I've also been confused. Because I shouldn't have to thank a man for hiring my professional skills. I shouldn't have to sleep with him to keep his business. You wouldn't manipulate a guy that way, Gray —"

"I don't fall in love with guys."

"And I don't fall in love with control freaks. Good-bye, Gray."

"Did you sleep with Llewellyn?" he shouted after her.

She turned. "Go home, Gray. I'll send the White Garden drawings to your wife."

Chapter
Thirty-Eight

When she got back to the Reading Room, Peter and Margaux were gone.

Jo stood in the doorway, staring at the carrel where she'd left the English don, the oilskin package, and Leonard Woolf's letter. Not even an empty coffee cup remained.

Of course. They had called in Gray to deal with her — *to persuade her to let this bizarre adventure go* — while they skedaddled with Leonard's bound volume. They were probably halfway to London by now. Or, Christ — why stop at London? They could be halfway to Fiji. The sky was the limit when you had an unknown Virginia Woolf to sell.

Jo sank down in a chair, a painful knot tightening in her throat. She'd probably be arrested for artifact theft, and she was close to weeping. Not just because Jock's notebook was gone — but because, despite everything, she had *trusted* Peter. Admired his authenticity. Mooned about his taste in functional buildings and the way his rolled shirtsleeves graced his wrists. It was so obviously, suddenly, how neatly he'd managed her — whisking her from Sotheby's to Oxford, where he'd succeeded in passing the first part of the manuscript to Margaux, then trailing around the countryside with her bits and pieces of clues until they culminated in a hole in Leonard Woolf's back garden. Making her actually *believe* he wanted to cook for a living.

Why was she always such a jerk?

She'd sacrificed her best career prospect — the White Garden — and a man who'd apparently *wanted* her, for a wild-goose chase with a charlatan in glasses. Hadn't she learned anything about men in her long life?

"There you are," Peter said briskly behind her. "We've moved downstairs to the Reference section. Hurry up, Jo — your coffee's getting cold."

"Funny Leonard should write that at the very end of the book," Margaux was saying. "About turning the page, and so forth. And looking for her in the garden. It's almost an exact quotation from his journal in the days following Virginia's death."

"The part about stupidity and selfishness

is what interests me." Peter's finger trailed across the page. "That used to be read as Leonard's admission that he kept Virginia alive against her will — by thwarting her attempts at suicide. But I'm thinking now it might have more to do with the bonds of Apostle friendship."

"Could do," Margaux agreed. "But these finds will turn all *sorts* of academic assumptions on their heads. Makes one positively *giddy* to read them."

"Is that why you agreed to call Peter?" Jo asked. "So you could get first crack at the material? Is that what Gray promised you?"

There was a pregnant pause. Jo waited for Peter to defend his ex-wife, but he was merely frowning at Margaux.

"Naturally," Margaux said crisply. "And as you're the one who called *me* this morning, and require *my* help, I think you should shut up about motives, don't you?"

"Gray?" Peter said. "How does your bloody client know Margaux, Jo?"

"Former client," she corrected. "He just fired me."

"*Hell.*" Peter grasped her shoulder. "I'm so sorry. Really, Jo —"

But she was looking at Margaux, who was suddenly far less defiant.

"Peter darling, can you *ever* forgive me?"

He groaned. "Don't tell me. You slept with this Westlake moron, didn't you?"

"Of course not!" Margaux protested, with an attempt at dignity. "But I ran into him at Sotheby's, and when he understood I knew you, he asked me to . . . keep him informed. If you got in touch. So I *did*. But now I'm with you again, I can't *bear* to have any secrets from you, sweet."

She reached impulsively for his hand. "I've . . . *missed* you so, darling. Truly I have. It hasn't been the same since we split. Don't you *hate* it?"

"I've hated a lot of things," he answered quietly. "But this isn't the place to talk about them, Margaux."

"You're right. Of course." She gave him a brave smile. "We'll have *loads* of time later. What matters now is our find."

"*Our* find?" Jo repeated.

"Look," Peter said patiently. "We haven't much time. Let's concentrate on the text, all right? And try to learn what we can from it?"

Neither woman answered.

"Jo?" he said.

"Okay."

"Margaux?"

She held his gaze for a smoldering moment and then said, "A few things leap out.

Little things, but hallmarks of Virginia's style nonetheless. The quotation from *The Wasteland,* 'Come under this red rock,' would fit, of course; T. S. Eliot was a friend of the Woolfs' and the Hogarth Press was one of the first to publish him. Then there's her reference to Westminster, or the men of Westminster; that's drawn from one of her short stories, about a young woman writer who's despised by a politician she meets at an evening party. Westminster came to symbolize for Virginia everything she hated about male dominance, convention, the establishment world she regarded as hostile to art —"

"She refers to Harold Nicolson that way."

Margaux glanced at Jo. "Of course. He was a *man.* And a government official. Virginia mistrusted both on principle, even those she regarded as friends. Maynard Keynes would fall into the same categories — he was the ultimate Westminster man."

"That helps us tie the work to Woolf," Peter said, "but it tells us nothing more about how or when she might have died."

"What we've got to reckon is the time frame." Margaux peered at the screen of her Reference computer terminal, all business. "I've jotted down key dates. We assume Virginia was alive at Sissinghurst on the first and second of April, correct? Because this little book tells us so. And we know her body was found in the River Ouse on the eighteenth of that month. She was cremated three days later, somewhere on the south coast — Brighton, I think."

"That was quick," Jo observed.

"Quick and dirty. Only Leonard was in attendance. The bastard."

"No Vanessa?" Jo demanded, astonished. "Not even Vita?"

"Not even the odd mourner hired off the street for the sake of appearances," Margaux retorted. "Leonard informed no one of the funeral arrangements. He could never bear to share Virginia with anybody — and so of course he deprived her of the memorial service she *ought* to have had, among the people who knew and loved her best. *God,* how I despise that man."

"Oh, now, Margaux —" Peter began.

She turned on him furiously. "Don't start, Peter! You *know* how he stifled her genius — lived to control her — and when at last she *abandoned* him in death — escaping by the only means in her power — he was so angry he got rid of her as quick as a dead cat. *Don't* start."

"Very well." Peter was looking at Jo. "We can assume Leonard buried her ashes in solitude, too. Along with a few other things."

"Where exactly was the body found?" Jo asked.

Margaux rolled her eyes in frustration. "Do you know *nothing* of academic method? One must at least *attempt* a certain logical order. Try not to interrupt. Try to focus on the *dates*." She swept back her hair impatiently and knotted it with a pencil. "From the second to the eighteenth gives us nearly three weeks to play with, which is far too much to be of any use — but I think we can narrow it down. Vita helps."

"How?"

"She wrote a letter to Harold describing a visit she made to Leonard Woolf, at Monk's House, on the seventh of April."

"That would have been . . ."

"The Monday following this account." She tapped the slim bound volume. "It's clear from the tone of Vita's letter that Virginia was missing again — no longer at Sissinghurst, and nowhere to be found. Vita had driven down to Rodmell to condole with Leonard. Listen —"

She scrolled through a text pulled up on her screen. *"The house full of his flowers and all Virginia's things lying about as usual. . . . Her scribbling-block with her writing on it. The window from which one can see the river. I*

*said Leonard, I do not like you being here
alone like this. He turned those piercing blue
eyes on me and said it's the only way. . . .
They have been dragging the river but have
given up the search."*

"Christ," Peter murmured. "Must've been
awkward, that visit. Vita knowing Leonard's
wife had left him, and exactly *why,* and
Leonard knowing that Vita had failed to
keep her safe. The guilt in the room!"

"Yes, well, everybody's lousy with guilt
after a suicide," Margaux said indifferently.

Jo shifted in her chair. "They gave up
dragging the river, but all the same the body
was found. What happened on the eighteenth?"

"It was rather creepy. Four teenagers from
Lewes were having a picnic in a field. They
spied a log in the river and decided to throw
stones at it. Only it wasn't a log. It was
Virginia."

Jo closed her eyes. "How far from Rodmell?"

"No distance at all." Margaux glanced up
from her computer screen. "That's the
creepy part. The meadow where the kids
were picnicking was below an old Georgian
farmhouse called Asheham — a house the
Woolfs had lived in and loved. Virginia
rented it for years before she lost the lease

in 1919, and they bought Monk's House instead. They used to walk from Asheham to Rodmell across a bridge, at Southease."

"So when she left Sissinghurst," Jo suggested, "Virginia could have gone to either place. Home to Monk's House — or maybe to Asheham. Would she have felt safe, there? Home, but not exactly home?"

"Who owned the house in '41?" Peter asked.

"A cement firm," Margaux said, "which took possession in the early thirties and destroyed the surrounding landscape with their quarries. The value of the property declined as a result and Asheham was eventually abandoned, though I'm not sure exactly when. And of course during the war, so many country places were requisitioned — for troop billets, and training, and so on."

"Men in black cars," Peter said distinctly.

The back of Jo's neck prickled. "And now?"

"Oh, the house is gone. Demolished a good ten years ago. But if we could *move on* from the bloody house —"

"What you're saying is that Virginia left Sissinghurst sometime between the second of April and the seventh, when Vita went to see Leonard," Peter said.

"Exactly. Five days."

He lifted his glasses and rubbed his eyes. "Harold Nicolson's vaguely menacing letter to Maynard Keynes was dated April fourth. That would be —"

"The Friday before Vita's Rodmell visit," Jo supplied. "Harold would have been at Sissinghurst for the weekend, again."

"He tells Maynard that Virginia's his guest, and that he has her notebook," Peter recited. "So she must still have been with the Nicolsons on Friday the fourth."

"— But gone by Monday, when Vita saw Leonard Woolf."

"Which means Virginia left . . . when? Saturday? Sunday?"

"Saturday," Margaux said decisively. "Once she knew Harold wrote to Keynes and tipped her hand, she had to get out immediately. She understood how vicious these people were. Harold wouldn't believe it, of course, and Vita was always so vague — so lost in her own world . . . but Virginia knew she had reason to fear them. Burgess and his lot. So she ran. The Nicolsons might have hoped for news of her, Saturday and Sunday — but by Monday, Vita's off to meet with Leonard."

Jo considered all this. It fit as neatly as a jigsaw puzzle; but there was something wrong. "Why did they assume she was dead?"

"Sorry?" Margaux said, as though Jo were a half-wit who must be humored.

"Why did Vita *condole* with Leonard, as you put it? Why drag the river? Virginia had run away before. Why not assume she'd gone to London or Timbuktu? *Why act as though she was never coming back?*"

"Because they knew it was true," Peter said quietly. "Think about it, Jo: how would Virginia manage to escape from Vita and Harold Nicolson, who were determined to save her? She must have had an accomplice. Someone who drove her to the train. Or all the way back to Sussex, for that matter. A person who would tell the Nicolsons exactly what happened, in the end —"

"Jock," Jo said.

CHAPTER
THIRTY-NINE

"Did I disturb you, Nana?" Jo asked.

It was barely six A.M. in the Delaware Valley, but Dottie was an early riser. She suffered from insomnia, a liability of old age, and often sat up in the middle of the night reading. Jo could imagine her: half-glasses poised on the bridge of her nose, faded pink nightgown beneath a sensible bathrobe, hair in pin curls. Her hands ropy with veins where they held her book.

"Sweetie!" Dottie cried. "Are you calling from England?"

"Yes, and I'm using a friend's phone, so I'll have to make it quick."

"Are you having a good time?"

How to answer that question?

"It's certainly been interesting," she said faintly. "I have loads to tell you. But I called with a question, Nana. About Jock. Did you know he worked at Sissinghurst when he was young?"

"Sissinghurst? Where *you've* been working? I had no idea. What was he doing there?"

"Gardening. It must have been right before he joined up. Do you have any idea when that was — when he ran away to the army and lied about his age, I mean?"

"Well, it was 1941," Dottie said doubtfully, "but I couldn't give you the day and hour. Summer, I think. He used to say he decided to fight Hitler when the Russians did. If I'm remembering right, the Nazis invaded Russia in June. Did you learn anything about his letter? All that talk about the Lady?"

"I'm still working it out. Listen: Have you found anything else since I left home — anything of Grandpa's, I mean? Something he wrote, maybe? Or . . . I don't know. Anything that you can't explain?"

There was a brief pause.

"No," Dottie said, with that same doubtful tremor in her voice. "— Not that any of *his* writing would be of help. He wasn't in a mood to tell us much. I loved Jock dearly, Jo, but I wonder how well I actually knew him. He wasn't himself in those last days. I mean, you wouldn't have said he was religious, now, would you? Never went to church at all. And if he *were* getting that way — thinking of his Maker, and so on, and turning to the Lord — why take such an awful step as kill himself? Churchgoers call it a sin. It doesn't make sense."

"But Grandpa *wasn't* religious —"

"I know! But I found the oddest thing in his tool shed the other day. You said you wanted his old things, remember — and they have to be valued by an appraiser. It's part of the settlement of the estate."

Disgust, now, in Dottie's voice; left to herself, Jo thought, she'd have thrown everything in black trash bags and left it all by the curb. *Estate.* An archaic word, better suited to the people who'd employed Jock Bellamy.

"What did you find, Nana?"

"A small statue," she said. "Of the Blessed Virgin. And you know he wasn't Catholic, Jo. It's the oddest thing."

They drove down to Sissinghurst, all three of them packed into the Triumph, on what Peter freely admitted was a hunch. "But if we'd waited for solid evidence," he said, "we'd never have got this far."

It was possible, Jo knew, that they'd reached the end of Virginia's trail. It was more than likely they would never learn how or why she met her death. But they had so little left to lose.

"There's everything to gain," Margaux remarked sensibly. "Push on, and at least we may solve a mystery. Besides — why not spend the final hours of a swift November day in the most beautiful garden in Kent?"

They arrived just before closing time. It was curious, Jo thought, how strong a sense of homecoming she felt as the car approached Cranbrook, and the exterior of the George Hotel came into view. This corner of Vita's world had come to mean too much to her: a link with her dead grandfather, a link to a barely glimpsed past. She would give anything to spend another week trolling with her laptop through the castle garden, absorbing the rich sights and scents as autumn came to a close. But this was Sissinghurst's last open weekend of the year; as of Monday, it would go dark until March.

She directed Peter around to the greenhouses, and with no small feeling of trepidation, led him and Margaux toward the Head Gardener's office.

"Is Imogen here?" she asked one of the staff gardeners who was busily watering some cuttings set out in trays.

"She's over at the test border," the young woman said. "Just behind the Powys Wall."

The test border was a disciplined proving ground for new perennials. Imogen planted specimens that interested her there, and watched them for a few years before deciding whether they merited a spot in Sissinghurst's beds. They found her deadheading a clump of pale green Echinacea — a type Jo recognized as Coconut Lime — with the withered stalks lying about her Wellies like sheaves of threshed wheat. She glanced up as the little cavalcade approached, and scowled.

"Not again!"

"Hello, Imogen," Jo said. "I owe you an apology, and I've come to make it. I'm truly sorry for all the trouble and worry I've caused."

Imogen studied her skeptically, then thrust her clippers in a pouch that dangled from her belt. "Yes, well, words are grand — but where's the notebook, I'd like to know? In the hands of the bloody *experts*. I don't know how I'm going to explain it all to the Trust —"

"What I did was wrong," Jo interrupted. "I took advantage of your kindness and went off on a wild-goose chase. If I can help set things right — talk to people at the Trust, or to The Family —"

"Good God, no," Imogen retorted,

shocked. "You've done enough damage."

"I can vouch for the fact that you weren't involved," Jo persisted. "I can shoulder the blame."

Imogen's eyes narrowed; she glanced at Margaux Strand and said, "You put her up to this, didn't you? And who the hell are *you?*"

Peter gave her a wry smile. "One of your hated experts."

"Has he got it all sussed out, our Marcus? Does he know whether Woolf really wrote that daft diary?"

"Not yet," Peter replied.

"Ah." She tugged off her garden gloves. "Then until he informs me of where we stand, I'm barring the lot of you from the premises. Can't be too careful. Something else might go missing." There was belligerence in her voice; and something else. *Pain.*

"Imogen . . ." Jo reached a hand toward her. "We're here to ask for your help."

"And from past knowledge of my stupidity, you assume you'll get it. I've reformed, however. Cheerio!"

"I rather think," Margaux intervened pointedly, "that you ought to listen to her, love. Remember what Graydon Westlake said? That we should all *work together?* Lest any of us *suffer individually?* You'll find words to that effect in those papers you signed."

Jo murmured, "So Gray got to you, too —"

But Peter interrupted her. "What papers?"

Margaux turned on him. "Ones your precious auction house dredged up. Outlining exactly who owes what to whom. I get sole academic access to the Woolf manuscripts, in exchange for my expert opinion. Imogen gets to look like the saint who made the discovery, instead of the git she is."

"And Jo?" Peter said hotly. "What does Jo get?"

"Immunity from prosecution. — Which is quite enough, I think, for somebody who's bollixed things up as much as she has."

Peter stepped toward her. "Marcus agreed to this?"

"Marcus drew up the papers." Margaux studied him coolly. "I would never have signed, of course, if I hadn't assumed you knew all about it, Peter. Before you ever left London with Jo. I thought I was simply doing what you *wanted* — what you'd arranged —"

"Oh, for the love of —" Imogen snorted contemptuously. "You've been hand in glove with those rogues in London, dearie, for the better part of the week. Sugarcoating their nastiness. Simpering in their laps. Don't try to lie about it now. You'd roll your Manolos in pig shit and wear them to Prince William's wedding if it got you what you want. So what do you need, Jo? I'm in a mood to disappoint our Dr. Strand."

"We'd like to examine the statue of the Little Virgin," Jo told her. "We'll probably have to move it."

"Move it!" Imogen was appalled.

"Lift it, anyway. Would you or Terence be able to help?"

They waited until the very last paying customers had been waved through the turnstile at the garden entrance. One of these recognized Imogen as the Head, and was inclined to linger in order to interrogate her on rose replant disease; but happily the old gentleman's daughter, who'd driven him down from London, was impatient to be gone and broke off his chat with a peremptory "Come along, then, Dad. You'll be wanting your tea."

Jo felt a scattering of rain against her cheek. She glanced around, at the Top Courtyard and the arch to the Lower one; at Vita's Tower soaring against the farmland and the Weald. The day had turned lowering and gray. No matter how many days in the future she might visit Sissinghurst, in spring and sun, she would remember it best as a creature of autumn, rising from a skirt of mist, as mythic as Avalon and as lost to time.

"Ter!" Imogen bellowed into her hand radio. "You're wanted in the White Garden." She flicked Margaux a glance. The don's lips were turning blue from the chill. "Cozy enough for you, Dr. Strand?"

They followed her, broad-hipped and sturdy as a field marshal, across the Lower Courtyard. Peter's fingers grazed Jo's as they walked. "Can you feel her? Virginia?" he murmured. "She's watching us."

The Yew Walk was shining faintly with the rain. As they turned into it, again Jo had the sensation of descending through a tunnel, no relief from the dark hedge pressing in on either side until the sudden deliverance of the doorway cut into the green wall. The entrance to the White Garden.

The rose arbor was directly ahead of them. Terence stood by it, his arms slack, a hessian square filled with perennial cuttings at his feet.

"Eh, Miss Bellamy," he said, with obvious pleasure. "I thought you'd done with us."

"Never so lucky." Imogen sighed. "Ter, these people want to examine the Little

Virgin. I'm here to make sure she's not tampered with. You're to do a bit of heavy lifting."

Terence shrugged, and pulled on the gloves he'd tossed near his tip bag. Jo glanced at Imogen, who inclined her head dismissively and took no step farther; after a second, Jo turned left along the slate path and then right, onto the pavers that led to the Little Virgin. The others followed.

She was standing as she had for sixty years, face almost obscured by the weeping pear.

Jo stopped short, gazing at the dull gray figure. Peter studied the Virgin for a second, then reached out and touched the gunmetal skin. "This wasn't always here, is that correct?"

"Has been since the making of the White Garden," Imogen returned, "the bones of which were laid in '49 and '50, on the site of the old Priest's House garden. The roses that used to be here were moved up to what was the *first* kitchen garden, near the Yew Rondel — it's called the Rose Garden now. If you're asking where the statue was before all that —"

"We know," Peter said. "Virginia told us. It was just to the north, outside this bit's hedge. But you couldn't see her legs from the path because of a drop in elevation. I understand why Vita moved it; the Virgin ought to be surrounded by white."

Imogen scowled at him. "This whole scheme was worked years after that Woolf woman died. It's got nothing to do with her, nor the statue neither."

"How wrong you are," Margaux said sweetly.

"What do you lot think to find?"

"Something that was hidden before the statue was moved," Jo said, "in a place only a gardener would know. It's a hollow lead casting, right?"

"If it were solid, nobody'd ever budge the thing. Terence," Imogen said, "I gather these fools want you to tip the lady over. Can you do it without breaking her neck?"

Peter helped the undergardener shift the Little Virgin gently toward the slate path. The lead was slippery with rain and the slim figure heavy. Imogen swore audibly as the statue descended earthward, but in a matter of minutes it rested facedown on top of the hessian bundle, cushioned by the season's last cuttings.

"Here." Peter tossed Jo his penlight. She knelt near the statue's base and flicked on the beam.

The interior of the statue was narrower

than she expected, and fluidly formed; a cleft in a manmade rock. At first she saw only lead, convoluted as it hardened in the mold so long ago; and then she noticed, far up in the torso of the figure, what looked like pillow stuffing. She reached her hand inside the aperture and pulled a bit of it out.

"What's this?" she asked, handing it off behind her.

"Wool," Margaux said. "Vita kept sheep, you know; she used to send knitting yarn to Virginia."

"Stinks to high heaven," Imogen observed. "Wonder how long it's been in there?"

Peter was watching Jo. He had noticed that she was pulling more of the stuff out of the Little Virgin, the penlight abandoned by her knees. "What's behind it?" he asked.

"A bundle of some kind," she said. "A wallet, maybe. Or, no —"

She withdrew her hand. She was clutching a roll of brown leather, tied with twine.

Wordlessly, Imogen pulled her shears from the pouch at her waist.

Jo cut the bundle free. It dropped at her feet like a severed hand.

"A garden glove?" Peter crouched beside her.

"There's something inside," Jo said.

CHAPTER
FORTY

It was a roll of paper, tied with more twine. Fingers shaking, Jo slipped the string from the roll.

"Careful," Margaux said sharply over her shoulder. "There'll be damp."

There was damp. The pages — each no bigger than the palm of Jo's hand — were closely scrawled in lead pencil that had faded over the years. She played the penlight's beam over them — it was now quite dark — and said, "It looks like Jock's handwriting."

"Let's go inside," Imogen said brusquely. "You can't read that out here. Ter, take care of the Virgin, will you?"

Peter helped right the statue before they left the White Garden. Jo waited; it did not seem fair, after their long hunt, to steal a march on Peter. She kept the bundle of paper swaddled in the ancient glove as they trekked back to the Powys Wall.

Terence parted from them at Imogen's office. "If there's nothing else, I'll be off. . . ."

"Go on, then," Imogen ordered.

Jo reached for him impulsively and hugged him. "If you ever give up your dream of L.A., I'd be happy to see you in Delaware. And thanks, Ter. For all your help."

"S'nothing. Come by the pub later and we'll pull a pint." He grinned at them and disappeared in the direction of the greenhouses.

Jo set the garden glove carefully on the staff table. Peter peered at the bundle.

"Cigarette papers. Can you believe it? Must've been the only paper he had. Did your grandfather smoke?"

"Not to my knowledge."

"Everybody rolled their own during the war years. Even Vita," Margaux observed. Then her expression changed. "My God — I bet those *are* Vita's cigarette papers."

"— The habit of stealing being one that runs in the Bellamy family," Imogen said dryly. "But don't admit it too loudly. You'd have to hand over that packet to the Trust."

Peter glanced at Jo. "You can decipher the script. Why don't you read this aloud?"

"I'll make tea," Imogen suggested. "It's downright cold now we've turned the corner to November. Sorry I've nothing stronger."

It was a peace offering; and she seemed remarkably unconcerned about setting limits on their access, now they'd actually found something in the Little Virgin.

Jo drew out a chair and took the first small sheet between her fingers.

2 April 1941

The worse bit about living on your own is that there's nobody to talk to. If it were home, I'd say, Da the Lady's come and asked me to keep something for her, and he'd say, Give it here, then, Jock, there's a good lad, and that'd be an end to it. Or Mum would say, Poor old dear, she's a bit wanting in the upstairs, isn't she? You'd best tell Miss Vita. And so I'd go and do that. But there's no one. I could write to Mum and ask but I'd never write to Da; he'd be that put out at me acting foolish. When you're man enough to work and live on your own among the gentry, you're man enough to know what to do with the puzzles they put in your hands.

Besides, I like the Lady. She's daft, right enough, and she looks like a walking skeleton when you see her across the garden, but there's a look in her eyes when she talks that makes you listen. I was asleep when she came to the barn door tonight but I got up and pulled my trousers on because it seemed like she needed help. That's the other reason I don't like to write to Mum — she'd call it indecent, the Lady looking for me like that, after the Family'd gone to bed. If I can't write to Mum I might as well write to myself, so says I. Maybe then I'll sort it out.

Jock, she says, standing at the foot of the hayloft stairs with her hair all wild and her fur coat on, will you drive me to the station?

At this hour, ma'am? I says. It's gone past ten, and there'll be no trains till morning.

She looked around her then like all the demons of hell were after her, and ran out of the stable. That's when I pulled on my clothes and went after.

She was hurrying down the drive to the road. I'd no business telling the gentry what to do, but I didn't like the look of her, nor her being all alone in such a state, and I reckoned Miss Vita would be angry if I said I'd seen the Lady go and lifted not a finger to stop her. I caught her up and said, Now, ma'am, can't it wait till morning, and she said I'll be lucky if they don't find me before then. I said, Who? But she didn't answer, just turned round wild-like and clutched my jacket with her hands. Jock, she says, Don't ever trust the men of Westminster, no matter what they offer. Westminster men lie.

Do they now, I says, as though she's talking how deep to plant bulbs before the first frost. I'll be sure to keep that in mind. But it's five mile and more to Staplehurst, and a long enough wait for the first train. Do you stay warm inside, ma'am, and I'll come find you at first light. You'll be much more comfortable in the pony trap, or Miss Vita's car.

Why do you call her that? she asked. Not Mrs. Nicolson, but Miss Vita?

It's what we all called her at Knole, I says. I'm a Knole lad, born and bred.

She's not to know, the Lady said, nearly in tears. She's not to know. It was a terrible mistake to tell Harold. I've written it all down.

She tapped something she had under her arm, and I saw it was a copybook, like we used in school.

That's all right then, I told her, like she was a little child. If you've wrote it all down. That'll keep till morning.

I made so bold as to take her by the arm, and turned her towards the house, thinking that if I talked to her gentle-like she might come back the right way so I could settle her and get Miss Vita to call Doctor. But she dug in her heels and shook her head and said I can't stay in this place, I'd be a fool to stay here now Harold's gone.

What, I says, with me and Hayter and Miss Vita what can handle a gun, and that Home Guard fellow posted in the tower? You're safe as houses, ma'am.

Don't lie to me, Jock, she says too quiet.

I put my hand on her arm again. If you go I shall have to rouse Miss Vita. It's as much as my place is worth, you leaving and me saying no word.

She seemed to fall in like a wilted flower at that, her shoulders hunching and her head drooping on her thin neck, and I was afraid she'd started to cry. I asked if she was all right and she said in a kind of whisper My head aches so, it's the voices clamouring, every hour, they never stop no matter how much I plead.

That sent a chill up my spine and I said, I'll get Miss Vita. But the Lady swayed where she stood and I had to reach for her, sure enough, before she swooned. Come along, I said, trying to keep the scared out of my voice. You have a liedown and we'll set you to rights.

411

A slow walk back to South Cottage, me holding her upright and her breathing hard. I looked at her face once and it was dead pale, shining like a ghost in the night, though there was no moon. When we reached the door I rapped on it, hard, and rapped on it again.

Jock, she says faintly, I'm not well. Take the book, Jock. Keep it safe.

She fainted then right enough. But it was Miss Vita who put the Lady to bed, and Miss Vita who kept the book, sending me about my business once I'd helped her carry the Lady upstairs.

I'm not easy in my mind. Not liking to fail her.

Miss Vita gave me a shilling, and said as how I was a good lad and to say nothing more about it.

She threw the deadbolt on the cottage door as I left.

4 April 1941

I fetched Mr. Harold from Staplehurst this afternoon, him coming down as usual for the Saturday and Sunday. Very absent-minded he was, and Is the Lady still unwell? he asks, as soon as I've seen his traps into the cart. He'd had a letter from Miss Vita, seemingly, them being the sort to write to each other every day. I told him I hadn't seen the Lady since Wednesday night when she'd had her fit, me being that busy with turning the kitchen garden, but I hoped as she was on the mend. He called me good lad as he stepped down from the box, but when I carried in his things I heard him talk low to Miss Vita. Quite out of her head, Miss Vita said, and it's clearly a return of the old trouble; do you think we should write to Leonard?

I've written to Maynard, he says. That should settle her.

When they saw me they fell quiet and I hurried with the bags, not liking to put my nose where it wasn't wanted.

I hope they have her book put by safe. Maybe it's fretting after it that's driven her out of her senses.

5 April 1941

I was up with the light this morning, knowing full well how Mr. Harold is when he's down for his two days, wanting to dig in his bit of garden. He was before me, all the same, smoking his pipe on the steps of the Tower, which is sandbagged and barricaded by the Home Guard and even Miss Vita barred entry. Very natural Mr. Harold looked, a proper gentleman in his old tweed jacket and flannel bags, and the smoke curling about his head. He bid me good morning, and said something about the beds in the Lime Walk, and I made to move on, me hoping to thin the peas, when he said, You did well to come to Mrs. Nicolson the other night. If anything like that should happen again, be a good lad and do the same, won't you? And I said as how I hoped the Lady was faring better. He said I am sure we shall have her on her feet in no time. And then — for the life of me I couldn't say why, or what moved me to do it — I says, very bold like, I hope as her book is kept safe. She was that worried about it.

Mr. Harold takes his pipe out of his mouth and looks at me as though my face had gone blue. Quite safe, he says. Provided no one talks when they shouldn't.

I hope I know how to keep a secret, I says, on my dignity; and how to value the trust of my betters. I pick up my barrow and turn for the kitchen garden when Mr. Harold says, I have set an angelic host around it, and lifts his pipe to the sky.

I gave no sign I knew what he meant. But it's clear as daisies. He's hid the book in Miss Vita's tower, where nobody can come nigh it.

I felt better after that. The two of them worked in the garden, and at tea time the Lady took a stroll among the roses, which is just starting to leaf. There was colour in her cheeks and no wildness about her looks and I thought, No harm done that I can tell.

Until bedtime, when she came looking for me again.

Jock, she whispered, standing right over me so I was scared half to death. Jock, you must help me.

What is it? I says, sitting up with the sheet to my neck.

I can't stay here any longer. If I stay here I shall die.

Now, ma'am, I says, don't you think you ought to speak with Miss Vita?

Please, Jock, she says. I've no one I can trust. Please help me.

I asked her to turn around while I pulled my clothes on and then I got her back down the stairs as fast as I could. It not being seemly for a lady of her quality to be up in a hayloft.

Ma'am, I says, the only way I can help you is if I call Miss Vita now. Or Mr. Harold. You must know how it is.

Call Miss Vita and you will kill me, she says.

I tried to speak, but no words come. There was something in her eyes — that look like a cornered animal — that made me listen. She was terrified of Miss Vita and Mr. Harold. I was sending her for help to the very ones she feared.

Lord, ma'am, I said. Whatever is amiss?

They're good people, she said, but they don't understand. I place them in danger the longer I stay here. I know things I shouldn't. They're like children, they don't see the risk. They're supremely uncon-scious. They write letters to men who put guns to people's heads.

Wild talk, and none of it any sense. What danger could such an old lady know? But I saw as how she was that scared. It was like throwing her in gaol, to call for Miss Vita.

Keep her talking, I says to myself. Keep her talking a while, and maybe one of them will hear. Maybe they'll come for her. And you won't have to do nothing.

I need to get to London, she says, like a woman in a fever. As quick as may be. You could take me now it's dark. In the pony trap. I'd go myself, only I don't know how to harness the pony.

The missus can't spare me for so long, I said. Nor the trap for so far a trip as London.

Then take me to the station, she says. I don't mind the wait. There will be a train soon enough. Please, Jock.

And she holds out a guinea, and presses it in my palm.

Now, ma'am, I says, there's no call for that.

Take it, she says. With my thanks.

So I harnessed the pony. He didn't half like it at that hour of the night, neither. And we set out in the darkness, me driving slow as slow and hoping all the time that Mr. Harold would hear the sound of the trap wheels and come shouting after. But he didn't. The South Cottage where they sleep is far enough from the cow barn. Only the Home Guard in the tower, maybe, saw us go; and it's not his place to sound an alarm for anything but Germans.

A chill night, and no moon. Close to midnight, maybe. There won't be a train until half six, I told her. She asked how long the drive to the station would be. Maybe an hour, I says. You'll have a fair wait, in Staplehurst.

But as it happened, we never got so far. Just past the hillock near Cranbrook

Common there was a car. A big, black monster with no running lights on account of the blackout, driving fit to bust. The road's tight as a glove and the hedges high and the beast was on us before we knew what we were about. I doubt the driver even saw us before he hit, his big black fender taking the side of the trap at a mad clip, the pony shying and plunging, and me without a prayer of saving us. The Lady screamed and clutched at my arm but it was no good, the whole trap was over, and the poor horse caught in the traces and screaming, too.

I was tossed in the hedge when the trap overturned, and took a knock on the head; lucky, I suppose, not to break my neck. But it took me a moment to get up and when I did, I saw the car had stopped. There were gentlemen in proper long coats and trilby hats and dark gloves, and they'd got out of the car to see what was amiss. But the pony was my job; lying on its side, legs kicking, and that awful screaming. I went to its head and felt in my pocket for my knife, to cut the traces — but I'd forgot the knife in my room back home. I tried to soothe him, thinking if he was calmer I'd be able to get the harness off him. One of the gentlemen came over

to help. Sat on the horse's head while I
worked the straps. Unpleasant, he was —
What kind of fool drives a gig at this hour
of the night? he asks, impatient, like I'm
the village yokel that knows no better.

The Lady had to reach the station, I says.

We'll take her on, he tells me, as I free
the horse and get him onto his knees. It's
the least we can do.

I saw, then, that another of them had her
by the arm and was half-carrying her to
the car.

Ma'am, I called out. Ma'am, are you all
right?

But she made no answer.

Fainted, the fellow next to me said. But
she'll be fine. Sorry for your trouble. And
he shoves a pound note in my hand.

The pony was dead lame. I had to leave
the trap and walk him home, a mile or
more.

I went straight to South Cottage when I
got there and roused the master. Such a
time I hope never to live through again —
Miss Vita, with her face set like stone, and
Mr. Harold more quiet than I've ever
known him. Worse, that was, than if he'd
raged like Da when the drink's on him.
Miss Vita looked at the horse and Mr.

Harold told Hayter he'd have to walk out with us in the morning, and look at the trap; and then he says to me, as I stand with my cap in my hand, Did you get a look at the car's number?

I shook my head.

Pity, he says.

But they was from London, I offer.

They would be, he says.

And turns away without another word.

Monday, 7 April 1941

It is certain now that no one answering to the Lady's description took the first train Saturday morning from Staplehurst station, nor the last. No one like her has been seen in all the Weald, as far as Mr. Harold can make out. He's asked the police and looked in at hospital. The telegraph has been fairly singing her name, and how she looked.

The earth has swallowed her up.

Today, Miss Vita is to visit the Lady's sister at a place called Charleston, and then drive to her home which is a monk's house. She has asked me to come and tell her people what I saw and know. When the trip is done Miss Vita will take me back to Knole — I am in disgrace. I am that sick with losing the Lady, and losing my place, that I wish I were dead. I tried to help but did only harm. I cannot tell Miss Vita she feared to stay at Sissinghurst, for she wouldn't understand and would probably be affronted. But she did not see the fear in the Lady's eyes.

To me Miss Vita says only You are a good fellow, Jock, and will be much missed; but your mother will be wanting you at home, to be sure. You are safer in such times with your family.

I am not missed and I will not be safe.

I will go for a soldier. Da will say it's all I'm good for.

Maybe she is all right and got wherever it was she was anxious to go. Maybe we will find her sitting at home when Miss Vita drives down to Sussex. Maybe it is not my fault that everything went bad and the pony was put down and the gig chopped up for firewood. But I feel in my heart that it is all my fault. I live that time — the car coming round the curve in the dark, the horse screaming, the feel of the hedge as it came up to strike my cheek — over and over, whenever I shut my eyes. And the Lady, not speaking or looking, as they dragged her away.

This bit of writing should be kept safe.

For Mr. Harold, maybe, who might want it someday. I will set an angelic host around it. For the Lady.

Jock Bellamy

CHAPTER
FORTY-ONE

"*Extraordinary* is a word too often applied to items that pass through an auctioneer's hands," Marcus Symonds-Jones observed as he looked around the conference table in Imogen Cantwell's office, "but in this case I would argue the term is merited. One such find would be notable — even if unattributed to an author. Two must be remarkable; but to have *three related documents,* two of them written by Virginia Woolf, is a discovery of the rarest order. When one considers the contribution the find provides to English history and literature — I think we may justly call it priceless."

"Priceless," Gray Westlake repeated as he rocked precariously on one of the Head Gardener's folding chairs. "That's hardly the best choice of word, Marcus. Say *priceless,* and I walk out of here."

"I think it's *exactly* the right word," Jo countered. "I wouldn't part with my grandfather's diary for any amount of money. It's too personal. And I want my grandmother to read it."

She had summoned Gray last night by phone while Peter contacted Marcus. The two men drove down to Kent together that morning in one of the Connaught's black cars — wary, but incapable, in the final instance, of refusing temptation. Marcus greeted Peter as though he were a cross between Jesus Christ and a corpse He'd just revived; Jo suspected Marcus couldn't decide whether to fire or promote him. Peter's complete lack of interest in the outcome of the question added to his offense.

For at least an hour after finishing their perusal of Jock's diary the previous evening, they'd sat talking around the same table in Imogen's office.

For a while, Jo simply listened to the others, her emotions brimming with the plunge into her grandfather's past. It was painful to feel what he'd felt, to share his anxiety, to weigh the decisions he'd been forced to shoulder too soon. In the crabbed writing on the cigarette papers, Jock was a familiar stranger — not the hale old warrior she'd known, but a tentative and lonely boy, struggling to act like a man. He'd hated himself for failing the Lady that night on the London road; but how much worse must he have felt when Virginia's body was finally pulled from the Ouse? The diary couldn't tell Jo. But she understood that the death had scarred her grandfather beyond repair. He'd abandoned his work, his family, his life — and run away to war. Looking for a swift and violent end.

"Are you okay, Jo?" Peter asked.

She shook herself out of her reverie, smiled at him, and said, "What troubles me is that we still don't know how Virginia died. Was she thrown, was she pushed? Or did she jump in despair?"

"She was killed in the car accident," Peter suggested, "and her body dumped off the bridge at Southease."

"She was brought back to Leonard," Margaux said darkly, "who refused to waste a perfectly good death notice."

Jo shook her head. "I think she was silenced by the men of Westminster, who drove out to find her after getting Harold's letter. They were clever enough to take her down to Sussex, where the world already thought she'd gone into the water."

"Harold and Vita knew otherwise," Margaux objected.

"Harold and Vita were in the midst of a war." Peter toyed with his mug of tea. "The Double-Cross Committee — the German agents run by MI5 — were a critical reason England defeated Hitler. Harold worked for the Ministry of Information; he knew far more about intelligence work than Virginia did. He may have weighed her loss against the fate of the country — and decided not to push things."

"That's such a sexist statement," Margaux said furiously. "I can't *believe* you sometimes, Peter. You think it morally sound to sacrifice a genius —"

"Harold tried his best to save her." Peter's voice was mild. "When he failed, he could have got himself killed, too, by protesting too much. He decided instead to go on."

"— Defending his Lime Walk and his English spring," Jo murmured.

"Aren't you glad they're still here?" Peter shrugged. "He'd sent the truth about Blunt and Burgess to Maynard Keynes; if nobody wanted to believe it — that was hardly Harold's problem. He wasn't the sort to expose his fellows."

"Lest they expose *him*," Margaux shot back. "But *murder?*"

"We'll never know whether it was murder," Peter reminded her gently.

"We know," Jo said.

Before they left Sissinghurst that night, Peter placed the cigarette papers, Leonard's letter and book, and the biscuit tin in a plastic bag. Imogen sealed it with tape and they all signed it with a black marker; then she photographed the bundle and locked it in her office safe.

"I can tell The Family I was in on the find with a straight face, now," she said with exultant relief.

Marcus Symonds-Jones was looking at Jo this morning as though she were a particularly recalcitrant child. "I don't think, you know, that you're in any position to make demands. Given your extraordinary behavior in recent days. The people at this table are all that stand between you and prosecution."

Jo smiled at him. "Did you learn that trick of intimidation from Gray? I suppose you'll offer me a document to sign, now."

"As a matter of fact —" Marcus lifted a sheet of paper from the agenda before him. "I have it here. You relinquish any claim to these items in exchange for a leniency I only *hope* we can guarantee. I have not yet consulted the Trust or the Nicolson Family

427

— God knows what penalties *they* might enforce — but we will try to do our best by you, Miss Bellamy."

"How fortunate, then," Peter interjected, "that we consulted The Family ourselves."

Marcus paused. He glanced at Gray, who was studying Peter with an interested expression.

"That's why we thought it best to meet here, in the garden, where the papers belong," Peter added quietly. "The Family were delighted to learn from Imogen that she'd unearthed a number of treasures related to Sissinghurst and its more famous occupants; and they felt we might be interested in a final document that has come to light." Peter paused, aware that the room had gone silent. "A poem, to be precise, written by Vita Sackville-West and found after her death."

"Where?" Margaux demanded. "In the Tower? I swear, there's more bloody stuff up there than anybody realizes. The Trust just *sits* on it."

"The Family, not the Trust, found this particular poem — and to them, it was inexplicable. But they kept it safe."

"Inexplicable?" Gray repeated. "In what way?"

"In the way that any piece of a puzzle is

meaningless without the rest. The poem is entitled 'In Memoriam: White Garden.' It's dated April 1941."

"That's when she published her Woolf poem," Margaux exclaimed.

"Spot on," Peter agreed. "Vita wrote 'In Memoriam: Virginia Woolf' for the London *Observer* that April. This poem — the one found in the Tower — would appear to be a companion to it. A more intimate lament, if you will, that she suppressed. Dr. Strand, can you recall any of the published poem?"

Margaux pursed her lips and closed her eyes, lost in thought for a few seconds. Then she intoned: *"So let us say, she loved the water-meadows, / The Downs; her friends; her books; her memories; / The room which was her own. / London by twilight; shops and Mrs. Brown; / Donne's church; the Strand; the buses, and the large / Smell of humanity that passed her by . . ."* Margaux's eyes drifted open. "Vita goes on to compare Virginia to a moth, fluttering against a lamp. And then she closes with:

How small, how petty seemed the little men /
Measured against her scornful quality.

We feminists *love* to quote that bit."

429

"What do you think of it? As poetry, I mean?"

"Not *entirely* successful." Margaux was enjoying her moment on the stage. "Vita seemed torn between a private tribute and a public one, the need to mourn her friend and the need to ensure Virginia's place in the English canon. That tension's evident in the verse —"

Marcus shifted irritably in his seat. "Yes, yes, all very delightful I'm sure — but to what does this chatter tend?"

Peter drew what appeared to be a simple sheet of writing paper from a manila envelope and placed it gently in the middle of the table.

In Memoriam: White Garden

I said she was a moth, fluttered spirit,
    delicate;
That bumped against the lamp of life. No
    mention made
Of how they tortured her, prey to
    nameless fears,
With such exact descriptions of the night:
Its quality, deception, unnumbered shades
    of grey
Crept in to suffocate the plangent souls
    she loved.

The glow of blanchèd flowers and pale
 birds
Her sole security for sleep.
O Virginia, whose cobweb fingers trailed
Among our thorns, jabbering in tongues
 and fractured
Semaphore, your madness is a comfort to
 us now.
What sense you made of bowler hats and
 bombing runs,
The water meadows drown; it will not
 stand for long
against the ministry of lies, the soporific
 song
we mutter in our darkened rooms, mere
 lullabies
before the final sleep.

I told you not to meddle. Not to worry
 your poor head.
I should have held you up as sane
Before the men, instead.
Fatuity, indifference; a bitter, soul-deep
 blight —
A weariness with war and bombs
And blackout shades pulled tight.
And when I paid attention —
You had slipped off, in the night.

White clematis, white lavender, anemone

and rose
The lists go on and on, my dear, remorse
  that barely shows.
I've planted you a garden here, against
  the pitchy black;
Pure white, my virginal, my owl; pure
  white,
Now just — *Come back* —

"It's an apology," Jo murmured, "and a farewell. Isn't it, Peter?"

"The Family tell me they would like this poem included with the other documents — the notebook, Leonard Woolf's bound volume, the cigarette papers. Their preference is that these finds remain in England, in an archival setting, and they're hopeful of consulting, through the Trust, the curators of Monk's House to reach an equitable solution for all parties concerned."

"Excellent," Marcus managed, with a visible effort at recovery. He tore at the cap of his Montblanc pen. "Just give me the best contact number, won't you, and I'll take it from here?"

"I've been empowered to act as broker between The Family, the Trust, and the University of Sussex," Peter continued inexorably. "The bulk of the Woolf papers are housed at Sussex, you see. The Family is desirous of placing these items with the rest of the Woolf collection, so that scholars" — he inclined his head toward Margaux — "might have the greatest ease of access. They've offered the notebook to the University at an exceptionally decent price, and the University is considering the acquisition. Jo Bellamy has agreed to *lend* her grandfather's papers for an indefinite period of time."

"Scholars?" Margaux repeated. "That's not what I stipulated. I was promised sole access!"

"We have documents, Peter!" Marcus spluttered. *"Signed."*

"— By no one with any real authority in the case, unfortunately. But don't piss your drawers, Marcus — you're not out of it altogether. I have here a letter" — Peter resorted once more to his manila envelope — "signed by representatives of both the Trust and The Family, requesting the completion of Sotheby's in-house notebook analysis and the return of the materials to Sissinghurst. The auction house will, of course, be paid for those services — out of the proceeds of our private sale."

There was a breathless silence as Marcus scanned Peter's letter. Then he tossed it on the table in disgust. *"Bugger."*

"As I said — you were set up." Gray rose from the table. "Jo, send me your accounting and any drawings you've got, once you're back home. With the holidays coming, Alicia's time is tight — but maybe in January you can meet us in Manhattan to discuss the plant list."

"That'd be great," she replied.

"Now, if you'll excuse me" — Gray inclined his head at Imogen Cantwell — "my plane is waiting at Gatwick. Marcus, you'll catch a train back to London, of course?"

The door closed soundlessly behind him.

"You nasty, underhanded, backstabbing *sod.*" Marcus made a show of gathering his papers and agenda, pique in every movement. "I'll see you sacked!"

"But first," Peter said, "you'll tell me where the notebook is. With Beevers in Watermark, or Finegold in Bindings?"

"Beevers," Marcus spat.

"Right, then." Peter smiled all around. "I'll just give him a call. Margaux — you might want to share Marcus's taxi to Staplehurst. There are trains on the hour. Imogen, you've been more than generous — but may I beg the use of your phone? My mobile battery's quite dead, I'm afraid. Jo — I shan't be a moment. Wait for me, will you?"

■ ■ ■ ■

She left Imogen to set her perpetual kettle to boil, and walked out into the garden. It was barely ten o'clock, a full hour before the gates of Sissinghurst would open; Paradise was left to herself.

Tomorrow was Saturday, the last Open day of the year. By Monday the castle grounds would be dead quiet, a few shadows dancing against the pale green panes of the propagation houses, a few barrows trundling down the slate paths. Mist, curling at the foot of Vita's tower. An angelic host. But by Monday Jo would be back in Delaware.

She paced slowly up from the Powys Wall through the Rose Garden fading now into dormancy; through the heart of the massive Yew Rondel, to the cross path that led through the opening in a brick wall, past leafless magnolias and a tool shed, into the Yew Walk.

Severe simplicity. Restraint. A vanishing point that beckoned.

She had never strolled entirely alone between these green walls. The fragrant yew seemed to whisper in the morning mist: *Come back. Come back.* Or was it Virginia they called?

The entrance to the Lower Courtyard opened on her left. She glanced at the steps spilling down from the Tower, the sweep of lawn and the bare bones of clematis, and walked on.

Her heart, she found, beat faster as she turned for the last time into the White Garden. As though a specter awaited her there. She would always look for Jock, now, in the shadows beneath the arching roses.

She stopped short, her gaze drifting past the arbor and its fading canes to the wrought-iron gate beyond. Jock had never seen this, though he'd been part of its dreaming. What had he feared, when he learned she was coming to Sissinghurst? That the careful web of lies he'd upheld for six decades in silence — the myth of Virginia Woolf's suicide — would explode in his face? Publicity? Flashbulbs? Accusation? The loss of the fragile peace he'd found among his tools in the Delaware Valley?

He'd been the only one of Sissinghurst's ghosts still left alive. The only one the world could interrogate. The one who faulted himself most for failing the Lady. And so he'd made his choice, Jo thought: to go silently into that great good night, rather than face the endless questions. She understood, now, that his choice had never had anything to do with her. It was no failure of love, no unanswerable reproach. It was Jock's bow to an obscure past he'd hoped would remain buried.

"Grandpa," she whispered as she turned into the path that led to the Little Virgin, past the mottled silver of eryngium and crambe, "I'm sorry for all your pain. I think for a while now I've shared it. But I'm telling you, my dearest: You did your best. You tried your hardest. And you've taught me that's all any of us can do."

"Are you really going Sunday?" Peter said quietly behind her.

She turned. "That's what my ticket says. Did he fire you?"

"I gave a month's notice. I want to be around until the Woolf papers are safely housed; I don't trust Marcus. Four more weeks of indentured servitude on behalf of a good cause — and I'm free. Here." He pressed a sheaf of papers into her hands. "I made that for you. A photocopy of Jock's cigarette papers. So your gran can read them. Imogen let me borrow her copier."

"I . . ." She looked up at him shyly. "So *grateful* to you, Peter. For everything."

"Don't be. I owe you a good deal more — the commission for this bit of work, for instance. I've got plans for the cash."

"Do you?" she said, slipping her hand through his arm. "Would they happen to include buying me lunch?"

" 'Fraid not," he said regretfully. "I'm promised to Margaux. We're to discuss our future, you see."

"Oh." She faltered. "No, actually, I don't see. Or maybe I hoped . . . but it's okay. I understand. I really do. She's . . . a remarkable woman, Peter."

"She's a virago," he said cheerfully, throwing his arm around Jo and steering her back down the path. "And don't tell me, in your endearing American way, that you're a Gemini yourself. Margaux's a screaming vulture, and I want nothing more to do with her in my life."

"I'm so glad," Jo whispered into his sweater.

"You haven't asked me what I'm doing with my cash."

"Opening Peter's Place?"

"Could do. But first I intend to have a bang-up Christmas. You've never seen Sissinghurst in the snow. Neither have I. But I'm thinking the village needs a good Michelin two-star. With an organic potager. We might hunt for a property together."

Her steps slowed. She looked up at him.

Peter was studying her as though she were

438

a piece of vellum or an illuminated page; something authentic he was afraid to touch.

"We might do almost anything at all," he said, "and I'd be happy. Go out, stay in. Eat. Drink. Make love —"

And as he took her in his arms, the great ghostly barn owl — *Life! Life! Life!* — dipped its wings over the Little Virgin, and soared away over the White Garden.

■ ■ ■ ■ ■

The White Garden
A Novel of
Virginia Woolf
STEPHANIE BARRON

■ ■ ■ ■ ■

A Reader's Guide

A NOTE FROM THE AUTHOR

Lawrence Block once famously said that fiction writing is nothing more than "telling lies for fun and profit." I have a habit of making things up, quite often about people who lived perfectly good lives of their own, people who would be furious to think they were the objects of my embellishment — Jane Austen, Queen Victoria, Virginia Woolf. But then these people, whose every word and act already seemed part of the public domain, died. And my imagination had its way with them.

The White Garden is a case in point. The idea for it took hold during a particularly bleak period in my life when I seemed to be writing only about death and violence. People I loved were dying, too. My mother began her slow descent into the terrible losses of Alzheimer's disease — she remained present, but increasingly unrecognizable. One night, her old self came to me in a dream, as it often does, and my aunt — a horticulture judge who loved gardens — was with her. My aunt had been gone for years, but the two of them were arm in arm, companionable and chatty as always, and they were intending to walk around Sissinghurst. *Come out into the garden, Francie,* they said; and so I followed them into the White Garden.

There's something restorative in writing about growing things when the world is dying around you. I imagine that Vita Sackville-West understood this, and that it is one of the reasons she survived so many upheavals — and perhaps a reason that Virginia Woolf could not. In thinking about these two women, and their relationship to such things as words, and flowers, and violence, I was riveted by a singular moment in their long mutual friendship — the moment it was broken forever, the moment they literally fell out of touch on the banks of the River Ouse. The three weeks that elapsed between Virginia Woolf's disappearance and the discovery of her body must have been difficult ones for everyone who loved her, Vita in particular. That period of silence, of unknowing, was tantalizing to me; I began to consider an alternative in which things were different, the inversion of what history believes to be true.

The White Garden is fiction, all the same. I hope its readers will enjoy exploring the possibilities it suggests, and forgive its inevitable license.

Anyone wishing to learn more about Sissinghurst should immediately obtain a copy of Adam Nicolson's book by that name (*Sissinghurst,* HarperCollins U.K., 2008), the most heartfelt, poignant, and lyric tribute to home that anyone could possibly write.

Francine Mathews
aka Stephanie Barron
Denver, Colorado
July 29, 2009

READING GROUP QUESTIONS
AND TOPICS FOR DISCUSSION
FOR
THE WHITE GARDEN
BY STEPHANIE BARRON

1. *The White Garden* is about uncovering long-buried truths. Is this a noble cause, or do you believe that the past is not meant to be dug up?

2. Have you ever discovered something about your ancestors after their death?

3. Why do you think Jock hid his secret from even his wife and granddaughter?

4. Who do you think the journal ultimately "belongs" to?

5. Out of all authors, living and dead, whose journal would you most want to read and why?

6. Both Virginia and Jock take pains to write their stories down. What power do you think is given to writing words down?

7. Who in the book do you believe is responsible for Virginia's death? Do various characters share responsibility?

8. Do you agree with Peter in his criticism of the idea that "writing is akin to madness"?

9. Does Jo ultimately fulfill her goal of learning more about her grandfather?

10. What do you think can be revealed about a person through how they tend a garden? What do we learn about Jock? About Vita? About Imogen?

11. Do you think Grayson truly loves Jo? Do you see parallels between how he treats Jo and how Leonard treated Virginia, per the way Margaux describes him?

12. Do you think being a part of the immensely talented Bloomsbury group contributed to Virginia's death? Would Virginia have been healthier as an "outsider" artist? Was it a benefit or a detriment that Vanessa was also part of the same group?

13. To whom does the White Garden mean the most? What does it mean to that character?

ABOUT THE AUTHOR

Stephanie Barron is the author of the stand-alone historical suspense novel *A Flaw in the Blood,* as well as the bestselling Jane Austen mystery series. As Francine Mathews, she is the author of *The Cutout, The Secret Agent, Blown,* and *The Alibi Club.* She lives near Denver, Colorado, where she is at work on her next novel in the Jane Austen series, *Jane and the Madness of Lord Byron.*

The employees of Thorndike Press hope you have enjoyed this Large Print book. All our Thorndike, Wheeler, and Kennebec Large Print titles are designed for easy reading, and all our books are made to last. Other Thorndike Press Large Print books are available at your library, through selected bookstores, or directly from us.

For information about titles, please call:
(800) 223-1244

or visit our Web site at:
http://gale.cengage.com/thorndike

To share your comments, please write:
Publisher
Thorndike Press
295 Kennedy Memorial Drive
Waterville, ME 04901